...**inters** lives in Salt Lake City, Utah. With canyons and high alpine meadows full of wildflowers, she never runs out of places to explore. They, plus her favourite vacation spots in Europe, often end up as backgrounds for her romance novels—because writing is her passion, along with her family and her church. Rebecca loves to hear from readers. If you wish to email her, please visit her website at rebeccawinters.net.

Ellie Darkins spent her formative years devouring romance novels and, after completing her English degree, decided to make a living from her love of books. As a writer and editor, she finds her work now entails dreaming up romantic proposals, hot dates with alpha males and trips to the past with dashing heroes. When she's not working she can usually be found running around after her toddler, volunteering at her local library or escaping all of the above with a good book and a vanilla latte.

CAPTURING THE CEO'S GUARDED HEART

REBECCA WINTERS

THE MILLIONAIRE'S ITALIAN INVITATION

ELLIE DARKINS

MILLS & BOON

CAPTURING THE CEO'S GUARDED HEART

REBECCA WINTERS

MILLS & BOON

Dedicated to my dear siblings.

I came from a family of six children,
five girls and one boy.

Everyone should have come from a family of
six siblings as marvelous and great as mine.

CHAPTER ONE

THE PARISIAN JUDGE of the Third Civil Division—the man otherwise referred to as President of the Land Court—tapped his gavel.

"In the case of Causcelle vs. Mercier, the court finds for the plaintiff."

Yes!

"The defendant will pay the penalties for fraud. If opposing chief counsels will meet with me in chambers, this court is adjourned."

Thank you, Monsieur President.

Anelise Lavigny had won her first case for the Causcelle Corporation and couldn't be happier. Soon she would call her father, Hugo Lavigny, and tell him the good news. Three years ago her father had become good friends with the world-famous Louis Causcelle. Apparently they'd met through business, but she'd never learned why their relationship had become so important to him.

After graduating from law school, she'd gotten her start working as an attorney in her father's office. He was known for developing polymers and electronics. Yet she'd only been working for her father a few months when Louis Causcelle came to her father's business and offered her a position at his corporation. She would be one of the attorneys for the hotel division. The Causcelle empire was worth billions and had been touted as one of the top five that drove the French economy.

Her parents immediately urged her to consider joining Louis's corporation. They told her they thought it was an honor that Louis had sought her out. Her parents assured her she'd be an asset at Causcelle.

In a way their encouragement had surprised her because they'd been very protective of her since the death of her fiancé. They'd done everything to show her their love and shield her from the intrusive press since her father was a prominent man. She'd leaned on their support. It went without saying that because she was their only child, they'd all been very close. Maybe a little too much?

Winning the case today had given her more confidence that she'd made the right decision to work for Louis Causcelle. Anelise had to admit to a surge of excitement at becoming more independent. She liked the feeling and enjoyed living on her own.

Serge Thibault, the chief attorney in Causcelle's hotel division and her immediate boss, nodded to her that she should leave without him because he'd be a while. Under the circumstances she'd go to her apartment to eat before she went back to the office.

Anelise left the courtroom of the Palais de Justice

with her briefcase and headed for the company limo
waiting for her across the Boulevard du Palais bridge.

A delightful May afternoon brought out the usual
hundreds of tourists visiting the Ile de la Cité, where
the Palais de Justice was located in the heart of Paris.

The boat-shaped island in the middle of the
Seine River contained much of the history of the
city of lights. Never could she forget she was walking over the ground of the former royal residence of
the kings of France. One could still visit the Sainte-
Chapelle, built in the thirteenth century by King Saint
Louis. The sacred place was known for its exquisite
stained-glass windows portraying Biblical scenes.
So much history…

She savored her surroundings as she climbed in
the limo and asked the chauffeur to take her to her
apartment in the Marais area of Paris. It contained
the gorgeous stone buildings and cobblestone streets
that made her feel she was living in a more romantic
time in France. The Causcelle family owned several
properties there. One was a sprawling, former two-
story royal palace that had become their corporate
headquarters.

A block away stood another former royal palace
that had been modernized. Various members of the
large Causcelle family lived there at times, including Louis Causcelle when he was in town. A staffed
kitchen provided their meals. Louis called it the *palais*.

He'd insisted that Anelise stay in the vacant suite
on the main floor where his eldest daughter stayed

when she came to Paris. Louis had insisted Anelise move there, so she only had to walk a short distance to work. Otherwise, she'd have to commute for a half hour from her parents' home in the posh sixteenth arrondissement.

Joy, joy.

After losing Andre Navarre in a fatal car crash eighteen months ago, she hadn't thought she could be happy again. He'd brought such love into her life, for him to have died at the scene had sent her into shock for days. She withdrew from people and hadn't wanted to finish law school. Her dreams of being Andre's wife and working with him when they traveled had died with him. Her darling Andre who'd just graduated in engineering no longer existed.

The media had exploited the crash because she was the daughter of multimillionaire Hugo Lavigny. They'd intruded in her life, even speculated that his death might have ended a promising career in law for her because of her heartache. But they callously suggested that it didn't matter because she would inherit her father's money one day.

When Anelise had read those cruel, disgusting words, she'd been sickened and angered by them. How dared they? That comment roused her out of her grief long enough to finish up her degree, but many nights she'd cried, most of them longing for him.

Thankfully enough time had passed since then that she didn't feel that way today. This new position at Causcelle had pulled her from that dark place and given her fresh focus. Ferreting out the fraud in the

Mercier case meant Louis Causcelle wouldn't regret hiring her. Not yet anyway. Not if she could help it.

Her limo driver drove her through the courtyard, past the fountain and around the side to the main entrance. She got out, thanking him before she hurried past two more security guards and entered the building.

A fiftyish male guard at the front desk of the entrance monitored who went in and out. She couldn't help but notice an attractive brunette having a heated conversation with him. Something was wrong.

The flustered man nodded to Anelise. "Your father called and hopes you'll phone him when you can, Mademoiselle Lavigny."

That's right. She'd turned off her cell in court. Her parents, especially her dad, were anxious to know how her first case had gone. "*Merci*, Guy. I'll do it now." Anelise started walking down the hall to her suite when she heard footsteps behind her.

"Wait, Mademoiselle Lavigny!"

She turned around as the other woman hurried toward her. Anelise thought she recognized her as a French television star featured in some drama series. She couldn't recall its name or that of the actress.

The *vedette*'s brown eyes with long dark lashes did a quick inventory of Anelise. "I take it you live here."

"Yes."

"How did you accomplish *that*?" She folded her arms like a schoolteacher waiting for an explanation from her naughty student. It sounded like the woman wanted to move in here. Guy must have told her she would have to be invited. Anelise was surprised the star hadn't asked her agent to help her.

The more she thought about it, the more she wondered why this woman felt she had a right to access an apartment here. This place existed strictly for the Causcelle family and their friends. Maybe the woman *was* a friend. A very special friend, like a former lover of one of the Causcelle men perhaps?

One finely arched brow lifted. "In other words, you won't tell me."

Good heavens. The woman really was upset. "I don't know what it is you want."

"A suite, of course, but the man at the front desk is no help."

"This isn't a hotel. I'm afraid you would have to talk to the head of the Causcelle Corporation."

"Is that what *you* did?" Her peremptory attitude might explain why Guy had seemed out of sorts. "Isn't he as old and impossible as Methuselah?"

Not Louis Causcelle. He was young at heart. Anelise liked him very much, but none of this was her business. "He's a wonderful man. If you'll excuse me, I need to make a phone call."

The minute Anelise entered her apartment, she ordered room service and freshened up, then called her dad at his office to explain what had happened in court.

"As you know, I discovered that the agent for the Mercier Company failed to transfer the stock certificates in a timely manner following the merger with

Causcelle. The discovery resulted in a six-million-euro settlement for us."

"That's my daughter! I'm so proud of you I could burst."

She'd never heard him so happy. "Thanks, Papa. I'm pretty excited about it too."

"What's the rest of your day like?"

"I'm going back to work, but I'll be over tonight to see you and Maman. *A bientôt*."

The landline rang as Nic Causcelle emerged from the shower in his suite at the *palais*. He'd just flown into Paris on the company jet from Chalon Champforgeuil in eastern France. It was the closest airport to the Causcelle ancestral home in La Racineuse fifteen miles away. His father, Louis, had become ill and would be living there from now on where his married daughters and their families would take care of him.

As for Nic, his father had put him in charge of Causcelle Hotels, a job he didn't relish. He much preferred continuing to work with his brother Raoul in the other divisions of the corporation here in Paris. They included exports, manufacturing, luxury cars and a trucking firm. But with their other brother, Jean-Louis, having left the family ten years ago to serve in the military, it meant either Nic or Raoul would be required to head the hotel business from now on.

Their father had flipped a coin. Nic called heads, Raoul tails. Up came heads. Raoul wasn't happy about it either. The two brothers were thicker than proverbial thieves and enjoyed working together. Nic couldn't understand why his father didn't ask their cousin Pascal to take over, but it didn't happen. At least Nic and Raoul would do business in the same place. And they both slept here in the *palais* so they could see each other, but only coming and going, unless they arranged for time off to be together.

He walked over to the phone and picked up. *"Oui?"*

"Pardon, Nicolas. Welcome back. It's Guy in the lobby. Mademoiselle Lafrenière has just been here asking about you again. She'd like to move in here. I told her that wasn't possible. It's not the first time she has asked, if you know what I mean."

Unfortunately, Nic *did* know.

"She thought you were coming back to Paris last week and has been here every day to inquire. She expects a call from you."

His dark brows furrowed. "Do you have the number?"

"Yes."

"Give it to me and I'll take care of it. *Merci*, Guy."

Once that was done, he hung up. Babette Lafrenière. That was all he needed. An actress with stars in her eyes and so ambitious, it oozed out of her. He'd met her over a month ago at one of their car dealerships while he'd gone there to straighten out a managerial problem.

The middle-aged manager, Pierre, always went overboard when Nic or Raoul met with him. On this day he was so dazzled by the TV star who'd come to look at the luxury cars, he couldn't contain himself introducing her to Nic. The second she set eyes on him, she ignored the manager and wanted Nic to do the honors of helping her with her purchase.

She had a brazen side to her nature, asking him to take her for a ride in the Bugatti she'd decided to buy. Her exotic kind of beauty couldn't be ignored, but her hunger for everything turned him off and he excused himself.

Somehow—perhaps through the car manager— she'd found out where he lived. Poor Guy at the desk had been haunted by her phone calls and visits ever since. Nic needed to do something about it today, but would leave it until after he'd been to the office where his father had worked for years. Once he'd said hello to everyone in his capacity as their new CEO over Causcelle Hotels, he would call Mademoiselle Lafrenière and say something that would put her off for good.

After dressing in a suit and tie, he left the *palais* and started walking to the office. A way off he noticed a light brown-haired woman with slender curves in a two-piece dark blue business suit headed in the same direction. She carried a briefcase and her hair had been caught back in a tortoiseshell clip, but he couldn't see her face.

Something unique about her had drawn his attention. She walked with a spring in her step on those long legs of hers, seemingly excited, maybe happy even because it was Friday. How would it be to feel like that?

To his surprise she entered the Causcelle Corporation and went right up the stairs as if she knew exactly where she was going. More curious than ever, he didn't use the private entrance with the elevator that took him straight to his office. Instead he walked behind her to the hotel division that took up the whole second floor. She entered the reception area of the front office and shut the door.

Within seconds Nic opened it quietly and heard the voice of George Delong, the executive assistant to Nic's father for years. The man could run the place blindfolded. *"Bon après-midi,* Anelise. Any good news?"

"We won!"

"Felicitations!"

"Merci."

"Where's Serge?"

"Talking with the judge."

His gray brows lifted above his glasses. "While you've been gone, our new boss has come back from his vacation in La Racineuse."

"New? What do you mean? Where's Monsieur Causcelle?"

Nic came all the way in. "I'm right here."

She wheeled around, catching him off guard because she was lovelier than he could have imagined. Her sea-glass blue eyes stared at him out of an oval face that needed no makeup.

George got to his feet looking surprised that Nic had appeared at all. "Mademoiselle Lavigny, may I present Nicolas Causcelle, the new CEO of Causcelle Hotels and son of Louis Causcelle."

Lavigny? It all made sense. She had to be the daughter of Louis's friend Hugo, the one he'd mentioned the other day back in La Racineuse. Nic thought back to his father's friendship with the other man. Odd how none of their family had ever met Hugo, but Nic's father kept his cards close to the chest on occasion.

Since Nic had called off his engagement to Denise Fournette two years ago, Nic's father had been urging him to find the right woman next time and get married. But Nic didn't trust his own judgment where permanent relationships were concerned, and those words had fallen on deaf ears.

For some reason his father had hired Hugo's daughter to work here once his doctor had told him he must retire. Nic had the suspicion something was going on he didn't understand. Why had his father suddenly decided on *her*? No doubt she had the right qualifications, but he had to admit to being curious.

"Mademoiselle Lavigny? It's a pleasure to meet you."

"And mine, monsieur." She acted all business.

"If you'll come with me to my office, we'll get acquainted." He turned to his father's assistant. "It's good to see you, George. We'll talk Monday morning after I meet with Serge."

"Tres bien."

"Bon weekend."

Anelise followed the attractive man who constituted one of the amazing Causcelle identical triplet sons born twenty-nine years ago. Their births had made headlines throughout France and Europe. They'd been famous from day one for being children of the foremost billionaire in France.

His sons would inherit everything Louis Causcelle owned, from hotels, transport services, trucking chains and elite cars to manufacturing companies. Their photos were constantly in the media and newspapers, but she'd never met one of them in person. She found that odd. Why hadn't Louis ever introduced his children to her parents?

According to Anelise's father, the triplets had been courted by royalty throughout Europe. They came from an old aristocratic family with property in eastern France deeded to their family back in the 1200s by Philip II. Their genealogy made them a source of great envy and constant targets of publicity.

The fact that they were handsome as Adonis and unmarried would make them desirable to every female, available or not. But no male possessed her deceased fiancé's dark blond looks and green eyes. Just remembering him brought a pang to her heart. She had to keep fighting this longing when she thought of him in order to maintain a professional front in front of the staff and now her new boss.

Anelise walked past the suite where she worked. Through another door she saw the other attorney, Helene Garnier, a woman in her fifties Anelise had met through Louis. She liked the older woman Louis had praised. Moving on, they entered the suite at the end of the hall where Louis had interviewed her after hiring her, but the moment was surreal.

The tall, solidly built male with wavy black hair led her to his inner sanctum. He indicated a chair for her and sat down at the desk where his father had once reigned. His vibrant black eyes missed nothing as they studied her beneath equally dark brows.

To think this son was now the head of the hotel division where she worked... Anelise couldn't comprehend it. He didn't know her from Adam. Now that she'd done well on her first case, she'd felt on a little firmer ground with Louis Causcelle, but no longer.

"My father was worried about the Mercier case, but evidently you found the lie in the details in time to stop the merger. I couldn't help but overhear you tell George you won your case. That will please my father."

"Thank you. He's been very kind to me. Would you please tell me what has happened that he's no longer the head?"

Nic sat forward. "Does that bother you?"

She didn't look away. "Frankly, I'm very disappointed. I was looking forward to working for him. My father says he's such a brilliant man and I'd learn so much."

"He isn't happy about leaving the company either, but he has a bad heart and is on medication. The doctor insisted he retire and stay home with our married sisters and the rest of our extended family."

"I'm so sorry. Is it permanent?"

"I'm afraid so."

She lowered her head. "How sad. I enjoyed our meeting before he hired me a month ago."

"I'll let him know about your triumph today."

"Thank you."

"Mademoiselle Lavigny, do you mind if I ask you what convinced you to join our corporation, other than our fathers' friendship?"

"Oh, not at all. I was keen for a fresh environment after working for my father's company. You know, something new and challenging. Th-that's what I've been needing," she stammered.

"My father told me you lost your fiancé. How long ago?"

"Over nineteen months now."

"I'm very sorry."

"So am I, but I've been making a new life for myself. This job offer thrilled me because the Causcelle Corporation has always had a brilliant reputation. But it's more than that. Your father came to my father's company to talk to me and I was so surprised. When I met him, he was so charming and personable, I felt like we became instant friends. He can tell a tale like no one else, and he drew me out of myself.

"When I told him about my life growing up without siblings, he pulled a photo out of his wallet and showed it to me. He said, 'Try living with these!' It turned out to be a picture of you and your brothers. You stood there in a pasture in shorts and tops with a cow near you."

"He *showed* you that photo?" The man sounded surprised.

"Yes, and I can understand why. I've never seen cuter three-year-old boys who all looked exactly alike. I told him I would have loved some brothers like that. He spoke fondly about your older sisters too, and he teared up when he talked about all of you.

"I told him my mother couldn't have more children after I came along, but she'd wanted a large family like his. He began to weep and wished your mother had been alive to see how wonderfully you've all turned out. If ever a father loved his family, he loves you. Do you mind telling me where that picture was taken?"

After a long silence he said, "Near the Causcelle Fromagerie. It's located on an ancient piece of property near the family château in La Racineuse where we raise Montbeliarde cows for cheese making."

"Like that cow I saw in the background of the picture?"

"Exactly. Those are the red-and-white pied cattle used for dairying and cheese making from the Haute-Saône/Doubs region of France. They descend from the Bernoise cattle. Did you know they were brought into France in the eighteenth century by the Mennonites?"

"I had no idea."

"Those cows produced milk that made the cheese my great-great-great-grandfather Auguste first sold at market. Cheese was the first product of the family business."

She couldn't hear enough. "The beginning of everything! No wonder my father always insists on buying Causcelle cheese. I love it too."

"That's true loyalty. My father would be delighted to hear it."

"What was the second product?"

"You mean he didn't tell you after your long conversation?"

"No." She chuckled. "But I could have listened to him all day if he'd had the time."

He eyed her through narrowed lids, as if he were trying to figure her out. "Auguste rode his horse to market to sell the cheese. When he'd made enough money over the years, he bought a cart to carry more cheese. Rather than a product, you could say that his method was the precursor to the trucking business his son Francois began to develop in eastern France."

"And so on and so forth down through the years to the present." She smiled at him. "What is *your* contribution to this chain of remarkable events?"

When the light went out of his eyes, Anelise knew at once her question had brought an abrupt end to their conversation. His hard, chiseled jaw tautened. "It stopped with my brothers and me."

"How can you say that after what I've learned about all of you?"

His eyes had clouded over, confusing her. "The story isn't fully written yet, is it?"

"You mean—" Anelise stopped, suddenly feeling terrible. "Forgive me if I touched on something so personal for you. When your father talked about his family, he spoke with such pride."

"But?" he questioned, surprising her. "You didn't finish what you were going to say."

"It doesn't matter."

"I think it does."

She took a deep breath. "I'd rather not."

"Please. I'd like to hear."

"He conveyed such a sadness over your brother who joined the military. Forgive me for saying anything."

"No problem. Go on. I want to hear it all."

Anelise feared she'd made a mistake mentioning the photo. She sensed a well of sorrow in him. "He told me he'd been so upset when your brother joined the military, it caused an estrangement that never healed. He sounded heartbroken about it. After he'd wept, he admitted it was his one of his many regrets that he hadn't been kind to him when he signed up."

She stopped for breath. "He wished he'd had the chance to beg his forgiveness, but feared it was too late." Anelise hadn't known Louis was seriously ill when he'd hired her, but she did now and it all made sense. Louis had feared dying before seeing his son again. "Before our interview was over, your father prophesied that each of his sons would take the Causcelle Corporation to new heights. Of that I have no doubt."

Her words seemed to have affected Nicolas Causcelle in ways she didn't understand. His silence had turned into brooding and a frown appeared, as if he were upset. Again she felt sadness radiate from him and his reaction made her uneasy. Perhaps he wanted to be alone. She stood up.

"I apologize for taking your time. Please know I'm truly honored to be working for your company. Please give your father my best. Tell him I'll miss him and the talks I would have enjoyed."

Anelise turned and exited his office. Whatever had been bothering him lay deep seated inside him. She wished she knew what had troubled him. When she reached the front desk at the other end of the hall, she was astonished to see the same self-absorbed woman who'd confronted her earlier at the *palais*.

The TV star standing at George's desk stared at Anelise with a stunned expression. "What are *you* doing here?" The woman's rudeness was off the charts.

George got to his feet. "Mademoiselle Lafrenière, may I introduce you to Mademoiselle Lavigny, one of our new corporate attorneys."

Shock registered. "*You're* an attorney?"

Anelise smiled. "It's a surprise to me too." She turned to George. "We met earlier today. Now I can put a name to her face."

"Mademoiselle Lafrenière is an actress you may have seen on the *Paris Noir* TV series," he informed her.

She eyed the other woman. "How exciting for you, mademoiselle. I'm sorry, but I don't watch much television. Now, if you'll excuse me, I have work to do before I leave." Anelise felt the other woman stare daggers at her as she turned to go to her office down the hall. More than ever she sensed this woman had been in a relationship with one of the Causcelle sons. She just didn't know which one.

CHAPTER TWO

NIC HADN'T MOVED a muscle since Mademoiselle Lavigny had left his office. With furrowed brows, he thought over the conversation with the new and beautiful young attorney. More curious about her than ever, he looked up her résumé on their personnel file. She was twenty-six and would be married by now if her fiancé hadn't been killed.

Interesting… His father knew how to manipulate better than anyone he knew. Had he decided to dangle her under Nic's nose with marriage the outcome? Why not hire her to work under Nic? Clever. He had to admit she was tempting bait, but no way would he allow that to happen!

Her faint flowery fragrance still lingered in the air…subtle, but there.

A part of him didn't want to believe his parent would endeavor to play cupid with him and Mademoiselle Lavigny. But after meeting her face-to-face, Nic realized his father had been so enchanted by her, he'd confided in her regarding very private family matters that included his mother. He'd even told her about his regrets over the way he'd treated Jean-Louis. He'd even wept in front of her, yet he'd always been such a private person around most people.

Nic's father had never talked to him or Raoul about his sorrow at hurting their brother. Had her engaging personality prompted his father to be open because she was a naturally friendly person who invited confidences? Maybe her warmth reminded him of his friend Hugo and he felt close to her because of it.

What was it between his father and hers that had bonded the two men three years ago? Did she know something Nic didn't, and was more than willing to try and seduce him for Louis's sake? If so, she made a superb actress. But after his mistake in getting engaged to Denise, he couldn't deal with another relationship. As for Mademoiselle Lafrenière...

Now would be the time to phone the annoying starlet and get this over with. But as he reached for the landline phone, George buzzed him. In a low voice he said, "Nicolas? There's a Mademoiselle Lafrenière here to see your father."

My father?

"I told her to be seated. She says she's a friend of yours."

Speak of the devil. His hand tightened on the receiver. "She isn't a friend of mine or our family. Tell her my father has retired and send her on her way. I'll call her later."

"Tres bien."

Nic hung up and left the office through the private elevator to the rear exit of the *palais*. After the short walk to his living quarters, he phoned the starlet on the *palais* line that had to go through the switchboard. He left a message for her to call. A half hour later Guy told him she was on the other line. He thanked him and clicked on.

"This is Monsieur Causcelle."

"At last. I was beginning to wonder if I'd ever hear from you, Monsieur Causcelle. Or can I call you Nic?"

Enough of her pointless flirting. "I've been out of town."

"So I understand. You're a hard man to track down. Since you're back, let's have drinks together. It's a Friday night and I don't have plans. Anywhere you say."

Nic suppressed an epithet. "I'm afraid that would be impossible. I'm permanently involved with someone else." It was the one statement he felt would put her off, even if it wasn't true.

"Ooh, that sounds serious."

"Very."

"It wouldn't be you've gone back to your former fiancée after all this time, would it? Or is this woman the formidable young attorney at Causcelle Headquarters who has brought you to your knees?"

Formidable? An interesting choice of words. What did the starlet know about Mademoiselle Lavigny? He closed his eyes in quiet fury. "I hope you're enjoying your new car, Mademoiselle Lafrenière. Best of luck in your career."

He hung up, not giving her a chance to say anything else, and phoned his brother's office on the main floor at Causcelle's. Nic needed to talk to him about his conversation with Mademoiselle Lavigny.

Raoul's assistant told him his brother was on the phone with a client. Nic left the message that he had arrived home and hoped Raoul would come by after he left work.

A half hour later, there was a familiar knock on the door of Nic's suite. "Come on in, *frerot*."

Raoul appeared. They gave each other a bear hug before sitting down in the living room.

"How does it feel to walk in the old man's shoes?"

Nic eyed his brother. "Weird. I'll never get used to the idea and prefer working with you the way we always have."

"I don't like it either."

"It's been a strange day and I haven't even lived through the first one yet. Do you remember our father telling you that he'd hired a new attorney?"

"You must mean his friend Hugo's daughter. He mentioned it to me on the phone."

Nic blinked. "That's the one."

"I take it you met her."

"Yes. She'd just returned from court. It seems she won her first case."

"That'll please Papa. What's she like?"

He rubbed the back of his neck where the nerves bunched up. "I'm still trying to figure her out."

"I guess you know our father invited her to live here at the *palais*."

"He *what*?" Nic shot to his feet. "I've been in and out of Paris on business and know nothing about that."

"Mademoiselle Lavigny has been here for the last month. Corinne told me because Papa invited her to move into Corinne's suite. I thought you must have known."

No. Their oldest married sister hadn't said a word. Was that on purpose because she was in on their father's plan to get Nic married off? Nic had been the first triplet born, and still single. "So, Mademoiselle Lavigny is living downstairs…"

"As far as I know."

It made sense. "That's why I saw her walking to headquarters earlier." *In the same direction as himself and giving off vibes that had drawn his attention.*

"Well? Aren't you going to tell me about her?"

"How much time do you have?"

"I have no plans for tonight." Raoul flicked him a curious glance. "You seem upset, Nic. What's going on?"

"More than you know. Today I believe I've seen the fruition of a well-thought-out, ingenious plot our father has been working on since I broke off with Denise. But there's more, much more. It has to do with Papa and Jean-Louis."

"Now you've really got me curious."

After Nic called the kitchen, he related to his brother what he'd learned.

"Papa actually *told* her about his fight with Jean-Louis?"

Nic nodded. "She said he wept over it and would give anything to ask his forgiveness, but feared it was too late and he'd never see him again."

Bewildered, Raoul got to his feet. "I didn't know father was suffering over it. He's never said a word to me."

"Nor me."

"Why would he tell Mademoiselle Lavigny something so personal? I don't get it."

'I don't either. I'm going to phone Corinne and find out if he told her or our other sisters." Nic pulled his cell phone from his jacket pocket.

"Good idea. Put it on speaker."

The two of them talked to their eldest sister, who swore neither she nor their sisters knew anything, but in a way, she was glad he was suffering. "Jean-Louis didn't want to work for the family business and took a way out by joining the military. Papa should have understood."

"Agreed," Nic murmured. "Do you ever hear from him beyond the once-a-year Christmas card with no address that we all get?"

"You know better than to ask me that. How about you and Raoul? Has he shared something with you because you're his blood brothers in every sense of the word? We sisters aren't his triplet siblings. Jean-Louis is as bad as Papa in the Sphinx department."

Corinne had that right. The Sphinx was always inscrutable. They'd all been hurt by his ten years of silence. "Just once I wish he would break down."

"I miss him and know you do too, Nic. Wish we could talk longer, but I've got to go. Papa is calling for me. Talk to you soon."

"Thanks, Corinne. Give him our love. Let us know

if there's anything you need." Nic clicked off and stared at his brother. "Are you thinking what I'm thinking?"

Raoul nodded. "The doctor says Papa is on a downward spiral. We should try to contact Jean-Louis and let him know about his condition before it gets worse."

"Since he's never answered our mail or emails, I think we should hire a private detective to find out exactly where he's serving and get word to him while there's still time. Serge has contacts and will know the right person for the job."

"Let's call him now, but tell him we don't want Papa to know what we're doing."

"D'accord."

Nic phoned Serge, who gave him the name of Claude Giraud, a man who'd been in the French secret service and would know how to trace their brother. Once the call had been made, they waited for him to come to the hotel and meet with them in Nic's suite.

"We appreciate your coming on such short notice," Raoul spoke first. "Our brother has been away from the family ten years. He's purposely stayed away and you need to know why. He didn't want anything to do with our family business."

Nic joined in. "We've been known as the trium-virate all our lives and are always in the news. Jean-Louis couldn't take it and we don't blame him for his feelings since we feel the same way. The combination of relentless media exposure, intrusion into our private lives and being treated as if we were all one and the same person was too much for him."

Monsieur Giraud nodded. "So, he joined the military to get away."

"Yes, but our father couldn't handle it from the beginning. He had dreams for the three of us, but Jean-Louis dropped out of business college in Paris where we were all studying. He threatened to join the army and Papa almost had a coronary, but that didn't stop our brother. He left for good and the two of them have been estranged ever since."

Claude shook his head. "How tragic."

"Yes," Raoul agreed. "The silence has been very effective. We don't know where he's deployed, let alone how to get word to him. Our mail goes to an official military mailing address. We'll give you that address. He's never answered one letter we've sent over the years."

"We receive a yearly Christmas card from him, and that's it," Nic supplied. "Now the situation has grown serious because our father is ill and the doctor says he won't recover. Raoul and I want Jean-Louis to know Papa is grieving over the pain he caused ten years ago. I know in my gut our brother has been suffering too. If you can locate him for us, we'll be forever in your debt."

"Money is no object," Raoul added in a solemn tone.

"Be assured I'll do everything possible. I'll let you know the instant I have the news you're waiting for. Do you know the date he joined the army?"

"October fifth or sixth, ten years ago."

"Possibly from Paris. That gives me a starting point. I'll find him."

"Thank you," they said sotto voce.

After Claude left, Nic turned to his brother. "Why don't I order dinner for both of us? Then I want to talk some more about Mademoiselle Lavigny."

Anelise studied the next case sitting on her desk and decided to ponder it over the weekend. An hour later she left headquarters and walked to the *palais* to reach her trusty blue Peugeot in the rear parking area. Her parents were expecting her.

She got in and wound around to the courtyard, where she saw a red Bugatti. It didn't surprise her that the TV star sat at the wheel obviously waiting for someone. No doubt that had to be Nic Causcelle or his brother Raoul. Louis had told her both his sons lived here at the *palais*.

Anelise drove past her and turned onto the street headed for her parents' home in Passy. She loved its cobblestoned streets and tucked-away museums.

Later over dinner she told her parents everything that happened after she left court. "I have to admit I'm shocked that Louis has been forced to retire."

Her father shook his head. "It doesn't surprise me. He's worked nonstop for years to build up his corporation and should have slowed down a year ago. Now he's put his son Nicolas in charge. What do you think of him?"

"I'm afraid the more pertinent question would be what he thinks of me."

Her mother Anne cocked her head. "Why do you say that, darling? You won your first case. That should have impressed him."

"He complimented me. If only I hadn't said anything else."

"Explain yourself," her father interjected.

"Oh, I made the mistake of telling him how much I loved the photograph of the triplets his father showed me from his wallet. It was too personal a remark and I'm afraid it might have upset him."

"In what way?" Her mother sounded perplexed.

"I asked him about the cow in the photo, and that comment led me to pose more questions about the beginnings of the Causcelle empire. It was then I felt a sadness coming from him. Maybe I had intruded too much and he regrets having to work with me."

Her father shook his head. "Nonsense. Something else has to be going on with him. Kind of like the way you sometimes get when someone asks you about Andre." Anelise knew her father was right about that. "Nicolas is too aware of his father's shrewd business sense in hiring you to question it. Give the office politics time."

"You're right." She got up from the table. "I've learned one thing. Never get into anything personal with him again."

"Then you're happy to be there?"

"I hope I will be, Papa."

Her mother looked concerned. "You sound exhausted."

"I am. It was a long day at court. Thank you for dinner and always listening to me." They'd had to do too much of that, and it was long past time she functioned on her own.

She gave both of them a hug, then hurried out of their home to her car. As she drove, she thought she noticed a red Bugatti a few cars behind her. Traffic was heavy, but it might be the same one she'd seen in the *palais* courtyard.

Anelise eventually arrived and pulled around to park. Through the rearview mirror she saw the red car come around, then pull out again. She didn't think this could be a coincidence and felt a frisson of concern. But by the time she rushed inside, she was too tired to think. An early night sounded heavenly. If only Andre were inside waiting for her...

Over the weekend she did some research on the next case and worked on it all day Monday at the office. There'd been no sign of the new CEO. At five, Serge walked in with a strange smile and shut the door. It surprised her since he normally displayed a sterner demeanor. In his hand he held a newspaper. "You and Nicolas are a pair of dark horses. Why didn't you tell me?"

She felt that knot of panic in her stomach. It was kind of like a PTSD reaction to the unexpected after experiencing the fallout after Andre's death. "What do you mean?"

"Stop pretending, Anelise." He grinned and put the

newspaper in front of her. She looked down and noticed an article on the lower half of the second page of *Paris Now*, a lowbrow, alternative afternoon paper. The headline stood out.

"New Love for One of the Bachelor Billionaire Triplets?"

Her gaze fixed on the piece that followed.

For the second time in two years, gorgeous, hunky billionaire Nicolas Causcelle is off the market! All female hopefuls will have to look elsewhere now. Insider sources report that his former fiancée, Denise Fournette, is "devastated" that Causcelle has found love again so soon after brutally casting her off. Sadly she didn't have the financial means to make the grade for a Causcelle.

His new lover is reputed to be media-shy Anelise Lavigny, only child and daughter of multimillionaire Hugo Lavigny. In this case it took money to capture money. Mademoiselle Lavigny was said to be "inconsolable" after losing her engineer fiancé Andre Navarre in a car crash only nineteen months ago, but this liaison between two of France's biggest commercial dynasties seems to have soothed her pain. Who says money doesn't talk?

The Causcelle triplets have long been the target of scheming mamas. Although since one of them seems to have disappeared off the face of the earth, that leaves only two delicious men

*to snap up. Good luck, Mademoiselle Lavigny.
One has to wonder if the golden boy has staying power this time, or if he'll cast you away
in the end.*

Anelise read the article twice while the scorching
heat of fury crept through her entire body. She took
a deep breath and shot to her feet, handing the paper
back to Serge, who was waiting for a response with
a gleam in his eyes. "Someone must hate Monsieur
Causcelle or me so much they were willing to risk
a slander suit in order to get this lie printed for the
whole world to read."

The gleam disappeared. "I'm very sorry."

"So am I. Is Monsieur Causcelle in?"

"He's on a conference call."

"I'm leaving now. Will you tell him I wish to talk
to him when he *is* available? This is my cell phone
number."

"Bien sur."

The moment he was gone, she pulled her purse out
of the drawer and left the building, sizzling with the
kind of rage she'd never known before.

Anelise had been forced to live with the intrusion
of the media for weeks after Andre's death. She'd
tried to hide away in order to grieve in private. But
being an heiress had made her fodder for the press.
The coverage dwelled on her financial assets and
made a mockery out of the most painful experience
of her life. To bring Andre's name into this article and
hurt his family again was unconscionable.

As for the article about Nic Causcelle, it was a major hit piece that had done more damage than a nuclear bomb. Not only was the lie about the two of them horrific, but to expose his former fiancée, and allude to their missing brother was criminal! Both her life and his had been served up to the public like a feast on which millions of people would gorge.

You could print a denial, but no one would care or believe it. By ten tonight the news about the two of them would be all anyone talked about. She refused to stand for it!

She hurried inside her suite and tossed her suit jacket on the couch. The whole thing was so ugly, there was only one thing to do. Anelise would resign immediately and move to Orleans, where she could get an attorney position with the company owned by her mother's family. They manufactured foods and beverages under the name Sabayon et Fils. Living there she would be out of the limelight and could visit her parents on weekends via the A10. It was only an hour-and-a-half drive.

Before she did anything else, she phoned Serge. Forced to leave a message, she said, "I can't work for the Causcelle Corporation a second longer. You know why. I'll turn in my resignation to Monsieur Causcelle, of course. I just wanted you to know I'm making arrangements to leave Paris. Thank you for all you've done for me."

For the next hour she packed her bags, gathered her belongings and took everything out to her car. She'd drive to Orleans tonight in case reporters had already camped on her parents' doorstep waiting for sight of her. Thankfully the author of the slanderous announcement hadn't mentioned her connection to her mother's family and their business interests. Anelise ought to be safe. *For now anyway...*

En route she phoned her parents and told them what had happened. She planned to stay at a bed-and-breakfast in Orleans where no one would know her. At least not for the moment.

"It hasn't been on the news yet."

"Wait till the ten o'clock news, Papa."

"Darling—you can stay with your *tante* Marie."

"No, Maman. I wouldn't do that to her. I'll be fine and will call you when I'm settled." Anelise needed privacy right now.

"Do you think this was retaliation because you won that suit?"

"I don't know."

"It sounds like someone wants revenge," her father exclaimed.

Anelise shuddered to think anyone could be that evil. "I promise I'll call you in a little while. Don't open your door to anyone. Love you."

Heavy traffic made it a two-hour drive. She ate at a drive-through and found a one-bedroom at a bed-and-breakfast where she registered under the last name Mattice, her mother's maiden name.

CHAPTER THREE

AT TEN TO 7:00 P.M., Nic ended the conference call with a Realtor who hadn't been honest with him. He intended to put Helene on the case, but she wouldn't be back in the office for several days because of a family funeral. It would keep until then.

After making a few notes on the case, he got to his feet intending to leave for the night when George buzzed him. "You received a call from Mademoiselle Fournette. She'd like you to call her when you get a chance."

Denise had called him? For the love of heaven, why? They hadn't spoken since their breakup two years ago. "Thanks for telling me."

Just then Serge appeared in the doorway. "I'm glad I caught you in time, Nicolas." The man looked flustered.

"What's wrong?"

"*This*, for one thing." He handed him a newspaper that had been tucked under his arm. "Read what's on the second page, bottom half."

Of course. More gossip about him. Was there nothing *new* anymore?

Nic opened the newspaper and spotted the article immediately. He thought he'd read everything that could be printed or put on TV about him or his brothers. But the evil, vindictive attack on three people in this article, including the reference to their missing brother and her fiancé's lethal car crash, wasn't like anything else.

This was new, all right, scraping the absolute bottom of the proverbial barrel of treacherous lies. The monstrous person who'd done this had tentacles that had reached the corrupt powers of *Paris Now*. Nic's head reared in fury.

"I'm sorry, Nicolas, but there's more. Mademoiselle Lavigny read it and has resigned. You were on that conference call earlier, so she left the office. She wants to talk to you when you're available."

He needed to catch his second wind. Denise's phone call was no longer a mystery. An epithet escaped. "Thank you, Serge." He handed him the newspaper. "I'll call her tonight. Under the circumstances, I won't be in tomorrow. Take care of things, will you?"

"Tres bien." Serge left the office.

One minute later Nic took off. All the way home his mind filed through the people who could have done something so unconscionable. As he entered his suite, Guy rang him.

"Nicolas? I thought you should know Mademoiselle Lavigny has vacated the building for good. She left the key with me."

That woman didn't waste any time. Who could blame her? "Thanks, Guy."

Once off the phone, it rang again. He checked the caller ID. "Thank heaven it's you, Raoul."

"I just got home and saw the article. This has to be the garbage from hell."

"In more ways than one. Denise is trying to reach me, and Anelise resigned to Serge. Not only that, she moved out of her suite."

"I can't say I blame her. What can I do to help?"

"That means a lot. Put out any fires that come your way while I phone Anelise wherever she is. Then I'll call you back."

"D'ac."

He put in a call and paced the floor, waiting for her to answer. It came after the third ring.

"Thank goodness it's you, Monsieur Causcelle."

He gripped his phone tighter. "I know this news has been devastating for you on several levels, Mademoiselle Lavigny."

"I'll be all right." There was no hysteria in her voice, which surprised him. "I went through this myself after Andre was killed. Money can be a curse once the press opens the floodgates. They didn't let up and couldn't think up enough hurtful things to tear me and my family apart, including Andre's. I wanted to run away and keep on running."

Coming from her background, she really did understand. He heard genuine pain in her tone, and sensed how much she'd suffered at her fiancé's death.

"It proves to me how difficult your life must be to live in the limelight, never knowing what will be thrown at you next. I'm so sorry for you and your former fiancée. The cruelty is unspeakable. I don't know how you've survived this long."

He gripped the phone tighter. "At times I'll admit it's been a horror story. Perhaps now you can see why my brother Jean-Louis opted out ten years ago."

"I *do* see. Now he's in another kind of horror story dealing with war." Her words touched him. There was more to her than he'd surmised. It brought out his protective feelings for her, which came as a surprise. "I'm glad you called so I can resign to you. Nothing else needs to be said."

"I'm afraid there is, but not over the phone. Where are you right now?"

"In Orleans."

What was in Orleans? He realized she wasn't in the mood to explain or answer questions. That was all right with him.

"Do me a favor and come back to Paris tomorrow morning. I'll meet you in the gardens at Malmaison at ten. It will give us time and privacy to talk. I'm afraid reporters are lurking everywhere."

"Isn't it full of tourists at that time?"

"Not tomorrow morning." The Causcelle Corporation contributed to the board. He would call the president and ask that it be closed until afternoon.

"I'll be there."

"Good. See you then."

After clicking off, Nic walked over to the window and looked through the shutters. Sure enough he saw a gang of paparazzi ranged outside in the parking lot. Anelise hadn't been far off when she'd worried about reporters being everywhere, even at Malmaison.

That settled it. He knew he needed to take immediate action to remove himself—both for his own security and so the staff here could feel at ease to do their job.

He reached for his phone and called the company that did the painting at the *palais*. He spoke to the owner, Adolphe, explaining there was an emergency. Would he send out a two-man team in their van immediately and come to his suite? They should pull up at the main entrance, and the night watchman would let them in.

While he waited, he changed into jeans and a pullover. Next, he alerted the night watchman, then called to arrange for a car to be waiting for him in front of Adolphe's business.

Soon he heard the elevator door open to his foyer and the two men walked in. "Thanks for coming. Here's a bonus for both of you." He handed them each a bill worth a hundred Euros. "Which one of you is the driver?"

"I am," said the younger Frenchman.

"Good. I need to borrow your hat and your jacket. I'd like you to stay here for ten minutes, then go back outside where a taxi will be waiting to return you to

Adolphe's. I'll be driving the van and your friend back to the business. Any questions?"

"*Non*, monsieur."

The driver handed over his jacket and hat, which Nic put on. Then came the keys.

"Make yourself at home." Nic looked at the other man. "Let's go."

By now it was ten to ten and dark as they left the building. The paparazzi, perched like buzzards waiting for a meal, didn't realize what was happening. They didn't catch on to the subterfuge as he and the other guy got in the van and drove to Adolphe's business. The car Nic had ordered was waiting there, with the keys under the front license plate.

Nic said good-night to the other man, who drove home in his car. Adolphe was still inside the business. Nic gave him the van keys, slipped him a two-hundred-euro bill and explained what was going on. The older man told him to use the facilities inside the next morning before leaving for Malmaison. After shaking hands, Nic went to a drive-through for food before going back to Adolphe's, where he parked around the back with the other vans.

First, he phoned Denise, who was furious and deeply hurt over the whole thing. He commiserated with her, then told her he'd find out the name of the culprit and get back to her. Next he called his brother. "Raoul? Do you think Papa knows anything yet?"

"No. I called Corinne to make sure she didn't let him watch the ten o'clock news or see the newspaper."

"I knew I could count on you. He'll hear about everything soon enough, but not tonight. It's strange. I thought he might have hired Anelise as a willing accomplice to play into his hands to get close to me. How wrong could I have been? She left town and the business so fast, I haven't caught my breath."

"What do you mean?"

"So much has gone on, I haven't had a chance to tell you anything." For the next few minutes he explained about Anelise's reaction and her resignation. "She went through hell herself with the paparazzi when her fiancé died. I can understand why she didn't even wait long enough to talk to me before resigning. I've been wracking my brain trying to figure out who was responsible for this outrageous piece of slander."

"Don't get me wrong, Nic, but is it possible she was so upset to find out Papa retired, she would do something like that? Is it possible she hopes to become CEO one day? Do you think that's why she got out of town so fast?"

Nic sucked in his breath. After hearing her pain earlier, the mere suggestion that she was after something else distressed him. "If that's true, then she's a very sick woman." *And I've lost my faith in people.*

"What about Denise? Is she so bitter that you broke off your engagement, she would go this far?"

"I don't think so. She called me a little while ago. I've never heard her so wounded and upset. I honestly don't think she had anything to do with it."

"Is there a lawsuit going on in the hotel department that has turned ugly?"

Nic ran a hand through his hair. "Not that I'm aware of."

"Well, I'm sure you'll figure it out."

"Our brother had the right idea to leave the family when he did. You know that?"

"Let's not go there, Nic. It's too painful."

"I wonder how long we'll have to wait until Claude locates him."

"Serge says he's the best," Raoul asserted. "That's good enough for me. Right now I'm more concerned with what's happened to you. Someone's gunning for you."

"You're right. Tomorrow I'm having a private meeting with Anelise out at Malmaison. Perhaps between the two of us we can come up with the name of the person who wanted to crucify me and smear the Causcelle name, and vilified two innocent women in the process."

"I'll help all I can."

"You think I don't know that? *Merci*, Raoul, but you should be in bed. I'll call you tomorrow."

After they clicked off, Nic lowered the back of the seat and closed his eyes, emotionally exhausted. Five hours later he awakened and slipped inside the building to freshen up. Knowing he wouldn't go back to sleep, he stopped at a café for coffee, then left for Rueil-Malmaison about twenty minutes away.

Soon he drove into the estate. Josephine Beauharnais had bought the land and the dilapidated manor before her second husband, General Napoleon Bonaparte, returned from his campaign in Egypt.

He'd been in a fury over the expense, but she'd used her money to restore the house and grounds. Malmaison meant "ill-fated home" in old French, dating back to the Vikings. Considering Napoleon's downfall, including his not being able to have babies with Josephine, Nic found the place well named.

As for Nic's own misfortunes, the one thing he'd learned in his life was that everything came down to money. Whether too much of it or too little, nothing else mattered and none of it brought happiness. He'd never been able to trust the women he'd been involved with. He would always have the deep-seated fear they loved his money more than him.

Like he told Raoul, their brother Jean-Louis had gotten completely away from it and all the sins greed and covetousness had spawned throughout history. Maybe it wasn't too late for Nic, who'd never felt so desolate. He wound around to the back area and saw one lone car parked.

Anelise hadn't visited Malmaison since she was fifteen years old. She remembered the black swans on the beautiful lake and the huge variety of roses. All of it originated from the inspiration of the Empress Josephine, who'd bought the château in 1799 and had created the world she'd born to in Martinique.

That visit had been a happy time for Anelise with her parents. But not *this* morning. There were no swans out and it was too early in the season for roses.

She supposed it was the isolation that prompted Monsieur Causcelle to suggest they meet here. Not knowing what to expect, she'd parked near the entrance. Once she'd officially resigned to him, it would be over.

A darkening sky meant there could be rain within a few hours. The elements matched her state of mind. She felt a horrifying emptiness inside. It frightened her to get this down after what she'd gone through losing Andre. The old adage that you could choose to be happy or unhappy had no meaning for her on this cool May morning. She couldn't bear the thought of losing her sanity again because the media was after her over the situation now. Maybe she'd just disappear.

A tap on the rear window jerked her out of her torturous thoughts and she turned around to see a tall man through the glass, his black hair disheveled. He wore a navy blue crew neck sweater and jeans, with a slight shadow on his jaw. At first glance she had a hard time believing it was Nicolas Causcelle. On Friday, the only time she'd ever seen him, he'd been dressed in a suit and clean shaven. She put down her window at his approach.

"I see you're an early bird like me and I appreciate it," he murmured in a deep voice. With shuttered dark eyes, he looked as if he hadn't slept for a long time. But it didn't take away from his unmatchable male potency.

"Only after being attacked in the news."

"It was an attack all right. That's what we need to talk about. Shall we walk over to the lake?"

Anelise swung her jean-clad legs around and got out. He had to be six-three. In her high heels at work, she hadn't noticed the difference in their height. But in leather sandals, her five-foot-six frame felt petite by comparison. They walked toward the water.

"When I talked it over with my parents, my father felt that the hideous piece in the paper announcing Andre's death all over again was an evil act of revenge."

He nodded. "I *know* it was, otherwise you and my former fiancée wouldn't have been mentioned."

"Agreed." She made sure her hair clip was in place, then eased her peach-colored sweater down lower on her hips. "Still, no matter how cruel the intention, you and I both have the satisfaction of knowing one thing."

"What's that?"

"The culprit willing to go to the press to humiliate you has to be living in a world of hurt neither of us can imagine."

He looked down at her. "That's a kind way of putting a malicious action."

"I've given it a lot of thought. No one would do something like that unless they were beyond desperate for your attention." She stared up into those cold bleak pools. "Do you know anyone fitting that description?"

"Millions of people and I know why."

She laughed softly, knowing it had been a foolish question. "Do you have a way of finding out who influenced *Paris Now* to print it?"

"I could, but I'd rather discover the source with your help. You found the problem in the merger at court last week and won the case. With your intelligence, it's possible we'll figure out the name of this wretched soul."

They walked along, listening to the birdsong in the trees. "Has this ever happened to you before?"

One dark brow quirked. "Raoul and I are in the news constantly, but this is something new."

"In other words, the article was personally vindictive in the most destructive way imaginable."

"*Exactement*, just like it was for you."

Anelise finally dared to say what was on her mind, but couldn't meet his eyes. "Forgive me if this seems impertinent, but it sounds like a woman. Have you been seeing someone who *wants* to be all important to you?"

He stopped walking. "If there were such a person, I would have dealt with her already."

She turned to him. "Since your father hired me, do you think another woman wanted the position I was given in order to get close to you?"

He rubbed his jaw. "I'm sure there are many female attorneys who'd like to work for us. But since I wasn't even a consideration as head of the hotel department when Papa offered you the job, that scenario doesn't fit."

Thoughts were firing in her mind. "Was your former fiancée an attorney?"

"No. Denise was a well-brought-up young woman of Parisian society my father felt would make me an excellent wife. I'll answer your next question before you ask it. Neither of us were in love, but I liked her better than any woman I'd met and thought we could make a go of it. It didn't work and she had an affair.

"That woke me up and I refused to go through life living a lie, not when both of us needed something more. So, I broke off the engagement. It was an amicable separation, but my father wasn't happy about it."

"Of course not. Has she seen the article?"

"Yes. We've talked about it and I'm convinced she wasn't the one who planted the story. Otherwise, she would never have gotten involved with another man in the first place. She needs to find happiness."

"So do you."

"We all do." Then she heard a sigh. "I'm afraid happiness is an elusive quality."

His lonely comment got to her. "I was happy with Andre. Truthfully, I can't imagine living with a man I couldn't love heart and soul, or who couldn't love me the same way."

He studied her face with new intensity. "Yours was a true love affair."

"Yes. Andre was my whole life."

"I'm sorry that happened."

So am I. "But it did." She smiled at him, wanting desperately to put the sadness behind her. "What I don't understand is why this person linked *my* name with you."

He cocked his dark head. "Do *you* have an enemy? Someone at your law school who was jealous of you? Serge said you were top in your class. He was very impressed."

"That's propaganda," she scoffed. "I guess we

could all name a person who would wish us harm, but I haven't the faintest idea who that would be."

His penetrating gaze found hers. "What about a woman who might have loved your former fiancé and lost him to you?"

Anelise shook her head. "There was no one else for either of us. After his death and my graduation from law school, I worked at my father's company for a few months. I felt I was friends with everyone in the head office. Then your father contacted me. As I understand it, no one knew about it until he offered it to me, so the position at Causcelle was never posted."

"Papa keeps his cards close to the chest. Your appointment came as a surprise to everyone."

"Monsieur Causcelle, is there—?"

"Drop the monsieur and call me Nic," he interrupted her. "Now go on. What were you going to ask?"

She shifted her weight as they stood on the gravel. "Do you think one of *your* sisters would have liked the position I was given? Perhaps even coveted it?"

He actually burst into laughter, the deep male kind. It was the first time she'd ever seen him smile or laugh. The man was incredibly appealing. "My sisters didn't study law and wouldn't be caught dead in a courtroom. They love the pastoral life too much. Papa knew it. However, when his triplets came along, he was determined to change all that. But it didn't work."

Anelise eyed him frankly. "In other words, he couldn't take the pastoral out of his boys either."

There she went again, speaking her mind before thinking how it would affect him.

"If you knew Raoul, you'd see a case in point."

"Forgive me. I should never have said anything. What about your extended family? I understand your father has a brother."

"Two actually. Our *oncle* Raimond, who heads the estate in La Racineuse and plans to die on the job he loves. The other one is our *oncle* Blaise. He's a professor of Latin and Greek here in Paris and uninterested in the family business, but his married son, Pascal, works with Raoul and me. We all get along great. Pascal is our age and a big entrepreneur like Papa."

"I can see that no one in your family is out to hurt you."

"But it's not beyond the realm of possibility," he added. "Keep thinking with that razor-sharp brain of yours. Together we'll come up with the answer."

"I don't know. Do I dare ask if Serge or Helene resent me coming into the company?"

He put his hands on his hips. "Those two were handpicked by my father years ago. They would never question his decision to hire you since I understand they told him they needed another person in there."

"I see." She spotted a bench in the distance and started walking toward it.

"Let's sit down and pool our resources, Anelise. Mind if I call you that?"

"Of course not."

He sat next to her. "I know you're planning to resign, but I'd rather you didn't. For one thing my father needed another attorney and you were his choice. I want you to have the chance to build your career here. We know that attack was aimed at me and I don't want it to be the reason you leave. I say we fight this thing through and eventually the guilty party will emerge."

"How do we fight when everyone will now assume we're a couple?"

"They'll assume more than that and you know it," he asserted, "so let's turn the lie into reality. Instead of my suing the paper and ruining them and the culprit in court, it might fun to let it stand. I have a plan. What would you think if we pretend to be madly in love? When we show up at the office tomorrow as an engaged couple, we'll convince them that money has nothing to do with our intense attraction."

Her head reared. It took a minute before her heart rate returned to some semblance of normal. "You're not serious."

A devilish smile curved a corner of his mouth, making him too gorgeous by far. "I can't think of anything more satisfying. This person who is out to destroy me won't believe their malicious joke has turned on them. You and I will be the nine-day wonder of the media and voted the most in-love pair in history."

"The press *would* print something like that." Her voice shook. "You're right. The headlines would be spectacular."

"The press will have a field day. Every article and photo of us together will plunge the dagger deeper into our adversary, making the backfire complete. During that time, we'll catch the person who thought they'd destroyed three people. When they see their ploy didn't work, they won't be able to stay quiet about it."

Anelise got up from the bench. "Your plan makes a strange kind of sense, but I need to talk this over with my parents first. If you don't mind, I'm going to drive back to Paris now and see them."

He walked her toward her car. "Call me from their home after your visit. If you decide not to go along with my plan, we'll think of another one. Let me give you my cell phone number."

She reached in her purse for her cell and he put his number in the phone. Once ensconced in the car, she looked up at him. "There's a lot to think about. I'm just afraid the paparazzi will already be installed outside my parents' home."

"It's possible, but I know you'll handle it." She took his comment as a compliment. "Thank you for meeting me here, Anelise. No matter what we decide, I feel better than I did when I drove in."

His trait of honesty could only be admired. So could his calm in the face of such a horrible situation. "I know what you mean. Expect a call from me in the next couple of hours."

A half hour later she found her parents eating lunch in their breakfast room. To her surprise and relief, their home wasn't under surveillance yet, but it wouldn't be long. That was probably because the press was still focused on Nic.

"You're back from Orleans!" her mother cried in surprise. "Just in time to enjoy a meal with us."

She sat down at the table. "I met Nic at Malmaison earlier this morning. We've been talking everything over."

"We've been talking too," her father interjected.

"He has a plan, Papa, but I told him I wanted to run it by you first."

"I'd like to hear it." His blue eyes smiled. "If he's the genius his father is, it ought to be a good one."

"Nic doesn't want to take the newspaper to court or find the person who had that article printed and sue them. He's not only asked me to stay on with the corporation, he would like us to pretend we're an engaged couple madly in love. His theory is that it will boomerang on the culprit responsible and we'll find out who it is." She looked away. "His suggestion is as outrageous as the smear piece in the paper."

"But very clever," came her mother's unexpected comment.

Her father started to chuckle. "Your mother's right, and I have my answer. He's Louis's son all right. It's the kind of thing he would have done himself."

Her mother nodded. "Those triplets have been chased and harassed for years. Nicolas has been in the news since his breakup with his former fiancée. The press has speculated who will be next. Nic has a real point. His pretend engagement to you will kill the endless curiosity about him. In time the journalists will concentrate on his brother Raoul, poor thing."

Anelise stared at both of them. "But *I* can't pretend to be his fiancée in order to keep my job."

"Of course not, sweetheart."

"We're strangers to each other. He's a troubled man, and—"

"You're still mourning Andre's passing," her mother broke in, reaching out to pat her hand.

"My dear daughter," her father began, sitting back in the chair. "Louis asked you to come and work for him for a very important reason. I never did tell you about the beginning of our friendship three years ago. It's time you heard our story."

Anelise had always wondered and sensed this revelation was of vital importance.

"I had stopped to eat at a café on the Rue Saint-Dominique in Paris when a man ran in with a gun and killed another man at the bar."

"*What?* How awful!" she cried.

"It was. After he disappeared, probably through a back door, the police came and everyone inside was detained for questioning. Two people said they thought *I* was the man who'd fired the fatal shot, but the gun was nowhere to be found."

"I don't believe it." Anelise shook her head, astounded.

"Another man stepped forward and told the police I *wasn't* the killer. He said he'd seen the man up close and the shooter was wearing an unusual signet ring with a snake on it. I was taken to police headquarters and there was a lineup. I swore on my life that I wasn't the accused man, but I was put under house arrest."

Her mother put a hand to her heart. "I lived in agony for a week. You'll never know how awful it was."

"For me too." Her father nodded. "The man who

swore I wasn't the accused man paid my exorbitant bail. A week later the killer, the member of a notorious gambling group who wore that ring, was found. And the man who stood by me was Louis Causcelle."

"*That's* how you met?" Anelise was incredulous.

He smiled. "Since that day, we've been good friends, but agreed to keep the entire incident private from everyone, even our families. Your mother was the exception. I gave him back the bail money. When I tried to give him the title to a business I had bought, he refused it. He said he didn't want a reward. But since he knew you were in law school, Anelise, he promised he would hire my daughter when you became an attorney as a form of recompense. He said he needed a brilliant one he could trust."

"I'm finally beginning to understand." Anelise's voice trailed. This was her father's unspoken plea that she go along with Nic's plan.

"Louis was such a good man and had a hard time after losing his wife," her mother interjected. "They had three daughters, and then she died giving birth to triplet boys. He's been a wonderful father. We're both proud of our children," she added. "I just hope Louis hasn't learned about that terrible article in the paper."

"I'm sure he has, Maman."

"Nothing escapes Louis," her father assured them, "but he knows his son will handle it. Otherwise, Nicolas wouldn't have been put in charge as CEO of the hotel division." He smiled at Anelise. "However, where you're concerned, you do whatever it is you feel you have to do in order to be comfortable. You're welcome to come back to work with me, or work for your mother's family. Maybe you'd rather do something else entirely different."

Oh, Papa. For once he was transparent as glass.

"Absolutely," her mother complied. "We're here for you always."

"I know that. You're saints."

Her parents laughed, but her thoughts were on Nic. Did *he* somehow hear the story behind their fathers' close relationship? Was that why Nic had suggested he and Anelise pretend to be engaged? Because he knew his father wanted to keep the promise he'd once made to Hugo? That was something she had to find out. She wanted to remain with the corporation for her own merits.

"If you two will excuse me? I have to make a phone call." She got up from the table and went into the salon.

Do whatever it is you feel you have to do in order to be comfortable.

CHAPTER FOUR

AFTER A SHOWER in his suite, Nic was shaving when his cell rang. He reached for it and wandered into the bedroom. It was Mademoiselle Lavigny. His pulse quickened before he clicked on. "Anelise?"

"Hello, Nic." She sounded strangely quiet.

"Are you all right?"

"That's my question to you. I don't know what I am. Before anything else, I need you to be honest with me about something important."

He frowned. "I'll do my best."

"Your father and mine met three years ago and became friends. Do you know the reason why?"

Her question was the last thing he would have expected. "I've always been curious, but I have no idea."

"That's the truth?" Her question penetrated his insides.

"I don't lie, Anelise, but it's clear you've asked me that for a reason."

After a slight pause, "I just learned about it today. Your answer has helped me make the most important decision of my life to date."

He gripped the phone tighter. "Which is?"

"If you want me to go on working for you and pretend we're engaged and mad about each other, I'm willing to do it until the culprit comes out of the woodwork."

Nic's tense body relaxed at her words. "It's the answer I was hoping for, but we need to see each other in person before we talk strategy. I'll want honesty from you too. Be prepared to tell me how and why our two fathers became friends. Will you do that?"

"I promise."

"Where are you right now?"

"My parents' home."

"Since you know the way to the *palais*, Guy will show you the elevator to my suite."

"But the paparazzi—"

"Don't worry. I've doubled security on the parking lot. I also added your name to the approved list at the desk. You'll be able to get in without being challenged or accosted. How does that sound?"

"I can't ask for more than that."

"*Bon.* We'll talk over a late lunch."

"Fine. I'll be there shortly." She ended their call.

He ordered a light meal, then alerted Guy and got dressed in a sport shirt and chinos. A half hour later the same woman he'd watched drive away from Malmaison entered the foyer from the elevator.

"Thanks for getting here so quickly, Anelise. No problem in the parking area?"

"No. I saw four guards."

"Good. I didn't know until Friday night that you'd

been living here for the last month. Come in the salon and make yourself comfortable."

Nic had enjoyed relationships with several women over the years, but he'd never entertained another woman in his suite, not even Denise. Though engaged, they'd maintained separate residences. He'd always needed some time alone in his life and this suite was the best place for him. Because of this latest smear article, his whole order of life had been disturbed in a brand-new way.

His only consolation for asking Anelise to go along with his plan rested in the knowledge that she'd lost her fiancé. Her emotions were no more involved with Nic than his with hers. Their one expectation was to expose the person who'd upended their world. Once discovered, they could put the ghastly incident behind them.

"I know you're as anxious as I am to get this over with." She found a place on one end of the sofa and sat back looking relaxed as she crossed her elegant jean-clad legs.

He sat down on a chair opposite her. "Before we go any further, I'd like you to keep the promise you made to me over the phone. What you said has aroused my curiosity."

Her gaze met his. "It's a touching story about both our fathers. I know my father would never have told me anything if that article hadn't been printed." The wistfulness in her voice, the hint of tears, got to him. In the next few minutes, she'd told him everything. "Since your father knew the same mind-blowing thing could have happened to him, he did everything he could to clear my father's name."

Astounded and moved by what he'd learned, Nic got to his feet and walked around the salon.

Anelise kept talking. "Your father is a saint, with a compassion rare to most people. It's no wonder my father has felt indebted to him and wanted him for his friend. It puts everything in a new light." By now she was wiping her eyes. "Who would ever have thought that was how the two of them met."

"Not in a million years."

"To see someone shot to death, and then be blamed for it. I can't comprehend it."

Nic sucked in his breath. "I'm still trying to wrap my head around the fact that my father testified over your father's innocence and paid his bail. If he hadn't come forward—if the real killer hadn't been caught—your father might have ended up in prison!"

She nodded. "You'll never know my father's joy when your father offered me the position, Nic."

"You became the sacrificial lamb."

"I'd do it again knowing what I know now. The important thing at this stage is to prove myself to you and your father."

"You already have by winning your first case."

No one in Nic's family knew the story. Yet his father had confided his pain over Jean-Louis to Anelise because she was Hugo's daughter. Nic felt shame, not only that he'd ever believed his father would try to force him into marriage, but that Anelise would be a part of that plan.

Louis had really liked Denise and had felt she'd make Nic a wonderful wife, but Nic searched his heart and knew his father had never pressured him to marry her. Nic had allowed his hurt over the problem with their brother to think the worst about his father, but Anelise's revelation had changed everything.

"I'm profoundly grateful that you've confided this to me, Anelise. Let's go in the dining room and start planning our next move while we eat."

He'd asked the waiter from the kitchen to set things up and got no argument from Anelise. She appeared hungry too while they enjoyed a chef salad and croissants.

"Are your things still in Orleans?"

"No. I only stayed there overnight at a bed-and-breakfast. I'd planned to work for my mother's family there, but you called so I came back to Paris."

"Where are your things?"

"In my car."

"I mean furnishings."

"At my parents' home."

He lowered his coffee cup. "I've given it a lot of thought and am proposing you move into my suite until we catch this person. There's a guest room that's never been used. Just so you know, Denise and I never lived together. It will be yours. Since everyone will think the worst anyway, it will make it easy for us to walk to work every day and discuss cases. It will keep the rumor alive until we want it to die down."

"I think it's a good idea that could work." She finished her roll.

He smiled. "Let's slip down to your car right now and bring up your luggage."

"I only have two suitcases."

"Heaven," he murmured.

She laughed as they left the suite and retrieved her belongings. Once back inside, he walked her into the empty bedroom. "Behold your new home. After you've freshened up in your en suite bathroom, we'll go shopping and celebrate our engagement at the revamped Jules Verne Restaurant at the *Tour Eiffel*."

Her head lifted. "When?"

"Tonight. What better time to nail the person who's waiting for me to retaliate?"

A smile lit up her face. "They'll never see *this* coming. Ooh, I'm glad I have my black dress with me. We know the press won't be able to contain their joy when you show up there. Give me an hour."

His dark brows lifted. "Only one? You're an amazing woman."

"Keep that thought while we get ready to convince our world audience it's a match made in heaven."

Nic chuckled and left her bedroom. Now that she'd agreed to go along with his plan, he was excited to begin the great deception. There was no time to lose. After changing into a black tuxedo, Nic phoned his brother.

"*Eh bien*, Raoul. You have no idea what has happened since the last time we talked." In the next few minutes he told him his plan. "We'll know if we've aroused curiosity when we watch the ten o'clock news tonight. I've already phoned Corinne so she won't let

Papa watch it. I should be home by eleven and I'll call to tell you more. Hang on to your hat."

"I'm already planted in front of my TV."

For the next hour Nic made a dozen phone calls in order to turn this evening into front-page news that would reach across Europe.

The last call went to the manager at Causcelle's luxury cars. "Bonsoir, Pierre."

"Monsieur Causcelle? It's an honor to hear from you. How can I help? If you need today's report, I have it here."

"*Non, non.* That won't be necessary. What I need is for you to ask Rudi to bring *la voiture noire* to the *palais.*" Bugatti's latest eighteen-million-dollar design was the new rage. "Tell him to leave it and the keys with the valet. I'll need it for this special night as soon as he arrives."

"Of course, monsieur. We'll get it ready immediately. May I ask why this is such a special night, or is it a secret?"

"It won't be one for long."

"How exciting. Enjoy it!"

"*Merci*, Pierre.

Nic could have called a dealership selling the twenty-eight-million-dollar Rolls-Royce Boat Tail, but he wanted to use his family business. Even more, he knew Pierre would tell everyone in sight. The man loved cars, but gossip was his major business. Nic imagined the paparazzi would already be here to take pictures when he and Anelise walked out to get in the car. This was going to be a fun night forcing the culprit from the shadows.

When he thought about it, he realized he hadn't had this feeling of sheer fun in years.

Anelise phoned her parents to tell them what she and Nic had decided to do. Both of them approved of his plan.

After hanging up, she hurried to turn herself into an ecstatic, love-struck woman engaged to one of the famous Causcelle triplets.

Once showered, she applied makeup. A little liner for her eyes, a pink frost lipstick and some blusher. She chose to wear her pearl earrings. Next came the dress. The only one that would work was a classic black sheath with spaghetti straps. She'd bought it to wear with Andre, but he'd died before she'd had the chance.

Until now she hadn't imagined ever putting it on, but this pretend engagement provided the perfect opportunity. Tonight she was glad she'd decided to hold on to it for an important occasion. She would combine it with her strappy black high heels and small black-beaded clutch bag.

After brushing out her hair that fell to her shoulders from a side part, she sprayed on a little fragrance. At last, she felt ready and opened the bedroom door. Her heart pounded as she walked into the salon, hoping she would live up to Nic's expectation of a Causcelle fiancée.

He stood near the couch with one hand holding

his phone. The coloring of his olive skin and vibrant black hair took her breath. He'd dressed in a black tuxedo and ruffled white shirt, the epitome of an unbelievably gorgeous man. A moan came out of nowhere to escape her throat. Nic must have heard it and their gazes connected. She felt him study every inch of her before hanging up.

"Forgive me," sounded his deep voice. "I've been waiting for Anelise Lavigny. Do you happen to know where she might be?"

She played along, enjoying his sense of humor. When she'd first met him, his serious demeanor had led her to believe he didn't possess one. "I think she left with a man named Nicolas Causcelle."

He moved closer to her. "You'll have to forgive me if I hardly recognize you."

"You took the words right out of my mouth."

His midnight eyes had come alive. "The only thing missing in this scenario is a diamond ring befitting your beauty. We'll take care of that after we leave here."

"I can hardly wait," she teased.

"Be aware of photojournalists watching our every move."

"I'll follow your lead."

A smile broke the corner of his compelling mouth. "Shall we go?"

They walked through the salon to the entrance hall and got in his private elevator. Anticipation for the night ahead with this unusual man left her a little breathless. But she came close to losing it altogether when they exited the *palais* and she saw a sleek black car parked outside the entrance.

If there were flashbulbs from the reporters photographing them, she never gave it a thought. Being with Nic made her feel protected. She'd lost her fear of the media. Right now her thoughts were on the ruse they were playing. She liked the idea of getting back at the press and had never been more excited.

Nic helped her in and walked around to get behind the steering wheel.

He flashed her a glance. "What do you think?"

Without conscious thought she cried, *"Holy Bugatti!"*

A round of deep male laughter poured out of him, the happiest sound she'd ever heard.

"Nic Causcelle—I think you're a new incarnation of Batman come to earth in a revolutionary Batmobile. Will we be flying to the Eiffel Tower?"

"Not quite." He still fought laughter. "We have a stop to make at ground level first."

He drove like Mario Andretti, leaving any reporters far behind in their wake. Before long they parked outside Xan, the most famous, expensive jeweler in Paris.

Anelise had seen pictures of the designer. She was an attractive blonde genius renowned for her unique collections that drew the rich and famous, kings and queens, from around the world. This was heady stuff. Anelise needed to be careful she kept her feet on the ground throughout this whole charade.

"Are you ready? This is it."

She glanced at him. "I'm dying to see what happens next."

"In your first life I think you were a private investigator."

"Maybe."

He levered himself from the driver's seat and came around for her. This time when she got out, he put his arm around her waist and ushered her inside. The elegant store had a few well-dressed customers, but the way he held her close to his hard body, she couldn't think.

Xan herself hurried over to speak to Nic and welcomed him like an old friend. "I'm honored you would come."

"I wouldn't have gone to anyone else. Xan? Please meet my fiancée, Anelise Lavigny, the love of my life." To Anelise's shock, he leaned close and kissed her on the mouth with surprising warmth, which she reciprocated. "We need a very special ring."

The woman smiled. "If you can tear yourself away from her long enough to come into my office, Nicolas, we'll figure things out."

Anelise blushed before Nic put his arm around her shoulders and followed the designer to the private office at the end of the store. She told them to sit down at the case in front of her. "After you called me, I gathered a variety of my favorites for you. Take your time looking. I'll be back. This will be the most important ring you'll ever wear." She left the room.

Nic clasped her left hand and lifted it to his lips. "What do you think? I want you to be happy."

They didn't have to pretend right now, but Nic had gotten in character and she didn't want to let him down. "All of these diamond rings leave me speechless. They're beyond my range of imagination."

She thought about the one-carat princess cut diamond ring Andre had given her. It sat in her jewel box at her parents' home. He'd picked it out ahead of time. She'd thought if she ever married one day and had a daughter, she'd give it to her.

Nic squeezed her hand a little tighter. "Which one draws your eye the most?"

"I admit there is one, but the diamond in that intricate gold setting is far too large."

Nic nodded. "It's the round solitaire set in white gold, isn't it? That one caught my attention first. I surmise it's eight carats. You have excellent taste, Anelise. Xan says the round shape brings out the most sparkle and brilliance of all the diamonds." He reached for it and slid it onto her ring finger. It actually fit!

Just then Xan came back. "Ah—you've chosen my favorite. Did you know the round shape represents eternal love? I've found over the years that those who love this cut are inwardly trustworthy, traditional and honest."

He nodded. "The ring found the right woman all right. We'll take it."

Anelise looked into those black eyes smiling at her. "Y-you mean it, Nic?" she stammered, hardly able to get the words out.

"It's made for you, *ma belle*." He kissed her with

passion right in front of Xan. Once again it was impossible to judge what was real and what wasn't. Her head swam as he touched one of her pearl earrings. "These are lovely, but tonight calls for the diamond earrings in the other case. I like the clusters."

Xan pulled out the tray while Nic removed the pearls and put them in his tuxedo jacket. The touch of his hands and skin on her body had sent darts of electricity through her. Did he know what he was doing to her? The designer placed the tray in front of them.

"Let me put these on you, Anelise. These represent eight carats of diamonds to match your ring," he whispered. She tried to sit still while he adorned her ears. Xan gave her a hand mirror to look into. They sparkled through her hair and she felt transformed.

"Perfection," Xan declared with genuine charm.

"One more thing. We'd like to see that diamond pave bracelet over there," he added. Xan brought it and he fastened it on Anelise's right wrist. It was dazzling in the light, causing her to gasp.

"Stay right there you two while I take a picture for my personal portfolio."

Anelise was so mesmerized, she couldn't have moved while the designer used her phone camera to snap them. On impulse Anelise kissed Nic first to thank him, and suddenly he was responding hungrily. She knew the other woman was taking pictures of that kiss too.

Once he relinquished her mouth, he helped her up from the chair and turned to Xan. "Thank you for your invaluable help and your artistry. This is a moment we'll remember all our lives. Now we have to leave or we'll be late for our own engagement celebration."

"Your business means the world to me." She walked them to the entrance of the store.

Half a dozen members of the press taking pictures had gathered around the car parked outside along with a crowd of spectators. Nic fielded the questions with a heartbreaking smile no woman could resist. As he helped her in, he gave her a swift kiss on the lips that would be caught by every camera.

The Eiffel Tower stood 1,063 feet tall on the Champ de Mars, not that far from the jewelry store. She noticed the seven thirty traffic moving toward it had grown heavier, but she couldn't take her eyes off the engagement ring and bracelet.

"It's hard to believe that some people can actually buy the kind of jewels I'm wearing. When I was in *ecole primaire*, we read a book that had a story about a boy who found a pile of jewels in the forest left by the fairies. Even on the page they seemed to sparkle. I kept the book and turned to that page over and over again for years, feasting my eyes on their brilliance and wishing I could handle them.

"Tonight, not a fairy but a man put sparkling jewels on my finger, wrist and ears. I know I only get to wear them for a little while, but I've been granted an old wish. When you conceived the plan to expose the culprit, I never dreamed I'd have the time of my life doing it with you."

He had to stop for a light and looked at her. "If you

want to know the truth, I've never had more fun and I find it astonishing that there's a woman alive this easy to work with, let alone please."

His words found their way inside her until they reached the parking area outside the famous monument. "It's a good thing I've already ordered dinner. From the look of the crowd gathering, we'll be lucky to make it before closing time."

"Except they wouldn't close knowing *you're* coming," she quipped. Together they made their way through people taking pictures and entered the exclusive electric elevator taking them directly to the restaurant. His strong arms went around her as they ascended, making her feel safe and cherished. *Remember this isn't real, Anelise. Don't get carried away.*

The maître d'hôtel met them the second they stepped inside. He fell all over Nic after greeting him.

"Marcel? May I introduce my beautiful fiancée, Anelise Lavigny."

"Ooh, la-la," the older man said with a twinkle in his eyes. "It's my great pleasure to meet you, Mademoiselle Lavigny." His eyes fastened on her ring. "May your union last forever."

He showed them through the room to the only table with a large floral arrangement and lighted candles. It had been centered at the window overlooking Paris. The other tables had been placed farther away to give them privacy.

Marcel moved the arrangement to one end so Nic and Anelise could see each other as they sat across from each other. "The wine steward will be right with you. Bon appétit. Let me know if there's anything you need."

"Everything looks perfect. *Merci*, Marcel."

Nic reached for her left hand and massaged her palm. "So far we've aroused the insatiable curiosity of everyone in this room including undercover journalists. By the time we finish dinner and leave, it's possible the person responsible for bringing us together will be among the diners."

"Let's hope so."

The sommelier poured the vintage wine Nic had ordered. He raised his glass and clinked the one she was holding. "To the most successful adventure of our lives."

Anelise couldn't help but smile. "May our triumph teach this person a lesson that will change their life, hopefully for the better."

"You think that's possible?" They both drank some. Over the rim of his glass, he stared at her. "I'm trying to decide what color of blue describes your eyes. In the candlelight they glow like sapphires, but in the jewelry store they reflected ultramarine."

"Mother says they're like sea glass. My father has always called them baby blues."

Nic smiled. "You *are* his baby."

She chuckled. "Your eyes are different in different lights too."

He leaned forward. "Black is black."

"Oh, no. Black is a shade, not a color, but it takes on many nuances. When I first met you, they looked a dull black like gunmetal."

"Seriously." She'd surprised him.

"Yes, as if you were worlds away. But when we sat in your office and I brought up some personal matters that I feared offended you, they turned black like India ink."

"What matters are you talking about?"

"The photograph and talk of your brother in the military."

He shook his head. "I wasn't offended, only surprised you knew so much, yet we'd never met."

"I'm truly sorry about that. Later at Malmaison your eyes didn't seem quite as stormy black. As for tonight, they're hard to describe."

"Try. I'm fascinated."

Her heart pounded in her throat. "Alive, like the velvety fur of a black panther in the moonlight."

At this point their Chateaubriand for two with béarnaise sauce arrived, interrupting her. The filet steak melted in her mouth. Crème brûlée followed for dessert.

"This has always been my favorite from childhood," he volunteered before eating every bit of it. She saw the schoolboy in him.

"I can tell. The black of your eyes is on fire. I love this dessert too."

"Your eyes have turned an exquisite azure. In future that's the color I'll look for to know how happy you are."

She took a quick breath. "How well do you think our ruse is working so far?"

Nic finished his wine. "As far as publicity goes,

we'll know a certain amount tonight when we get home and watch the ten o'clock news." He glanced at his watch. "It's recording now. The totality will be apparent tomorrow when we see the morning headlines."

To her surprise he got up from the table and pulled a white rose from the arrangement. Before she knew what was happening, he walked around to her. After kissing her shoulder, he tucked the stem of it under the spaghetti strap for everyone to see. The intimate gesture left her weak as a puddle. "Shall we go?"

Could she?

CHAPTER FIVE

ANELISE GATHERED AS much strength as she was able and got to her feet, clinging to the table until she felt stable. Nic slid his arm behind her waist and guided her across the room to the elevator. All eyes followed their progress. Some diners who must have known Nic nodded to him, but he concentrated on her.

They entered the elevator, but they might as well have been riding a meteor through the universe before reaching the ground. She'd lived in Paris all her life, but it had never appeared more magical.

Once outside the elevator she could tell the crowd of journalists and paparazzi had enlarged. With so many spectators, she couldn't see the car. Nic pulled her close and buried his face in her hair. "Is there any question we're getting more than enough splash?"

"It's so dreadful it's no wonder your brother ran for his life."

"*Dieu merci* we have an infallible method of escape."

She'd never been so thankful to reach the car. The crowd parted for them. Nic brushed her lips with his own before helping her in. After he went around to his side, he pressed the accelerator and they were off with a roar of the engine.

"Did you see the look on that journalist's face when we whizzed past him?" she cried. "I doubt he was able to get a picture until it was too late." Suddenly they both started to laugh, needing a release of tension.

Nic eyed her, his handsome face reflecting a happiness she hadn't seen until now. "He and a dozen others. What an amazing night, Anelise."

Indeed it was. The term "wined and dined" had taken on a whole new meaning she'd never forget. She turned her head to smell the sweet fragrance of the rose. He had no idea her body still throbbed from the feel of skin against skin.

When they arrived at the *palais* in record time, she blurted, "You really *were* a race car driver in another life."

His husky chuckle amused her. "Running away from the press may have made me an expert behind the wheel. But a racing career would only increase the media's coverage on me."

She nodded. "You're right. Tell me something. Even though you weren't born a singlet, what would you have pursued if you could have thrown off your business chains?"

Anelise loved it when he laughed. He unlocked the car doors. "A research scientist."

"Truly?"

"Cross my heart, but an explanation will take some

time. I'll tell you upstairs later. Several cars followed us in here and now I'm tired of us being the target."

With his help she got out. As she turned, she glimpsed the back of a red car in the periphery, but it took off behind two other cars so fast, she wasn't sure of the make.

He grasped her arm and they entered the building. A younger-looking security guard she didn't recognize was on duty at the desk. "Bonsoir, Monsieur Causcelle," he said while his eyes roved over Anelise with unabashed male interest. "Congratulations on your engagement. When I came on duty a few minutes ago, Guy told me the news. I'll be covering for him for the rest of the week while he's on vacation."

"*Merci*, Robert. Give these keys to the valet and please meet my fiancée, Mademoiselle Lavigny."

"It's a pleasure, mademoiselle."

"*Enchanté*, monsieur."

After that Nic walked her down the end of the hall and around to the elevator. When the door closed, they were finally alone.

"At last," she exclaimed as they rode to the second floor. "I don't know how you've lived with this kind of attention all your life."

"That's my question for you after watching Marcel and Robert swallow you alive."

"Don't be preposterous, Nic." The elevator door opened just in time for her to escape to the salon and hide the heat creeping into her cheeks. "I'll be right back." She darted through the room to her bedroom, where she could freshen up.

After removing her shoes and hose, Anelise took off the jewelry, including the ring. She laid everything on the dresser, including the white rose, and put her watch back on. From one of the drawers, she pulled out a pewter-blue top with matching sweat pants and put them on. Once she'd run a brush through her hair, she felt ready and walked into the salon in sandals.

Nic had to be in his bedroom.

No sooner did she sit down on one of the upholstered chairs than he walked in wearing gray sweats. With his tall, rock-hard build, the man looked superb in anything. He shot her a glance. "I'm glad you got comfortable too. Would you like a sherry or a brandy? Or maybe a soda? There's cola in the fridge in the kitchen."

"Nothing, thank you, but don't let me stop you."

"I'd rather watch the news."

"I'm dying to see what came of our night out."

He found a place in the middle of the couch and reached for the remote. "We'll catch the news from other stations first, then watch the recording." A second later, the TV came on.

"This is FT-2, and now we're here at the Jules Verne Restaurant in Paris where the famous Nicolas Causcelle is dining with his new fiancée, Anelise Lavigny. Though she looks like a film star who should be on the screen, she's the new attorney for Causcelle Hotels. Imagine having her looks and a brain as well. She graduated with top marks from the Sorbonne Law School."

As Anelise groaned, Nic turned to FT-1.

"All Paris is agog with the latest news. We're here at the Jules Verne Restaurant, where the fabulous Nicolas Causcelle has started a trend. You don't need to send your new fiancée a corsage. Simply pull a white rose out of the flower arrangement and slip it under the strap of her oh-so-becoming black dress. A match made in heaven."

Anelise would never forget that moment. "Please turn it off, Nic."

"Just one more. Let's see what's on F-3."

A video of them arriving back at the *palais* played on the screen. How did that get on the news so fast?

"And it's helpful to know they've both put their tragedies of a car crash and broken engagement behind them to find love again. We'll hope this second time around will bring them happiness. And who knows? Another set of Causcelle triplets? You can vote online whether they'll have three boys or three girls. No matter how long it takes, the winner will receive a new Bugatti of their choice."

She sat forward. "We're not even married, and already there are wagers on whether we'll have triplets and what kind!"

Nic flashed her a broad smile. "Are you ready for the recording?" With a click came the familiar music of a major channel and the voice of anchor Madelaine Corot.

"Ici, Paris! Welcome to the top-of-the-hour news. No. You're not hallucinating. The man who climbed out of that sensational black Bugatti at the Tour Eiffel *is none other than gorgeous billionaire Nico-*

*las Causcelle, one of the famous Causcelle triplets.
His stunning new fiancée is Anelise Lavigny, only
child and daughter of multimillionaire Hugo Lavigny.
Her mother comes from the wealthy Mattice family
of Sabayon et Fils Foods in Orleans. She's wearing
an eight-carat diamond among other jewels as they
enter the Jules Verne Restaurant. By now all eligible
and not-so-eligible females have gone into mourning.
Even I am still trying to catch my breath after that
kiss he just gave her. Stay tuned for more and you'll
understand why we're number one in the ratings!"*

"The press are impossible, Nic!"

"But tonight they did their job as never before."
He shut off the TV with another satisfied smile. "Our
evening turned out to be a colossal success. Now we
wait for our infuriated culprit to creep out of hiding.
Since we've eliminated every possible suspect, we'll
know the identity of this person right away."

She studied him for a moment. "While we've been
watching, an idea came to me. Do you know who's
in charge at *Paris Now*?"

"The paper is controlled by some major sharehold-
ers. Why?"

"Maybe you could ring one of them and ask them
to congratulate the journalist who got the scoop on
our engagement. This person might be so surprised
that you're not angry over the mention of your former broken engagement in their sleazy paper, he or
she will give away some vital piece of information."

Nic grinned and got to his feet. "Do you have any
idea how spooky you are? I was thinking exactly

the same thing while we were watching TV. There has to be some kind of radar connecting our thought processes."

"Or maybe someone above is on our side."

His black brows furrowed for the first time all night. "Like whom?"

"Your mother? She never got to raise you. It's possible she's looking over you, watching out for your welfare now that your father is ill."

"You think?" His disbelieving tone told her not to tread further, but she couldn't help it.

"Where was your mother born? I've been wanting to ask."

"La Racineuse," he muttered.

"I had no idea. I thought she must be another Marie Curie in the making."

"Non, non." He chuckled. "Delphine Ronfleur came from a farming family too."

"I should have guessed as much. She left her imprint on all of her children, even the last three she didn't get the chance to hold and love. Tell me more about your desire to be a research scientist. Where did that come from? What kind?"

"I used to think about the cheese we made, why it was so good people would keep buying it. Everyone said it was the milk from the cows. Why *those* cows? There had to be a reason, and research would help me understand."

"That's why you seemed to know so much about the cows. Didn't you tell your father about your interest?"

He lowered his head. "*Non.* Papa always said he needed his sons to help him run the business. We didn't fight him. After high school we were sent to business college in Paris and were hounded by the press morning and night. Jean-Louis suffered the most. He loved mechanics. Before we left La Racin-euse, he could repair every car, truck and farm machine on the property."

"Anyone who can repair machinery is a genius to me."

"*He* was! The guy loved working with his hands, but his college grades suffered. At that point he and Papa had bad fights. One day he announced he was leaving to go in the military. It sent our father into shock. Our family was never the same after that."

"How awful for all of you." She groaned.

"When I saw what it did to our father, I gave up my dream of science."

She looked at Nic through the mist. "What dream did your brother Raoul have to let go of?"

"Raising cattle and sheep. He spent a lot of time helping out in the pasture on our property. One time he told me David had it made being a shepherd before he slew Goliath."

"Obviously he meant it."

"There was never a question of that."

Just then Nic's cell phone rang. He took one glance. "It's Raoul. I promised him I'd call at eleven."

She checked her watch. "It's after that now. Please go ahead and return it."

"In a minute. We haven't discussed our plans for

tomorrow. What I'd like to do is visit my father with you. Do you mind if we leave here at eight thirty in the morning? Pack what you need. I don't expect us to return before Thursday. I'll ask the kitchen to send up our breakfast first, then we'll leave for the airport."

His request surprised her, but she'd love to see Louis again. Right now she wanted to do whatever Nic asked until this was resolved. "I'll be ready."

"Be sure to put that ring back on."

"I will. *Bonne nuit*." She hurried to her bedroom with so much to think about she'd be awake for hours. Tomorrow she'd find a book so she could press the rose. That had been a moment in time she'd never ever forget.

Nic turned out lights and walked to his bedroom before phoning Raoul. "I promised to call you, but the night got away from me."

"So I gathered after I saw you slip the stem of that rose under the strap of a certain black dress worn by one breathtaking woman. I took half a dozen swallows. So did any man watching and wishing they were in your place…"

He chuckled. "Cut it out. What else did you see?"

"Everything showing on the other stations. One did an interview with Xan, the designer. She flashed a picture of you kissing Anelise in a passionate embrace. It was supposed to show her new eight-carat diamond ring, but no one with hormones was paying attention."

"Give it up, Raoul."

"I'm not kidding and I'm not sure that you haven't escalated the press's interest in the two of you. I thought you wanted to get them off your back. It's better than the stuff TV has to offer. Any ideas on who did this to you?"

"Not yet."

"I don't hear you complaining in any way, shape or form if you follow my meaning. In the morning I think you'd better let Papa in on what you're doing. He always reads the *Figaro* with his first cup of coffee. There'll be headlines in every newspaper across France."

"I know. He'll be awake by six thirty. Anelise and I will fly there in the morning and stay overnight. I'll ask Corinne to get him ready for our visit. Raoul— before we hang up, I have something amazing to tell you. It puts a whole new complexion on everything."

"Even *you*."

"What do you mean?"

"There's a change in you, *mon frere*."

"Anelise revealed a secret to me no one in our family ever knew. It has taken away my negative feelings toward *Papa*."

"That sounds pretty miraculous."

"It is. There's a very specific reason our father hired Anelise and you won't believe why."

"Don't keep me hanging."

In the next breath, Nic told him everything. After hearing the revelation, Raoul blurted, *"Sainte Marie!"*

"My sentiments exactly."

"Our father kept hers out of prison!"

Nic clutched the phone tighter. "Anelise called Papa a saint. She praised him for raising us without Maman. I feel guilty over the years I've resented him for making us work in the business, and for his treatment of Jean-Louis."

"It baffles me that we never did know he suffered over losing him. Let's face it, we owe her a great deal for confiding in you."

"Agreed. Now you can see that if I had accepted Anelise's resignation, it would hurt him when what he wanted more than anything was to keep his promise to Hugo."

"It's all making sense, Nic."

"I also need to forgive Papa for trying to keep the business alive through us. He *did* need help, and he's no different than millions of other fathers."

"If you and I had deserted Papa and done our own thing like Jean-Louis, I don't want to think what could have happened to him."

Nic sank down on the side of the bed. "Neither do I. Anelise has been teaching me about forgiveness."

"What do you mean?"

"She feels sorry for the person who had that article printed in the newspaper. She doesn't see evil. It's her belief that person is in a world of pain deep down."

"Anelise could be right. She sounds like an extraordinary person."

"I believe she is, and the revelation about our father's suffering won't leave me alone."

"I know *I* haven't been easy on him for my own reasons," Raoul murmured, sounding far away.

"A lot of suffering has gone on, but right now we've got to find Jean-Louis and bring him home before it's too late for a reconciliation with Papa."

"I'll call Claude Giraud tomorrow and find out if he's learned anything."

"Let's keep in close touch."

They hung up and Nic got to his feet. Thinking about tomorrow, he phoned the office and left a message for George. Neither he nor Anelise would be in until Friday.

Before he got in bed, he called the Causcelle pilot and arranged for the private jet to be ready in the morning. They were flying to Chalon Champforgeuil. From there they'd drive to the château to see his father. After hearing Raoul's morose tone just now, Nic had more than one mission to accomplish there. A private one...

Six hours later he showered, shaved and dressed in a business suit and tie, the kind his father liked him to wear. Louis expected his sons to look professional rather than casual. Before Nic did anything else, he phoned Pierre's office and left a message for Rudi to come for the Bugatti. Since it had done its job, Nic wouldn't need to drive it again.

A waiter from the kitchen had delivered their breakfast and the morning paper. He sat down at the table to read while he waited for Anelise.

The first page showed a photo of him and Anelise riding up the *Tour Eiffel* with his arms around her. The headline read "Billionaire Nicolas Causcelle Captures an Exclusive Market." The accompanying paragraph continued on the quarter top half of the second page with another photo. This one showed him kissing the palm of her hand across the table at the restaurant. The caption beneath made him laugh.

"I'm glad you've found something amusing in the paper." A stunning Anelise had come into the dining room dressed in a light gray two-piece business suit with a strand of pearls around her neck. She sat down before he could help her and reached for the coffee he'd poured. "But I'm afraid to ask why."

"There's a photo of us in the restaurant." He handed her the paper, pleased she'd left her dark blond hair loose. Like silk.

Her head lifted and her gaze met his with a smile. "*Besotted?* Is that word even in use anymore?"

"It is now, and we're stuck with it." He chuckled while they ate their eggs and brioche in no time. "Are you packed?" Nic was excited to get going. He would be seeing his father again, this time through *new* eyes.

"My overnight bag is in the salon."

"Then I'll grab it and we'll head downstairs. I've sent for a limo to take us to the airport. I'm anxious to make sure the Bugatti has been picked up. First, however, I need to return these."

He reached in his pocket and handed her the pearl earrings he'd removed last night. "They'll match the necklace you're wearing."

"I was going to ask you for them. Thank you for remembering, Nic." She put them on.

"A gift from the man you'd planned to marry?" He knew next to nothing about her former fiancé.

She averted her eyes. "No. The necklace and earrings belonged to my grandmother on my mother's side."

"You look lovely in them. The ring looks great on you too," he said before leaving the table to get her overnight bag. He'd put his bag in the foyer. Once downstairs they walked down the hall and around to the entrance.

Robert stood to greet them. "Bonjour, Monsieur Causcelle, Mademoiselle Lavigny. Your limo is waiting."

"*Merci*, Robert. *Ça-va?*"

"I'm all right now that the Bugatti has been picked up. A lot of people have driven in and out of the private parking area all night. They would get out to take pictures and try to come in asking questions about you and your fiancée. The guards told them to leave the premises or they'd call the police."

"Well, it won't happen anymore. Thanks for doing your job."

"There was one huffy driver who told the guard she was a personal friend of yours and would wait here at the desk. He told her she couldn't stay and would have to move on. She got nasty with him, but finally left."

That set off an alarm bell inside Nic. But it was Anelise who asked, "What kind of car was she driving?"

"A red Bugatti."

"I've seen it around here before."

Nic looked at Anelise as pure truth flowed through both of them. He turned to Robert. "You all did the right thing and deserve a bonus. If she bothers the guards again, phone Raoul. He'll take care of it. We'll be back on Thursday. Hold the fort."

Robert grinned. "*Bien sur*, monsieur."

In another minute they reached the limo and climbed in the back with their overnight bags. Nic told the driver to take them to the small airport, then he looked at her. "You figured out the name of our culprit at the same time I did."

Anelise nodded. "Babette Lafrenière, the *vedette* from TV."

"That's the one. How do *you* know her?" He couldn't help but be intrigued.

"I don't, but I ran into her twice. Once in the reception area of the *palais* last Friday after court. And then in George's office later that same day after meeting you."

"The pieces are fitting together. Tell me everything."

She laughed. "Just now when Robert explained that the woman in the red Bugatti got nasty with the guard, I knew it was the same one who'd bothered Guy. I had just walked in from being at court and could hear loud voices. Guy looked totally frustrated. They were arguing about something. He called my name and told me to phone my dad. I nodded and kept walking to my apartment.

"Before I reached the door, she caught up to me using my name and said, 'I take it you live here.'

When I said yes, she demanded to know how I had accomplished it. When I told her I didn't understand what she meant, she got angry and said, 'In other words, you won't tell me.'

"I explained that I didn't know what she wanted. She snapped back at me with, 'A suite, of course, but the man at the front desk is no help.'"

Nic chuckled. "I wish I could see your exchange on video. I bet her meltdown outdid any performance."

"I'm sure it did. I told her it wasn't a hotel. She would have to talk to the head of the Causcelle Corporation. With eyes blazing, she asked if that was what *I* had done. Then she said in a patronizing tone, 'Isn't he as old and impossible as Methuselah?' All I said was, 'He's a wonderful man,' and I excused myself to go inside.

"A few hours later I went back to work where you and I met. After I left your office, I walked past George to say good-night and discovered her standing there. She looked stunned when she saw me and asked in a haughty voice what I was doing there. I've never known such rudeness.

"George hurriedly introduced me as one of the corporate attorneys. You should have seen the shock on her face. 'You're an attorney?' she cried.

"I tried to make a joke out of it and said it surprised me too." Nic burst into laughter.

"George promptly informed me I could see Mademoiselle Lafrenière on the *Paris Noir* TV series. I told her I thought that must be exciting, but I said I didn't watch much television and needed to leave for another appointment. I felt her staring daggers at me as I walked out the door. Not until I got outside did I realize how rude that must have sounded to her."

"You delivered the coup de grâce." Nic squeezed her hand that wore the diamond ring before he let it go.

She glanced at him. "How do *you* know her?"

"Over a month ago I was at our central car dealership on business. She happened to be there looking at the red Bugatti. Pierre, the manager, was working with her and introduced her to me. From that moment on she—"

"Forgot all about Pierre," Anelise interrupted, "and latched onto you. No doubt she wanted you to take her for the ride of her life and had it all planned out."

He sucked in his breath. "It didn't happen. Like you, I excused myself and left for La Racineuse. To my chagrin she found out where I lived, probably through Pierre, who talks too much. When I got back last Friday, Guy told me she'd been coming around the *palais* in hopes of seeing me. She'd kept calling nonstop to find out when I'd be back. I told him I'd take care of it."

"That explains why I saw her parked outside over last weekend," Anelise theorized. "I believe she even followed me to my parents' home on Friday."

Nic moaned. "Friday was a day to remember for a lot of reasons. Guy gave me her number and I called her when I went back to my suite. To make a short story even shorter, she asked *me* out for drinks. I told her I couldn't because I was permanently involved with another woman. That was something she couldn't fight."

"That was *your* coup de grâce, Nic."

"Or so I thought. Little did I know I'd uttered a prophecy about you and me without realizing it."

"What did she say?"

"Her comeback is imprinted in my mind. She said, 'It wouldn't be you've gone back to your former fiancée after all this time, would it? Or is this woman the formidable young attorney at Causcelle Headquarters who has brought you to your knees?'"

"The *what*?" Anelise cried.

"An interesting choice of words don't you think? I couldn't figure out how she even knew you. I told her I hoped she was enjoying her new car and wished her luck in her career."

Anelise let out a deep sigh. "Now that we know the truth, I want to learn a lot more about her. I packed my laptop. While we're in flight we'll do some research on her and see if we can find something helpful on her."

"Good idea. When we return to Paris, I'll contact Claude, the secret service agent who is doing another job for us because of what you told me. He'll help us get to the bottom of it."

CHAPTER SIX

"WHAT DID I SAY?"

"The revelation about my father's sadness over Jean-Louis couldn't have surprised me more. After I told Raoul, we both agreed we needed to find our brother and bring him home before it was too late for the two of them."

Again Nic grasped her hand, enfolding it. Though surprised, she didn't mind. Not at all. "You'll never know how grateful we are that you shared that with me. You're a wonder, Anelise."

She swallowed hard, deeply affected by his words and the way he looked at her as if delving into her soul. "I know it would thrill your father to see him again."

He nodded his dark head. "I'm counting on Claude digging up more information on Mademoiselle Lafrenière. I have to admit I'm curious why she has picked me out of all people to ruin."

Anelise rolled her eyes. "Aside from the obvious that she's attracted to you, I'm more concerned there's an ulterior reason for why she did this to you. She might be a real danger. That's got me worried."

"Don't worry too much. Not while we're home at La Racineuse."

Home. In his heart, she knew he'd never left.

Once on board the Learjet, she opened her laptop. Nic leaned closer to see the screen and she breathed in the scent of his shampoo. If she wasn't careful, she would lose her concentration around him. In a second, she'd looked up the social media sites to find something on Babette.

"Here's a Twitter account. Two hundred followers, Nic."

"I see she'll need a lot more to catch up to Juliette Binoche's millions of fans."

"It says here Juliette has been in sixty films. I'll look up more information on Babette." With a click, a picture of her appeared above a tiny article. "Elizabeth 'Babette' Lafrenière, twenty-four, a French-Canadian performer in the television series *Chaos.* She's single, and born in Quebec, Canada. No awards.'"

"French-Canadian?" Nic murmured. "She doesn't speak Quebecois."

"Maybe her family moved to Paris when she was a child and she lost her accent."

He shook his head. "There's no information here to help us, nothing that sounds an alarm. I'll definitely ask Claude to investigate her background."

She turned off her computer. "Before we reach your home, tell me a little about your sisters. Do they all live at the château?"

"No. Anne and Yvette have their own homes with their families on Causcelle property. The eldest,

Corinne, along with her husband, Gaston, and their children, Brigitte and Honore, have moved into the château from their home to take care of Papa. We've also hired a health care nurse, Luca Rives. However, my sisters come in to help and stay when Corinne needs a break. Raoul and I have already taken turns and will come when we can to relieve everyone."

"You have a wonderful family, Nic. Everyone should be so fortunate."

"You're right. This evening you'll have the chance to meet them at dinner. Tomorrow I'll show you around the property."

She glanced at him. "Will I see the cows that make the Causcelle cheese?"

"That's part of the plan."

"What's the other part?"

"I want to show you something that I'm thinking of turning into a business investment. You can help me decide if it's worth it."

"Now you've really intrigued me. Your eyes have the sheen of that panther I told you about last night." His male beauty had no equal.

"I'd better start wearing sunglasses."

"It's too late for that."

The fasten-seat-belts sign flashed.

A half hour later Corinne and her husband, Gaston Leclerc, met them at the entrance. After Nic hugged both of them, Anelise heard his attractive brunette sister murmur that their father had seen the news about the engagement in the morning paper.

"I thought as much." He walked Anelise through

the exquisite entrance hall to the drawing room. The seventeenth-century Causcelle château contained ceilings painted to reflect its history. What a glorious home! Louis had raised his family here.

When he'd sent his boys to business school in Paris, they'd been installed at the *palais*. They'd gone from one luxurious château to a modernized palace. Each son had his own suite, but Anelise knew it pained Nic that Jean-Louis's empty bedroom was still waiting for him here.

While she studied some tapestries on the walls, a balding Louis was wheeled in the room by his caregiver, Luca. Corinne introduced Luca to her. Louis, who'd given his bone structure and handsome looks to his sons, was impeccably dressed in a suit and tie as always. He looked well cared for, but his coloring and gaunt features told her he was failing.

"The guest bedroom is at the top of the stairs on the right, mademoiselle. You can freshen up there whenever you wish." At that point she and her husband left the room with Luca to give them time alone.

Anelise smiled at Louis and walked over to kiss his cheek. "When you hired me, I never dreamed I'd be seeing you in the surroundings where you were born. It's a thrill to be in your beautiful home, Louis."

He smiled back and reached for her left hand to look at the diamond ring. "I retired just in time and am pleased Nicolas had the good sense to snap you up before some other man did. Please—sit down."

Shaken by the comment when she knew Louis had no knowledge of why she was wearing the ring, she found a seat on a damask love seat near him. Nic leaned over to kiss his father. Suddenly she saw him hug him in a gesture she knew must have surprised Louis. "It's good to see you, Papa. You look well," he said in a voice full of emotion. Then he turned to sit next to Anelise.

Her pulse raced when he unconsciously enveloped her hand in his. She knew Nic wasn't acting right now. Raw emotions caused him to reach for her. He leaned forward. "Corinne told me you saw the announcement about our engagement in the *Figaro* this morning. We came as soon as we could to explain."

Louis gazed at Nic. "You're my son, all right. You knew what you wanted the moment you saw Anelise. That doesn't surprise me. Do you know I had my eye on your mother when I was seventeen years old? We were out in the pasture in the rain. I'd only met her the weekend before. Right then I told her she couldn't marry anyone else because she belonged to me."

Anelise let out a cry of delight.

"I had bought her an engagement ring with my savings. It was a simple band, not a diamond like the one Nicolas gave you, Anelise, but it did the trick. I put it on her finger a week later, and that was it!"

"Oh, Louis—" Anelise jumped up from the love seat to give him a quick hug. "How sweet and romantic."

Nic got to his feet. "I never knew that story, Papa. Unfortunately, I can't say our story is anything like yours. Our engagement is the result of *this*!" Anelise watched him pull a news clipping from his suit pocket. "Read the article, Papa. It appeared in *Paris Now* the other day."

Louis adjusted his bifocals to look at it. "Ah... *This* is why Corinne told me the newsboy hadn't come by yet."

"The second I read it, I phoned Anelise to meet me at Malmaison to talk it over."

"And you came up with the pretend engagement idea," his father blurted. "I would have done the same thing. Smoke out the culprit. The two photographs of you in the local paper here had me totally convinced you were in love. Well done, *mon fils*. The idiot who did this will come to no good in the end."

"Anelise believes this person is suffering more than we know," Nic confided, to her surprise.

"Of course they are! Have you figured out who it is?"

They both stared at each other before saying yes.

Louis chuckled. "If I don't miss my guess, it's a woman."

"No one is smarter than you, Papa."

"That's the first time you've ever said that to me, Nicolas."

The way Nic struggled to find the right words, Anelise knew he had past regrets and was in pain.

"Over the years I've left many things unsaid, Papa. I'm ashamed of that now."

This moment had turned into something too private. Father and son deserved time alone.

Anelise slipped out of the room to the foyer. The beautiful day compelled her to walk outside in the sunlight and wander around the grounds.

With each step, Nic's words to his father rang in her ears. *Unfortunately, I can't say our story is anything like yours.*

No, it wasn't.

Why did she feel so hurt? How could she feel anything when her world had come to an end with Andre's death?

Over the next hour she explored, but the farther she got away from the château, the more she realized a truth that shook her to the core. For nineteen months now she'd mourned Andre. Yet except for one moment, Andre hadn't been on her mind since Nic had swept into her life last Friday.

"Anelise?"

Surprised to hear Nic's voice, she wheeled around in time to see him running toward her. The sight of him caused her heart to thud, proving beyond any doubt that something earthshaking was happening to her.

He raced up to her and gripped her upper arms, breathing fast. She thought he was going to kiss her. *And she wanted him to.* "I'm sorry I was so long."

"Don't be," she begged him, trying to catch her own breath. "I know how important today is to both of you."

This time his black eyes blazed with light. "We discussed everything and made our peace. I told him we're going to find Jean-Louis and bring him home."

"I hope it's soon."

"So do I. He now knows it was Babette Lafrenière who started all the trouble. He said he was grateful to her. To quote Papa, 'She's the reason we're back to being father and son in the truest sense of the word.' Only more good can come out of this."

Her eyes smarted. Louis was a marvel. "As we've both acknowledged, your father is an exceptional human being."

Nic rubbed his hands down her arms before letting her go. It left her bereft and his touch had caused her to tremble. "He thinks you're an angel for going along with my plan, Anelise. More than anything he wants you to stay with us."

"You can tell him I want to stay because it's an honor for me. But only if it's what *you* want."

"If *I* want—are you teasing me? Don't you know you're the greatest thing that has happened to the Causcelle family?"

But what about you personally, Nic? With that question she realized she had lost her heart to him.

"I want you to look at the property I'd like to buy. First, we'll stop at a deli for a snack along the way."

"How far is it?"

"Only two miles from here. Let's walk around to the garage for the car."

"Why is acquiring it so important to you?"

"Not for me. For my father. It's been his heartfelt wish for three decades. If I could do this for him, it would mean everything to me. I'm counting on you being my good luck charm."

Good luck charm?

She'd like to be that for Nic, but when she looked down at the diamond on her finger, more longings welled up inside her. If this kept happening, she was in real trouble because these new feelings had everything to do with Nic, not Andre.

Nic drove them to the next little village and hurried into a store for some sandwiches and coffee. They were both hungry. When he got back in the car, Nic ate before leaving for the site while Anelise nibbled her sandwich more slowly as they drove through the countryside.

Anelise looked around. "Do you know after living in Paris, the pastoral setting and cows make me feel like I've landed in a perfect universe?"

"Now you know why my brother and I love to come out here whenever we can."

Within a minute they reached the other side of the hamlet where the remains of a burned-down church came into view. Nic pulled to the side of the road.

She turned to him. "Why did you stop here?"

"*This* is the property."

"I don't understand. Fire has destroyed it. When did it happen?"

"A year after my brothers and I were born."

"But there's been no war here."

"You're wrong, Anelise." His deep voice grated. "An ongoing war of a different kind has been raging in this region for a long time. Every so often violence erupts."

Anelise knew there was a lot more to his explanation than that. "You look so troubled. Can you tell me about it?"

Nic finished his coffee. "Twelve monks were living in this monastery at the time. Eight new priests had joined them the night before the place was set on fire. No one survived and no one was caught."

Anelise came close to choking on her food. "How ghastly—"

"My uncle Gregoire, a new priest and my mother's favorite brother, had just joined them the day before the tragic immolation occurred."

"Oh, no, Nic—" Tears rolled down her cheeks.

"*Dieu merci*, my mother had already gone to heaven the year before it happened. But Papa and Gregoire had been good friends. My father never got over it. Over the years he'd hoped the place would be rebuilt and he was willing to give money in Gregoire's memory, but nothing has been done about it for fear of more retaliation. He carries that sorrow as well as the loss of my mother."

She wiped her eyes with one of the napkins. "It only takes one person who's out of his mind to destroy the lives of others. I can't fathom such cruelty..."

He inhaled sharply. "I've thought about it for a long time. What I'd like to do is buy the property for my father and turn it into a hospital/hotel in Gregoire's memory. A person would go in for surgery, and a family member would get a room to be near to him or her during their convalescence. It would be free to anyone who needed help. I mean *anyone*! No restrictions.

"I would also have the chapel reconstructed for anyone who wanted a place to pray. In fact I'm thinking of buying a few other properties around France and doing the same thing."

What had Louis told her? He knew that one day his three sons would raise the corporation to new heights. A lump lodged in her throat. "That's beyond inspirational, Nic."

"It's been done in many places. But I'm afraid my proposal will get turned down over the same fear of retaliation. So what would you think if my plan included a research center as well?"

Research, the heart of Nic's dream. "Go on. I want to hear it all."

"I'm no scientist, but I do know that controlling disease due to pathogens that move between animals and humans has been challenging. Those pathogens have been responsible for the majority of new human disease threats everywhere, and a number of recent international epidemics.

"Currently, our surveillance systems often lack the ability to monitor the human-animal interface for emergent pathogens. Identifying and ultimately addressing cross-species infections will require a new approach. Those resources are hard to come by."

He knew all this while running the massive Causcelle hotel network? "You mean impossible except for someone like you. I think it's the most wonderful idea I've ever heard." Anelise understood exactly what he was saying. The depths to this man left her close to speechless. "It's a genius idea that only someone of your brilliance and generosity would even consider."

He stared hard at her. "Yet you still think it will be impossible to convince the owner to sell?"

"No, Nic. After what you've just told me, I believe

anything is possible. Where do you need to go to make your proposal?"

"Back to La Racineuse to talk to the archbishop of the region."

"Then let's try to arrange a meeting before we have to return to Paris."

The lines in his handsome face relaxed. "I doubt he'll be available, but hopefully the bishop will agree to give us some time today. With my scholarly attorney to support me, why not?"

Yes, she *was* a Causcelle attorney, but no scholar. She wished she didn't want to be anything more to him. Since their engagement, she feared that this pretense had started to become reality for her. Yet she knew their fake alliance was only temporary in Nic's mind.

His prophetic words came to fruition when they reached the church and he was told the archbishop was away on business. She felt Nic's disappointment. The secretary showed them into the office of the bishop, who greeted Nic warmly, and introductions were made.

Anelise listened while Nic explained his purpose for being there. The bishop listened and praised Nic for wanting to do something about the property where his uncle had died. He expressed his sorrow over all of it. She couldn't imagine Nic being turned down until he mentioned the idea of reconstructing the chapel part of the burned church. It would be nondenominational so anyone could use it to pray. At that point the bishop shook his head.

"A chapel of any kind would throw more fuel on an old fire."

On hearing that, she pressed Nic's arm and whispered, "Do you mind if I say something?"

"Go ahead."

She sat forward. "As Monsieur Causcelle explained, I'm one of the Causcelle corporate attorneys. What he doesn't realize is that I would have advised him against having any kind of chapel built inside. After what happened here, I agree it would be unwise.

"But what you don't know is that Monsieur Causcelle plans to purchase more properties to build hotel hospitals with research centers around France. All will be *free* to the patients and their families with no restrictions as to race, nationality or religion. The acquisition of your property would represent the first one."

The bishop's brows lifted in surprise. He gazed at Nic in wonder.

On a burst of inspiration, Anelise continued. "Each facility will be in honor of the men who lost their lives here, but it will be the Causcelles' secret with God." Having spoken, she sat back and felt Nic's hand grip hers almost painfully, yet she welcomed it.

"You're willing to do this in other parts of France too?" The bishop sounded awestruck.

"It's my father's wish and my hope for the future."

She heard the older man clear his throat. "I'll talk this over with the archbishop when he returns. I won't have an answer for a day or two. My secretary will call you at your corporate offices in Paris, Monsieur Causcelle."

"I can't ask for more than that, Your Reverence. Thank you for seeing us on such short notice."

"It's been my pleasure."

With her fingers crossed, Anelise thanked him and got to her feet.

Charged with emotions difficult to contain, Nic walked her out of the church to the car in the parking lot. Before he helped her in, he wanted to crush her in his arms, but had to hold back as other people were walking around. "Do you have any idea what just happened in there?"

She glanced at him with anxiety in those ultramarine blue eyes. "I'm afraid I overstepped another boundary." In the next breath she climbed in the front seat while he walked around.

"That's not true," he cried after getting in behind the wheel. "Your last words to him about my family's secret with God were the exact thoughts in my heart. I couldn't believe it when I heard you voice them. Instead of him turning us away like he's done to my father numerous times, he said he'd talk with the archbishop. You, Anelise Lavigny, accomplished something I didn't think was possible. It's a first step and I'm indebted to you."

"I refuse to take credit for anything. I saw his eyes, Nic. When I told him you were going to build these facilities in other parts of France—when he realized they would be free to anyone needing help—your words spoke to *his* heart."

Anelise quickly looked away from him. "I can testify that you *are* your father's son. Now I think we'd better go or we'll be late. Your sister said we'd be eating dinner early."

The last thing Nic wanted was to share her with anyone else, but Corinne had gathered the family around their father. "Let's not say anything about this in case nothing comes of it."

She nodded.

"Anelise? Tomorrow morning, I have something I have to do and will be away for a couple of hours. Just so you know, I'll be back in time for lunch."

"That's fine. If your father is up to it, we'll have a visit."

"He'll love that."

When they returned to the château, she disappeared upstairs and didn't come down until Nic knocked on her door. His other sisters and their families had assembled and greeted Anelise with warmth when they walked in the dining room. Nic had her sit down next to him.

Their father took over. "Nicolas has informed me that he and Anelise are not engaged, only pretending to be until they can speak to the person who had lies about them printed in the newspaper. What's nice is that Anelise works for our corporation, so she won't be leaving us."

"I've never seen such a big diamond!" This from sixteen-year-old Brigitte, one of Corinne's children.

Anelise removed the ring and passed it around so everyone could examine it. "It's huge!" Julie cried. She was Yvette's sixteen-year-old daughter.

"Your *oncle* has exquisite taste."

"Are you going to let her keep it, Oncle Nicolas?"

Good question, one that had kept him awake last night. "If she wants it, it's hers, Brigitte."

"I liked that black Bugatti I saw you driving on the news, Oncle Nicolas. When are you going to let me drive it?" Honore questioned. Corinne's fifteen-year-old son brought smiles to everyone at the table.

"Yeah," called out Theo, a son of Yvette's.

Nic grinned. "When you're old enough to handle such power."

"Was it fun riding in it, Mademoiselle Lavigny?" asked Anne's thirteen-year-old daughter, Lisanne. "I'd give anything!"

Before she could answer, Nic said, "She took one look at it and cried, '*Holy Bugatti!*'"

The whole room exploded in laughter, including Anelise. He couldn't remember when they'd ever been this happy as a family.

"It's true," Anelise claimed with tears of laughter in her eyes. "I was convinced your *oncle* was a new version of Batman." Her charm infected everyone, including him.

"I guess I'll have to drive it here one day and take you all for a ride."

"Yay!" the kids shrieked with excitement. His gaze sought Anelise's eyes. Hers shimmered like sea glass. He knew she was enjoying this too.

After dessert he whispered, "Would you like to take a short drive before bed?" He was aching to hold and kiss her.

"That sounds lovely, but I'm tired and plan to do some reading. How about tomorrow?" She got up from the table.

Nic rose to his feet. He fought to keep the disappointment out of his voice. "We'll do whatever you'd like."

"I'd love to see the *fromagerie* where the little photo of you and your brothers was taken."

He couldn't understand her fascination with that photo, but his question about it would have to wait. "I'll put it on our agenda."

"You have a wonderful family and I bet your father is anxious to spend some private time with you. *Bonne nuit*, Nic."

She thanked Corinne for the delicious lamb dinner and said good-night to everyone before leaving the room.

Nic watched her go. For reasons he didn't understand, Anelise wanted to be alone. Tomorrow he would get to the bottom of it. He turned to push his father's wheelchair to his suite on the main floor of the château. After a short visit because Louis was tired, Nic went to his suite on the second floor and phoned Raoul.

His brother picked up after the first ring. "Nic— I'm glad you called. I've been anxious to know how everything went with Papa."

"I buried the hatchet, and he wept with me. He

agrees on my pretending to be engaged to Anelise until we confront the culprit. I told him we've got Claude on the job looking for Jean-Louis. That's how it went."

"I couldn't be happier," his brother said in a husky voice. Nic had to hold back about the visit to the bishop until he had answers.

"Any news from Claude?"

"Not yet."

"I'll be back tomorrow night and we'll talk then. *A demain.*"

They clicked off and he went up to his room. When he finally climbed in bed, his mind kept returning to that moment at the table with Anelise. Until he'd asked her to go for a drive with him, he'd felt she wanted to be with him in all ways. Why did she unexpectedly pull away?

Nic tossed and turned, going over everything in his mind. There'd been so many moments where he'd felt a closeness with her. He'd never experienced those kinds of feelings with another woman. How could he forget her words to the bishop? She'd been so in sync with Nic's emotions, it was uncanny. He couldn't have imagined her sudden breathlessness when they touched, or the way she'd look through to his soul with those incredible blue eyes.

He pounded his pillow, trying to find a position so he would fall asleep, but it was a long time in coming. Relieved when morning arrived, he showered and shaved. Once dressed in a suit and tie, he left the château for the dairy. Since there'd been a breakthrough with the bishop, Nic hoped the same might be true with old man Dumotte, the head of the dairy, for Raoul's sake. Anelise had given Nic hope.

CHAPTER SEVEN

SUNLIGHT STREAMED THROUGH the château windows. Anelise got up to shower and change into jeans and a khaki blouse, always remembering to wear the ring. She tied her hair back at the nape with a scarf and went downstairs.

The Leclerc children had already gone to school. Though she enjoyed talking to Louis and Corinne after breakfast, Anelise kept waiting for Nic, who ought to be back from his errand by now. The fact that she cared so much alarmed her. She'd hoped morning would help her to think clearly about the situation with a man who wasn't her fiancé. To her chagrin, she realized Nic had become important to her in a way that frightened her.

As she'd told her parents, he was a troubled man with issues. He'd never loved his former fiancée. Maybe he couldn't love any woman. Perhaps the absence of a mother interacting with his father had affected his vision of marital love.

Neither Nic nor his brothers had married yet. That was why it would be ridiculous for her to get involved emotionally with a man who wasn't interested in her. Forget that he was one of France's most famous celebrities. In the end it could only mean heartache for her. She'd had enough of that with the loss of Andre.

The sooner they learned more about Babette Lafrenière's background and dealt with her, the better. Then this charade would be over. Anelise had promised to continue working for the Causcelle Corporation, but she'd find a new place to live on her own.

"There you are, *mon fils!*"

Nic had just walked in the salon to hug his father. Anelise's pulse came to life.

Corinne stood up. "Can I get you something to eat, Nic?"

"*Non, merci.* I ate earlier, and I've promised to show Anelise the countryside. We need to get going since we have to return to Paris tonight."

"Then you two go on and enjoy yourselves," Louis said, smiling at her.

"I've loved talking to both of you." Anelise got up to follow Nic out of the château to his car.

He helped her get in. "We'll drive north, then head back to the *fromagerie.* Sorry I was so long."

"Don't be. Did you accomplish what you needed to do this morning?"

"No."

"I'm sorry," she said when he gave no explanation. Something was troubling him. "While you were gone, your father and sister gave me a history of your family that kept me fascinated. You mentioned he has a brother Blaise who's a professor of Latin and Greek at the Sorbonne. How different could the interests of two brothers be?"

"The university life always appealed to him. His son, Pascal, a married cousin my age, runs a printing company in Paris and publishes many of his father's works while he helps me and Raoul. They and their families can't get enough of the big city."

"Paris *is* wonderful."

"Speaking of Paris, do you know you haven't told me about your life growing up. Where were you born?"

"In Paris. When I got older, I spent holidays with my mother's wonderful parents in Orleans."

"What about Hugo's parents?"

"They lived in Paris. Papa's mother died when I was seven. My grandfather passed away from the *grippe* during my first year in high school. I loved them so much."

His eyes found hers. "What about aunts, uncles and cousins?"

"Our families weren't prolific like yours, Nic. Papa was their only child, and my mother only had one sister who died soon after being born. But I'm not complaining. No girl ever had a more wonderful childhood than I did. My mother let me bring all my girlfriends home from school and have sleepovers. We used to play school. I ended up being the teacher and thought I'd grow up to be one."

"What happened that you didn't?"

"You really want to know?"

"I want to learn everything about the brilliant

woman my father hired. He's always had a sixth sense and knew he'd found gold when he found you."

She didn't dare take those words to heart, but they thrilled her nonetheless. "I was in my last year of high school and my father had a problem that not even his best attorney could solve. He had to ask around for someone exceptional and it cost him a fortune. One night I peeked in his study and caught him pacing. He looked at me and said, "You know what I need, Annie girl? If you go into law, you could be my attorney and help me when I get into trouble. No one sees a problem the way you do. You're a marvel.'

"I knew he was teasing, but I also knew he rarely brought his troubles home. It hit me then how much he carried on his shoulders no one knew about. I started thinking about what he'd said, and weeks later I made the decision to go to law school after graduation. I wanted to be able to help him one day the way he'd always helped me."

After a silence, "Did his attorney prevail?" Nic asked in an oddly thick toned voice.

"Yes."

He reached for her hand. "Thank you for letting me look into that Lavigny *tranche de vie*. The more I find out about you, the more I realize how remarkable you really are."

"If you're not careful, you're going to make me cry."

"Then we'll change the subject." He let go of her, but she wished he hadn't. "Take a look at the land around here. It's home to me and my siblings. Always will be. Do you know this is the only place in France that produces all the wine types? *Vin de paille, rose, jaune, rouge and blanc.* The quality of the soil makes the difference."

"After what you told me earlier today, you really should have been able to go into research."

"I'm not complaining. Not anymore."

The new understanding with his father had done wonders for his morale and she was happy for him. "Where are we going exactly?"

"I thought I'd show you a place most people never visit whether they're a native or a tourist."

"But *you* have, Nic."

"Our father made certain of it to further our education. It's a site called Seine-Source, the beginning of the Seine river. Since you've never been there, I thought you'd like to see where it starts out in a wooded area as a tiny trickle."

"The world-famous Seine a *trickle*?"

Her comment produced a chuckle. Before long they reached the spring and the artificial grotto above that comprised a dragon, a dog and a statue of a nymph called Sequana. "My *oncle* would tell you it's Latin for snake."

"The river does meander like one!" she murmured. "Jacqueline Francois immortalized it in the song called 'La Seine.' I've always adored the words."

"Do you remember them?"

"Only the ending. I think it goes, 'She sings her love for Paris because the Seine is a lover and Paris sleeps in her bed.'"

Nic pinned her with his intense gaze. "The author of those words had to be in love. You told me that your love for Andre was real. How did you meet him? Or would you rather not talk about him?"

"I don't mind." It didn't hurt, not anymore. "I had a law study group and one of the girls gave a party. She invited some other friends. Andre happened to be among them, an engineering student. He played a lot of tennis and asked me if I'd like to spend one afternoon away from the books and have a game with him."

"Which obviously you did."

She laughed. "We had many of them."

"He must have fallen in love with you on the spot."

By the way he was looking at her, and the throb in his vibrant voice, Anelise couldn't swallow, let alone talk. She wasn't thinking about Andre. Her mind kept visualizing the Seine swirling around Paris where she and Nic lay locked in each other's arms. This had to stop. "I guess we'd better get going."

"One more spot to see."

He drove south while he talked about the history of the area back in the 1200s. He knew everything! When they reached the large cheese-making plant, Nic parked near it. "We're facing the pasture where that photo was taken, but there are no cows right now. I'd take you on a tour of the place, but we have to pack and drive fifteen miles to the airport."

"I know." It was for the best, but she wanted to cry her eyes out for having to leave. Being with Nic had given her a new sense of confidence, and made her see some strengths that she'd never considered. He'd opened her eyes to a different sort of life.

"Tell me something, Anelise. Why were you so interested in the photo of this place my father showed you?"

"Not only the place, Nic. Most women think about being married and having children. When I saw those three adorable faces and realized your father had to take over from day one, it touched my heart. Both of your parents had to make sacrifices. She took care of your three sisters while she carried her sons in the womb. Your father did the rest. It's a success story beyond comprehension. That was the day I recognized the true meaning of the word *sacrifice*."

All went quiet until he let out a deep sigh. "You've made me look at everything in a new light. I'm more grateful than you know."

He'd just spoken the words in her heart. After that admission, he started the car and they headed for the château to get their bags and say goodbye.

She studied his profile, recognizing she wasn't the same woman who'd flown here yesterday. Stepping into Nic's world had changed her until she didn't know herself.

All Nic could think of during the flight to Paris was that Anelise would be going back to his suite with him. They would have total privacy. When it came time to work at the office, she'd be with him. Until they investigated Babette and decided what to do about her, he would keep Anelise to himself day and night for as long as he wanted. He didn't have to be in a hurry. She wasn't going anywhere.

The minute his driver had taken them to the *palais* and they'd reached his suite, she turned to him. "Nic? I hope you're going to contact that PI about Mademoiselle Lafrenière right away."

"First thing in the morning."

"Good. I have visions of her showing up in my office to confront me. That woman doesn't worry about boundaries."

Her comment gave him the impetus to tell her of his idea that had been percolating for several days. "While we're pretending to be engaged, I'm moving you into my office with me. If she comes barging in, she'll have to face me."

"No, Nic. You're the CEO. It wouldn't be right. Surely we don't have to go *that* far."

He eyed her. "You didn't hear all the things she said to me at the car dealership. Want to bet she won't show up tomorrow?"

She looked down. "No. I trust your instincts."

"Bon," he muttered with satisfaction. "It's settled. Now that we're back, please help yourself to anything in the kitchen while I phone my brother." Claude would be getting a call from him too.

"Thank you, Nic, but the food on the plane did it for me. I had a wonderful time. See you in the morning." She disappeared into her bedroom.

He stared after her until she shut the door. Frustrated with longings he'd never experienced for any woman, he charged into his room and changed into a robe.

His hand gripped his cell harder. "Come on, Raoul. Answer!" The phone rang five times before his brother picked up sounding drowsy.

"Eh bien. Are you still in La Racineuse?"

"We just got back. Have you talked to Claude?"

"No. He left me a message that he's out of town, but will call as soon as he has any information. Are you all right? You sound anxious. Is Papa worse?"

Nic took a quick breath. "For now, he seems fine. We had the most amazing visit of our lives and I've made my peace with him."

"Is that the truth?"

"I don't blame you for being skeptical."

"How did he handle that hideous article and your fake engagement?"

"He said he was glad it happened since it brought him and me together. But what I'd like to know is how *you're* handling the endless buzz, Raoul."

"It's all anyone talks about."

"I'm sorry."

After a brief silence, "Did you—"

"No luck," Nic cut him off.

A telling sigh came through the phone.

"Sorry, bro." Nic cleared his throat and changed the subject. "Do me a favor? As soon as Claude gets back to you, tell him to phone me. I have another job for him that's critical too."

"What's going on?"

"Guess who's our culprit."

"I can't imagine."

"Babette Lafrenière."

"I don't know that name."

Nic let out a laugh. "You don't watch much TV either. That's what Anelise said when she met her for the first time."

"Raoul—let me in on your joke."

"Babette is a *vedette* in some TV series. The information on the web says she's French-Canadian, but she gives no evidence of it in her speech. Anelise and I believe she could be dangerous. That's why I need to get in touch with Claude. I want her investigated before I decide what to do."

"I'll send him another message and ask him to get started on her ASAP."

"You're the best. *Bonne nuit.*"

Anelise brought the rest of her things from her office into Nic's. He'd had her desk and equipment moved early that morning. Now they sat opposite each other. He smiled like a cat who'd just eaten a bowl full of tuna. "I'm crazy about this arrangement. We can see each other every second."

As if she weren't aware of it and loving it. His outrageous comments made her laugh. They also caused her heart to ping throughout the morning. He ordered lunch and snacks for them. She'd never had so much fun in her life, on or off the job.

Nic had to answer more calls than she could imagine. Her admiration for his knowledge and business acumen continued to grow at an alarming rate.

At four, George buzzed Nic. "You have a visitor again," he said in a hushed tone. "She insists on seeing *you*." Eyes black as India ink sought Anelise with that I-told-you-so look. "Shall I call for security?"

"That won't be necessary, George. Walk her down the hall to my office."

"Tres bien."

Clicking off, Nic sat back in his leather chair. "Let's play her along and see what happens."

Anelise's hand tightened on the pen she'd been using to make notes on a possible new hotel acquisition. The numbers didn't add up. She needed more information on the demographics and needed to talk to Nic about it. "As long as I have your back."

"Is there any question of it?"

"Of course not, Nic. But I *am* concerned she's baiting you. She has no fear of reprisal."

"Which proves she's a threat. We'll figure it out. All you have to do is take your cues from me."

A knock on the door ended the discussion.

"Entrez."

When the door opened, Babette came in without invitation, but stopped when she saw Anelise and the diamond on her ring finger. "I asked to see *you*, Nic Causcelle, not the new attorney."

"I'm sure you know that Anelise is my fiancée and I can't bear to be apart from her." It had been all over the news. Knowing of her obsession, he couldn't tell if she was feigning ignorance or not, but it didn't matter. "How can I help you? Advice on another car perhaps?"

Her head reared. "I want to live in the *palais*. It's near the film studio where I can get away from my fans. There are times when I need peace. The security guards make it the perfect place for privacy,"

Anelise stepped in. "I'm afraid you won't get much peace if you live there, Mademoiselle Lafrenière. Nic can't make a move without someone out in the parking area shoving a camera or a microphone in his face. When I think about it, you must have tremendous confidence to perform for an audience the way you do and deal with all the adulation. I know *I* couldn't do it."

Nic smiled at Anelise. "As long as you remember *I'm* your doting audience, *ma belle*, nothing else matters." He sounded like he really meant it, and his eyes played over her with such a slow intimacy, it robbed her of breath. They might as well have been the only two in the room before he eventually stood up and transferred his attention to Babette.

"The *palais* isn't a hotel, Mademoiselle Lafrenière. It's the home where the Causcelle family has resided for over a hundred years. Only members of my family stay there when they are in Paris."

She glared at Anelise. "*She* lives there."

"Because my father made it possible. She's a special case and was installed in one of my sister's suites when he hired her to work for the corporation. Soon she'll be his daughter-in-law and he adores her." Nic sought Anelise's gaze once more. "So do I, and now she's living with me."

"And I love it," Anelise said in a trembly voice. It was only the truth.

The other woman glared at her with eyes spouting nonverbal vitriol. The actress hadn't yet figured out what was going on, not when she'd thought she'd destroyed Nic with her lies.

"My fiancée and I wish you luck in your career, Mademoiselle Lafrenière. Now if you'll excuse us, we're busy trying to get some work done." He walked toward the door and opened it.

Dead silence on the *vedette*'s part meant nothing had gone the way she'd imagined when she'd barged in. Anelise got the feeling Babette wanted to stomp her foot and start throwing things like the little girl with the curl. She did neither. With an imperious turn of her head, she marched out.

Nic closed the door behind her and took a few long strides to his desk to make a phone call. "Robert? Mademoiselle Lafrenière might be coming by. I've told her it won't be possible for her to move in. If she gives you any trouble, let me know." He hung up.

"What an amazing woman!" Anelise cried, trying hard not to laugh out loud. "Poor Robert if he has to tangle with her again."

Nic's features darkened. "She's bold beyond caring, Anelise. More than ever, we know she's up to something that could be criminal. She wants a lot more than a room at the *palais*."

"I know. I keep wondering what she hopes to achieve now that we've called her bluff. We haven't fooled her. No doubt she has more tricks up her sleeve and will now be ready to play them. I'm starting to get nervous."

"We've got security and you've got me. I'm Batman, remember?"

"This isn't funny, Nic. If anything happened to you—"

Something flickered in the recesses of his eyes as he stared at her. "Nothing will happen to either of us. Raoul has contacted the man who is looking into her background for us. It won't be long before we discover the truth. But I don't want to think about her right now. What do you say we quit for the day and drive out of the city for dinner?"

Yes, yes. "I'd love it, but before we leave, I'm trying to solve a problem with a case Serge assigned me. The figures don't match the asking price of this older hotel your father wants to buy. I'd like your opinion."

"Where is it located?"

"At the Quartier Saint Louis District in Versailles."

"Versailles? That's perfect. I'll have my car brought around and we'll discuss it en route. Once we've checked everything out, we'll do what Marie Antoinette did."

"You mean visit the farm and dairy when she could?"

He nodded. "Where else? It's my favorite place on the estate. We'll see the cows we didn't have time to see out at La Racineuse. Maybe some sheep too. The last time I was there they dressed up the sheep in ribbons."

"You're kidding."

He laughed. "Raoul considered that an insult because the farm wasn't a pretense for the queen. She'd loved it and wanted her royal children to love it too. I haven't been there in ages."

Neither had Anelise. Doing anything with Nic gave her an ecstatic feeling she wouldn't be able to hide from him much longer.

CHAPTER EIGHT

NIC DROVE INTO the town of Versailles and they reached the old Peacock Inn Hotel. Once a favorite spot in the reign of Louis XIV, it now appeared on its last legs.

"What's the financial history on the place, Anelise?"

"According to this report, the latest owner died without children. No one came forward to keep it in condition and it became a liability to the bank. They've had it up for sale for twenty years."

"Does it say why my father decided to buy it?"

"Yes. He received a favorable report from the chief engineer on the property. The foundation is solid and the ground stable. Therefore, remodeling could go ahead without problem. Serge added the following note about your father's reasons. 'It's near Louis XIII's former deer park, the Saint Louis cathedral and the King's Kitchen Garden.'"

"Papa loves his history."

"But I don't think he'll love the asking price. I've done research on the other real estate properties sold in this neighborhood in the last year. Their tax bases aren't high, yet none of the transactions reveal the sold prices. That goes against the public freedom of information act. I've a feeling the bank is asking for an exorbitant amount of money here."

"Naturally. With Papa as the buyer, they can make up for the taxes and money for improvements they've had to invest to hold on to it for the last twenty years. No doubt they've leaned on the owners of the sold properties to keep quiet."

"That's illegal, Nic."

"I suspect they're relying on an ancient law about this being part of a royal holding to support their position. If that's the case, we'll fight it. First you'll need to contact Jacques Beauvais in the Yvelines Ile-de-France Department."

"I'll spend tomorrow sending out information requests to him and we'll see what happens."

"Tell him we'll go to court if we have to before I sign anything. And now, I'm tired of thinking and want to enjoy the rest of the day with you." And the evening, *and* the night. All he could think about was being alone with her.

When they reached the mammoth château, visiting hours had ended. Tourists were leaving in droves. Nic held her arm while they walked through the unique grounds. Though beautiful, he preferred to watch her expression as she took it all in.

"Do you know the scroll designs of this garden around the water *parterre* remind me of stained-glass window outlines? Maybe Le Nôtre had them in mind when he created this masterpiece."

"Maybe," he murmured, but right now he was too fascinated by the way the sun brought out the different colors in her silky dark blond hair. Strange how he'd thought she'd had light brown hair when he'd first seen her walking to work.

They continued on toward the Queen's Hamlet and stood beneath the trees. "Oh, Nic… We're too late to visit the dairy."

He slid his arm around her womanly waist, wanting to feel her close to his body. "I'm disappointed too. We'll come back next week and make a day of it."

"Could we?" She turned her head and that's when their cheeks brushed, stoking the fire burning inside him. He pulled her into his arms. "Forgive me, Anelise, but I can't hold off any longer." In the next breath he lowered his head and covered those enticing lips that had been calling to him like a siren.

All day he'd imagined kissing her while they sat across from each other in his office. Now he had his heart's desire and didn't want it to end. He knew instinctively she'd wanted this too. Their transforming kiss grew deeper and longer. He wanted to carry her someplace and love her into oblivion until a voice called out that they needed to leave.

Nic had a hard time relinquishing her delectable mouth and body. A blush crept into her cheeks the second the guard on duty walked up to them. The man's eyes widened.

"It's *you*, Monsieur Causcelle!" His eyes swept over

Anelise with male appreciation. "Forgive me for intruding on you and your fiancée, but the gates closed at six and now it's seven thirty. I'll phone security to let you out."

"That's very kind of you. *Merci*." He grasped her hand and they retraced their steps across the grounds to the entrance.

"Even an estate guard knows who you are, Monsieur Causcelle," she teased.

Once past the gate he said, "I'm sorry, Anelise. You had me so enthralled, I didn't notice the time, let alone anyone else around."

"Neither of us did." She took a breath, seemingly to steady herself. "Even if you felt you had to work for your father in the business, I don't know why you didn't disappear years ago like your brother."

"I'm glad I didn't, otherwise I would never have met you." Her eyes widened at his words. After helping her into his black Mercedes, they left the parking area. "You have a knack for changing the subject when you're uncomfortable, Mademoiselle Lavigny. But I'm not going to apologize for what went on between us back there."

She didn't look at him. "I'm afraid it was inevitable. We've been virtually living together for a week. The night we got engaged I had a difficult time remembering that the way you kissed and held me wasn't real." After a pause, "You can understand why some film stars carry on off-screen for a while after playing the kind of romantic role we've undertaken."

For a while? Her admission meant he hadn't been

dreaming about the feelings they'd aroused in each other from the moment they'd met.

"Let's drive back by the Peacock. I saw a place where we could have dinner."

She turned to him. "Now who's changing the subject? You're spooking *me* if you're talking about the Creperie. I've been salivating ever since I saw it."

"There was no other place to eat." Their minds *did* think alike.

A few minutes later he pulled up in front of the small restaurant and they went inside. To his relief no one recognized him. He asked the young waitress for a table in the rear for privacy. She handed them menus.

Nic glanced at his and knew what he wanted. "Have you seen something that appeals to you, Anelise?"

"The Louis galettes sound delicious. They're stuffed with ground beef and eggs. I'd also like cappuccino, even if it isn't French."

The waitress came back. "Are you ready to order?"

"*Oui.* How large are the galettes?"

"One is enough for me."

"*Bon.* One for my fiancée, and two for me. Both of us want cappuccino."

"*A toute à l'heure,* monsieur." She walked away.

A smile lifted one corner of Anelise's mouth. "You've gained another admirer in your miles-long list. She couldn't take her eyes off you."

As long as Anelise liked looking at him, nothing else mattered. "I told her you were my fiancée."

"She didn't care I was wearing this ring. You're a regular hazard, Nic."

A laugh escaped. "Is that what you think about me?"

"Yes. You should walk around in a ski mask."

"That's fine. I'll only take it off for you."

"Nic…" Her voice had gone husky.

He loved the sometimes shy side of her.

Their food arrived. After eating one galette, he stared at her over the rim of his coffee. "I have an idea. Tomorrow's Saturday. I need to be in work for the day to catch up, but let's do something exciting afterward."

She'd just taken another bite of food and had to swallow. "I can't. It's my aunt's birthday. I'll spend the day at work too, but I'm driving to Orleans with my folks tomorrow evening and will be staying through Sunday."

The news that she'd be away from Paris for the rest of the weekend came as a blow. "Does your aunt know about us?"

"Everyone believes we're engaged, and I'll go on wearing the ring. Just be thankful you don't have to be dragged along to keep up the pretense."

This was no longer a pretense for Nic, but he didn't know what the hell to do about it yet. He finished the second galette, but it tasted like sawdust. "If you're ready, let's go."

By quarter to ten they'd arrived back at the *palais*. No sooner had they reached his suite than his cell rang.

She smiled at him. "I bet that's your brother. See you in the morning." She disappeared before he could stop her. He knew why. She didn't want to talk about that kiss near the royal dairy, but he couldn't stop thinking about it. From the first moment he'd seen her walking along the street, he'd felt an attraction that had taken over his whole world.

Since the evening that they'd agreed to get engaged, every look, touch and kiss had brought him to life. She filled his dreams. Within a week, his world had become a different place that exhilarated him. The thought of her not being in it for the rest of his life terrified him.

Anelise checked her watch. One thirty. Sleep wouldn't come. Not tonight. The reason for her agony slept in another bedroom. Much as she would like to blame it on anything but the truth, she couldn't.

Be honest with yourself, Anelise. You're in love with him, a man you've only known a week, but he's not in love with you.

Nic had admitted that his engagement to Denise hadn't been a true love affair. He'd let her go. The only reason he'd asked Anelise to play along with the fake engagement had to do with Babette Lafrenière. His hormones had nothing to do with love. In twenty-nine years neither Nic nor his brothers had married.

He and Raoul seemed to get along better than most married couples, and their greatest concerns involved their father and Jean-Louis. She needed to face it. Three devastatingly attractive, brilliant men, wealthy beyond comprehension, continued to remain single for a reason she didn't understand.

Anelise pummeled her pillow. No more living here in Nic's suite while she ached to be in his arms and kissed forever. After the party tonight in Orleans, she would come back to Paris on Sunday and get an apartment near the Sacre Coeur, a favorite area. She wouldn't sec Nic until she went to work Monday morning.

With her mind made up, she turned on her other side and prayed for oblivion. To her shock she awakened the next morning realizing she'd finally slept, but she'd be late for work. Thank heaven Nic had already left when she emerged from the bedroom.

After grabbing a cup of coffee, she hurried outside with her briefcase and practically ran to the office. Nic, freshly shaven, sat at his desk, already on the phone with someone. In a light gray suit and tie, he looked so handsome it hurt.

"Sorry I'm late, Nic."

He'd just gotten off the phone and flashed her a smile to die for. "You work too hard and should have slept all day."

"I couldn't. These request forms need to be finished and couriered by afternoon."

"I'll help you since Claude will be coming here at two to give us the lowdown on Babette."

"Oh—" she cried in surprise. "Did he say anything about her?"

One dashing black brow lifted. "Only that our suspicions are dead-on."

The news gave her hope the situation would be resolved in the next day or two. They could get on with their separate lives. She'd leave the *palais*, and move back to her own office. That way she'd only see Nic once in a while.

She got to work and before she knew it, the requests they'd worked on had gone out. Nic ordered lunch and then Claude arrived. With the introductions made, he put on his glasses and pulled some papers out of his valise.

"This is a fascinating case. First of all, she's been having a liaison with a journalist at *Paris Now*. The business printed on the internet is fiction. She wasn't born in French Canada. Her birth mother, now deceased eight years, was Eva Grenier, of Lyons, France. She had a baby out of wedlock.

"The daughter, Babette Grenier Hoang, is twenty-nine, not twenty-four. The birth father was the notorious Henri Duong Hoang from Vietnam. He was imprisoned in Turkey for robbery. Later released. Fled to Lyons, France, where he met Eva and got involved in a big gambling operation in Paris. He killed a man that didn't pay his gambling debt." Claude eyed the two of them. "That killing took place at the café-bar where both your fathers were eating."

"Nic—" she cried in astonishment. Their gazes met in disbelief.

"There's more," Claude continued. "The police caught up with Henri, who went to prison and died there three months ago from strangulation. According to prison records, Babette visited him there regularly.

"Several inmates testified that his daughter never forgave Louis Causcelle for helping the police put her father in prison. He identified the ring with a snake insignia. His daughter has the same design tattooed on her right calf. She knew her birth father was the killer, but she doesn't care.

"She has performed on TV, but in a minor role and the show was canceled. To my knowledge she doesn't have another job yet. She's living in rooms at the back of the Fusion Bar in Pigalle. Apparently she has an uncle in Lyons who works in a bar. Maybe there's a connection."

Nic rose to his feet. "She hates my father and has been planning her revenge. It makes horrific sense. Claude? I can't thank you enough for all you've done so quickly. You know you can name your price."

He got to his feet. "I'll leave this information with you. There's enough here for you to prosecute her for the lie in the paper. I only wish I had better news on your brother. I'm still working with one military man who I believe can tell us what we want to know about Jean-Louis. The minute I hear from him, I'll let you know."

After he left, Nic walked around and pulled Anelise into his arms. She couldn't deny him right now and they clung. "You were right about her. Our culprit has been living in a world of hurt neither of us can imagine."

"I can't comprehend what she's been through in her life."

"If I know you, you don't want her prosecuted.

Neither do I. Let's go back to the *palais* and decide what we're going to do. But first I need this."

He trapped her mouth with his and kissed her so hungrily, she could hardly breathe. This wasn't supposed to happen, not if he didn't love her. Afraid of her own feelings, she slowly eased away from him. A good walk back to the *palais* would help her work off the emotions riddling her.

Part of her felt great relief that they knew what had driven Babette's agenda and why. Yet the other part of her suffered pain because this meant there was no more need for the engagement. His desire for her didn't mean love. No doubt he'd kissed Denise with this much passion, enjoying the moment. But it wasn't enough for Anelise.

The whole purpose of the engagement had been to expose the culprit. Now that Babette had been flushed out, Nic no longer required Anelise's cooperation. The birthday party for her aunt couldn't have come at a more propitious moment. If she didn't get away from Nic this weekend, she'd never want to leave him.

Could there be anything more pathetic than to hang on to a man when you knew it was hopeless? Denise had been wise enough to figure out the truth in time to find love with another man who would love her back. Anelise knew deep down she'd never meet a man like Nic in this life, but she didn't want to live in constant pain because he couldn't return her love.

Carrying that thought to its conclusion, it meant she couldn't go on working for the corporation, even though it would hurt her father. Over the weekend she would explain the situation to her parents and hope they would understand.

"Where are you going?" Nic asked after they'd walked in the suite.

"To pack an overnight bag."

He frowned. "You can't leave yet. We need to talk about Babette."

She didn't want to go anywhere, but she had to get out of here for self-preservation. "I know. Give me five minutes first."

Five turned into fifteen before she entered the salon with a suitcase and sat down on a chair. Nic had made himself comfortable on the couch in shirtsleeves. He'd been writing what appeared to be a letter.

"You've been busy."

Nic looked up at her. "I thought I'd have this sent to her and would like your opinion." He handed it to her.

Great penmanship was a lost art these days, but not for Nic.

Chère Mademoiselle Babette Grenier Hoang,
My fiancée and I want to express our sorrow over the loss of your mother, Eva, and your fa-
ther, Henri. Your life must seem even more dif-
ficult to be told your series was canceled. We
have every hope you'll be asked to do another
one soon. God bless you in the future.
Sincerely, Nicolas and Anelise

Tears threatened, blurring her eyes. She put the letter on the coffee table and stood up. "Babette will be shocked out of her mind that you know everything about her and figured out she was the one who had the lie printed. The fact that you're not seeking retribution of any kind should silence anyone with even a modicum of decency.

"The journalist at *Paris Now* she's been seeing will tell her she's lucky to have received a gracious letter like that rather than a summons to appear in court. It's perfect, Nic." *You're* perfect.

"Your approval means a great deal since you were attacked too."

"Thank goodness it's over. Now I have to leave. My parents are waiting for me. See you Monday at work."

"You won't be coming back here Sunday night?"

She shook her head. "No. I have other plans. Now that we know about Babette, you should be able to enjoy your weekend. *A la prochaine.*"

Anelise left the suite so fast, Nic didn't have time to take a breath. But right now wasn't the time to stop her. He'd received several calls. One from the bishop, another from Raoul and one from his sister Yvette he needed to return. Maybe their father had grown worse. The letter he intended to courier to Babette could wait until tomorrow.

He reached for the phone and called her. "Yvette? Is it bad news about Papa?"

"I'm glad you called. No. This is about Oncle Raimond. It's very sad. He fell at the *ferme* today. Stefan got him to the hospital. The doctors say he has a bad case of ALS."

Nic groaned. Raimond was their father's younger brother by a year.

"As you know, he's been in charge of everything at La Racineuse for years. This news means the workers under him will have to manage. Unfortunately, there isn't anyone to do the job the way he has done it, and his son Stefan is needed at the *fromagerie*. Papa says you're in charge, Nic. Do you have any suggestions?"

Yes, and he was going to do something about it right now. "I've got several calls to make, then I'll phone you back with an answer."

"Bless you, *mon frere*."

After they clicked off, he scanned his phone list for his dynamo cousin Pascal and rang him. Ten minutes later he called him back. "*Eh bien, Nic—comment ca va?* Congratulations on your engagement. She's one gorgeous woman."

"You think?" They both laughed. Everyone in the family liked Pascal, including Nic. "I'm calling as the head of the Causcelle Corporation. Do you understand what I'm saying?"

After a silence, "I think I do."

"I was wondering if you would take over for Raoul at headquarters. I don't know for how long and I can't give you more than a minute to think about it."

"You're kidding me."

"I wish I were, but the situation is serious. I can't think of another person, let alone a family member, who could do Raoul's job and then some the way you could. But only if you want to."

He heard a slight intake of breath. "I'm your man."

"That's what I needed to hear. I'll call you back by the end of the evening to make it official."

Three seconds later he phoned Raoul. "I'm on my way over to your suite. Don't go anywhere!"

He left his suite through a side door and ran down the hall where Raoul stood waiting for him. "What's going on?"

Nic grabbed his brother. "I've got something to tell you, so just listen and don't say a word until I'm finished."

Five minutes later Raoul gave him a bear hug he'd always remember.

Nic knew what this moment meant to him. "While you phone Pascal and catch him up on what's important before you leave for La Racineuse, I'll phone Yvette with the news."

"Nic? I have no words." His emotions had overcome him.

After another hug Nic walked back to his suite and returned the bishop's call. He learned enough that he couldn't wait to talk the news over with Anelise. But she hadn't been able to get away from Nic fast enough because she was running from him.

He knew how her mind worked. Now that they'd dealt with Babette, she planned to give him back the ring and move out of his suite. She wanted to end the engagement, but he refused to let that happen.

The hours of the night went on forever without her

there. He kept busy until it was time to drive to Orleans on Sunday. It was located on the Loire River,
and he thought of the town as Jeanne d'Arc territory.
Following the map, he arrived at the beautiful home
of Anelise's family on her mother's side. The ivory-
toned *chatellerie* sat back in a wooded, sylvan park
near a large pond.

Her older blue Peugeot stood out among the luxury
cars assembled in the courtyard. Love of money and
titles didn't drive her. He'd only been with her for a
week, but knew in his gut she was his soul mate. Deep
down, he was sure she knew it too. They suited each
other and the woman never disappointed.

He got out of the car and walked up to the entrance.
A middle-aged housekeeper opened the door. *"Oui,
monsieur?"*

"I'm Nicolas Causcelle, the fiancé of Anelise. Will
you let her know I'm here?"

"Tres bien. Entrez."

He stepped inside the foyer and looked around.
The interior of the beautiful country manor reminded
him of his home in La Racineuse. Suddenly he heard
footsteps.

"Nic—" She sounded incredulous that he was here.

Anelise walked over to him dressed in a pale blue
chambray jumpsuit and heeled sandals. Her dark
blond hair floated around her shoulders. Talk about
a vision!

"Why didn't you tell me you were coming?" He
realized he'd shocked her by showing up like this,

yet her eyes shone an azure blue that told him what he needed desperately to know.

"The suite got lonely without you. I decided to surprise you. How's the celebration going?"

"It's over. We've just been in the sun room talking."

"A lot has happened since you left yesterday that I need to talk to *you* about. I'd like to tear you away. Can you leave now? I'll follow you back to Paris."

She hesitated. "I did have other plans."

"You mean about not coming back until Monday? Can't you change them? This is important."

"Does it concern Babette?"

"No. Unless something else happens, she's a thing of the past. I'm talking about news I received from the bishop, as well as an unexpected development in the family. If you're willing, I need your help and it can't wait until Monday."

She took a quick breath. "Of course, I'll do what I can."

"Thank you. Tell you what. I'll go out to my car while you pack. Once back at the *palais* we'll talk everything out." He started for the door.

"Nic—"

He turned to her, afraid she would change her mind if they talked any longer.

"About the bishop. Is it good news?"

"It might be. We'll see."

She dashed off and he left the house. When she didn't appear fifteen minutes later, he realized she was having a difficult time saying goodbye to her family. Nic was about to phone her when she came hurrying out and ran to her car with her suitcase. The sight of her caused him to release the breath he'd been holding. He could have phoned her to talk while they were driving, but decided against it in the heavy traffic.

When they reached the *palais*, he kissed her soft cheek before she climbed out, unable to stop himself. "I know you had other plans for this weekend. This means a lot to me. Thank you, Anelise."

"You don't need to thank me. I want to help you."

CHAPTER NINE

NIC'S APARTMENT HAD never looked so good to him
with Anelise planting herself on the couch. He ordered dinner to be set up in the dining room, but
would have preferred to grab her and kiss the day-
lights out of her. However, there were matters to discuss first.

He brought them both a cola from the fridge and
sat across from her. "Were your parents disappointed
that you had to leave?"

"Not at all. The only thing they were upset about
was that I didn't bring you in to meet the rest of the
family. I told them you were in a hurry. Now tell me
what's wrong."

Nic knew why she didn't want her family seeing
him. She was planning to end the engagement, but he
had news for her and took a long swallow.

"Raimond Causcelle, *mon oncle*, who lives in La
Racineuse, is a year younger than Papa. For years he
has overseen the whole place that includes the *fromagerie*, the livestock, the dairy, the farm, everything! Yesterday he collapsed and the doctors have

diagnosed him with a severe case of ALS. He won't ever be able to work again. There's only one person who can take over without a breath being lost. The man I'm talking about will do it in a heartbeat."

"Raoul," she cried out excitedly. "But he runs the other parts of the Causcelle Corporation here in Paris."

"He did until last night when he left for La Racineuse. I've hired our cousin Pascal Causcelle to take his place. I told you about him."

"Yes. You said he's a big entrepreneur."

Anelise had a photographic memory, one of the thousand things he loved about her. "He'll do marvelous innovations with our company. I'll work with him part of the time to help him. We've agreed it's temporary. But it might end up being permanent."

"Incroyable." She recrossed her legs. "Besides the fact that you're losing a brother, how will you be able to do *your* job if you're helping your cousin too?"

"Raoul and I will always be close, but now I have *you.*" He drained the rest of his drink while he let that statement sink in.

A confused expression broke out on her gorgeous face. "What do you mean?"

"For the next week I'm putting you in charge of the hotel division. George will be your backup. He can run everything and has for years. Papa relied on him from the beginning."

She almost dropped her cola. "But what about Serge or Helene?"

"Both are invaluable, but they don't have your brilliance or vision. You take one look at a project and see the merits as well as the flaws. You're like a quarterback in American football. Raoul and I watch our favorite teams every time we can in the autumn. Ever heard of Tom Brady? He looks at the field and knows where he's going to throw the ball before anyone else has even thought about it."

"A quarterback?" She laughed hard. "I've heard of everything now."

He sat forward. "Will you do it? I need you."

"I'm afraid Serge and Helene will be hurt."

Thank heaven they were her only concern. Her kind heart was another trait he adored. "No, they won't. That's because they trust my judgment and I trust *you*, implicitly. I realize it seems a huge responsibility, but I need you on my team, and I'll be there at the end of the phone if you need me. We'll keep my office just the way it is while we all work together. What's your answer?"

"I'm dumbfounded you'd consider me for this. As long as it's just for a week, I'll go to the office and try to wade through the work you do every day as if it's nothing."

"Is that what I do?"

Her smile melted him to the spot. "Yes. Effortlessly. All men should be so gifted."

"You've made this one very happy."

She put her empty can on the coffee table. "Nic? Don't keep me in suspense. I want to know what the bishop told you."

Nic's heart thundered. "He had a talk with the archbishop and they suggest I present a written, legal contract outlining my plans to their office right away."

Anelise jumped to her feet. "This means they're considering it! You must be thrilled out of your mind."

Almost. "There's just one thing."

"What is it?"

"It's about us." She looked away. "I could read your mind before you left for Orleans yesterday. We'd dealt with Babette and your eyes said there didn't have to be an 'us' now. We no longer needed to be engaged. That is what you thought. Be honest with me."

She nodded. "It must be a great relief to you."

"You're wrong. I don't want to get unengaged."

Odd how shock suddenly altered her appearance. "Why? I don't understand."

If Anelise only knew how he felt about her, but this wasn't the moment to bare his soul. It had only been a week. She'd never believe he wanted to marry her this fast. "I'm only asking that we stay engaged for a bit longer."

She sank back down on the couch without saying anything.

"What's wrong, Anelise? Is there another man you haven't told me about? Someone you're anxious to be with?"

"You know there isn't!"

"Since you've never talked about your former fiancé, does the memory of your engagement make you feel guilty about ours?" Nic didn't believe it was true, but he had to admit to a certain jealousy over the man who'd won her love.

She looked at him in surprise. "That's not it at all. Nic, if we stay engaged now that Babette's threat is over, it will be dishonest. If you remember, you told me you broke your engagement to Denise because you refused to live a lie when you weren't in love with her. I don't want us to live a lie either."

His body tautened. "That relationship was entirely different than the one you and I are in now. I'm asking you to continue as my fiancée for a specific reason." Long enough for him to convince her he couldn't live without her.

"Raimond's illness is forcing me to navigate through some rough waters. Our family doesn't need the added stress that publicity will create if the press learns our engagement is off. Your role as part of the team will be more credible with you wearing my ring. It adds an essential element of trust."

Again she got up. "I agree you've been thrown a curve you never saw coming and I do agree we should stay engaged for a while longer to avoid more press intrusion. The hierarchy of your corporation is undergoing drastic, major changes that are affecting everyone, including you. I *was* planning to look for a rental tomorrow so I could move out, but you're right. It would create more notoriety you don't need."

"Forgive me if it's asking too much of you. I'm sorry."

"No, no. I'm in this with you all the way. For your sake I'm willing to keep up the pretense until things calm down."

Relief washed through him in waves. "That's all I ask. Dinner has arrived. Let's go in the dining room. While we eat, we can draw up that contract to present to the bishop."

"Do you have specs of the project?"

"I've been working with an architect. They're in my bedroom. I'll get them for you." He came back to the dining room with three scrolls. "Take a look at these."

While they ate and talked, Nic's phone rang. It was Raoul. He picked up. "I didn't expect to hear from you tonight. How are things?"

"So bad you wouldn't believe it. Everything that could go wrong has happened. You need to get out here and help me. The sooner, the better."

Nic took a deep breath. He'd never heard Raoul this shaken. "I'll come first thing in the morning."

"I'll be waiting." He rang off.

Anelise stared at him. "What's wrong, Nic? You look ill. Is your father worse?"

"I don't think so. Raoul only said he needed help. It could mean anything. Let's work on that proposal and get some sleep. I want us to leave here at six in the morning."

Her eyes widened. "You want me to go with you? I thought—"

"I know I wanted you here, but this is an emergency. And while we're in La Racineuse we can visit the bishop. You're the attorney on this project. While you finish working on the contract, I'll phone George and Pascal. They're both going to have to run things tomorrow." He also needed to alert the pilot.

* * *

The next morning during the drive from the airport to La Racineuse, Nic told Anelise they would meet his brother at the hospital parking lot. When they arrived, she noticed the place was filled with cars and people. She had no trouble spotting Raoul, who stood out immediately.

This was the first time she'd seen him in person. From a distance they looked identical, but on closer inspection she saw differences. Nic pulled in by his car and they got out.

Raoul walked over to them. "Finally we meet, Anelise." The two brothers were definitely part of a set, but not the same. He kissed her on both cheeks. "Papa raves about you."

"Your brother thinks the world of you."

"It's mutual."

"I've wanted to meet you. I'm sorry about your father and your *oncle.*"

"Thank you. We all are. Raimond is worse than we thought and can't have visitors. Maybe tomorrow."

"I was afraid of that," Nic muttered. "More than ever it's important that you're here to take over. Don't worry about anything. Pascal has climbed on board without a murmur. Between you and me, I think he's perfect for the job."

"I couldn't agree more, but now we need to talk."

"That's why I'm here."

"I'll follow you home."

Anelise knew at once Raoul was disappointed

she'd come. "I have an idea. Since you have so much to talk about, why don't I follow you?"

Nic flashed her a grateful glance. "You don't mind?"

"What do you think?" She got back in the car and started the engine. The two brothers climbed in Raoul's car and took off. Friends from the cradle. With no siblings of her own, she couldn't imagine what that would be like.

When they reached the château, they didn't get out. Anelise didn't move either because she and Nic planned to drive to the church to see the bishop. That was the whole point of her coming here. She leaned back and closed her eyes, enjoying the light breeze through her open window while she waited.

When she felt a lingering kiss on her lips that she wanted to go on and on, she thought she'd been dreaming and opened her eyes. The breathtaking man who stood there was no dream. Her heart quaked.

"Wake up, sleeping beauty. We've a call to make on the bishop."

"Nic—" The car clock revealed she'd been asleep more than an hour. She moved over to the other seat so he could get in and start the car. "Tell me everything!"

"I will after our visit. Do you need to freshen up in the château first?"

"No, thank you. I'm fine. Even if I weren't, I'm dying to know what the bishop will say."

"You and me both."

After a two-minute ride, they reached the church.

Nic walked her into the bishop's office. "Come all the way in and sit down. I'm glad you're here."

"We are too, Your Reverence." He pulled the final documents out of his briefcase and laid them on the desk, then he gripped her hand. She loved it whenever he touched her. The bishop put on his glasses and looked everything over for a long time.

"You've been very thorough. These superb drawings of the new hotel and hospital preserve the majesty of the original church. I also see the area for the bovine research center. Interesting."

"We need more of them. New diseases spring up and always will."

"I'm intrigued you've given this so much thought."

Anelise sat forward. "My fiancé has always had a dream of being a research scientist."

The bishop smiled and put down the papers. "Well, my son, maybe your dream can come true indirectly." She felt Nic's tension. "Everything looks in legal order. I've been given permission to tell you that the property is yours upon this signing."

Oh, Nic—

The bishop put his signature and seal on the paper next to Nic's.

No matter the bad news from Raoul, this was a glorious day. She knew Nic was overcome and she squeezed his hand harder.

"My father will see this and be able to die with some peace."

"Some?" the older priest inquired. "What are you saying?"

"As you know, Jean-Louis has been gone these past ten years."

"Ah, yes. I'm sorry for his suffering."

"You've relieved a lot of it with this signing. The family can't thank you enough."

"Before you leave, I'd like to give you something that belonged to your mother's brother in the seminary. After your father came to us wanting to help rebuild the church in honor of him, I sent for this little book found in his belongings.

"Inside the cover he wrote words of a quote that will be precious to your father. It says, 'If my tongue cannot say in every moment that I love You, I want my heart to repeat it to You as often as I draw breath.'"

He handed the slim book to Nic. It was another moment she'd never forget as her heart streamed into Nic's.

After they left the church and got in the car, he turned to her. "Didn't I tell you that you were my good luck charm?"

"I wish I could fix all the other worries troubling you. Please tell me."

"Where to start."

"That bad?"

"Afraid so."

"Let's get the worst over with first."

Nic cleared his throat. "Claude called Raoul yesterday afternoon. He finally heard from a man who told him Jean-Louis was discharged from the army for multiple illnesses over two weeks ago."

"Multiple? How awful."

"He left his deployment in Africa and there's been no trace of him since. The doctors didn't give him much hope for surviving. He could be anywhere, but Claude won't stop looking for him."

This was too much. "I'm so sorry."

"It's all right, Anelise. Our family has a more immediate problem."

"What else is there?" She sat back, still trying to deal with the terrible news.

"Remember when I told you this area has been plagued with what you could call vendettas?"

She feared what was coming. "Yes."

"The torching of the monastery was only the beginning. Since then there have been a number of unexplained incidents affecting our family. Last night it happened again when someone lit one of the barns on fire. Thankfully some of the workers caught it from spreading in time."

"Nic—I can't believe it. Why do you think it happened?"

"I can tell you exactly why and who did it, but I'd rather talk after we get home." He started the car again.

This man she loved was sailing into rough waters all right.

Soon they reached the château and he parked the car. "Let's go upstairs to my suite where we can be private."

He hustled her inside before anyone saw them. After they entered his bedroom, he put a hand on her arm. She wanted to be more than a comfort to him.

She wanted the right to crush him in *her* arms. "If you weren't here with me right now, Anelise, I'd lose my mind."

Not you, Nic. She'd never known anyone who could handle everything the way he did.

"Do you need something to eat first, Anelise?"

She shook her head. "I'm not hungry yet, but maybe you are. That was a big meal on the plane. I just want to freshen up."

"The bathroom is right through that door."

"Thank you, Nic."

He walked over to the window and looked out on the estate while he waited for her.

"Tell me what you learned from Raoul." She'd come back in the room.

Nic turned to her. "The *grange* is the headquarters for all estate business. He has been there in meetings with the heads of the different services. Only one man didn't show up."

"You say you know the name of this arsonist?"

He nodded. "Old man Dumotte. He's the one in charge of the dairy." After a silence on her part, he said, "I can hear your mind working, Anelise."

She sat down on a nearby chair. "I have a hunch this has everything to do with your brother taking over."

"The truth is, Dumotte never liked our *oncle* Raimond. He's too much of a reminder of Papa and I know Dumotte secretly detests him."

"Why?"

"Dumotte is a man of strong principles that don't

fall in line with the way Causcelles think and run business. He barely tolerated our *oncle*, but Raoul represents our father, the man he's despised for many decades. For Raoul to show up from Paris to take over the estate has pushed him over the top. Dumotte can't handle it and had to do something destructive to let us all know how unhappy he is."

"So the barn fire is his latest declaration of war. Poor Raoul. To have to come home to a hornet's nest when there's so much sadness over your *oncle*'s illness is a nightmare."

Nic put his hands on his hips in a male stance. "Even if it's ugly, Raoul won't put up with it. This is his home where he wants to be and work, his birthright. All the estate workers love him. He'll never want to be anywhere else again."

"Yet the situation couldn't be good for your father when he hears about the fire. What can be done about Dumotte? He's a danger to everyone with his mindset."

"For the time being my brother will put him under surveillance. He's the one with the authority and the only person capable of taking charge with Raimond so ill. If he has to, he'll relieve Dumotte of his duties at the dairy."

"Don't you think if that happens he'll come after Raoul and try to get rid of him? You know what I mean."

"Of course, and knowing that man, he'll fight to the death to keep that job. He has money to hire an attorney."

"Oh, Nic—the man sounds dangerously unstable."

"True, and anything could happen if he's thwarted, but Raoul is taking this in stages."

He felt her searching gaze. "What are you going to do?"

"I can't do anything for Raoul at the moment, so I'm working on a plan for my own life."

He saw a look of anxiety enter those fabulous sapphire eyes. "What are you saying?"

"I'd like to run the Causcelle hospital research centers that are going to be built. The first one will be here, obviously. You weren't far off when you told the bishop it was my dream. With that signed document from the bishop, I'm thinking of moving here permanently."

She seemed to be in shock. "But who will run the hotel division in Paris? There's no one like you."

"As I told you earlier, you could run everything until I have found a successor, Anelise. You're phenomenal."

She slid off the chair. "Your faith in me is astonishing, but… I have my own plans too. Your mind seems to be all over the place right now."

"It's that kind of day. If you truly aren't interested, I have lots of second and third cousins who'd give anything to live in Paris and take my job. And right now I'm getting hungry. Let's grab a bite somewhere. After that I'll show you the place on the property where I want to build my own home. Then we'll leave for the airport."

She shook her head. "What has come over you?"

"Illumination."

"Do you know what kind of house you want?"

"Yes. Something very modern with lots of windows surrounded by nature where children can play and climb trees right outside."

Her face lit up. "I can't imagine anything more wonderful."

"If I do marry, it's possible I'll be the father of triplet girls or boys. And I'll make sure they dress the way they want, figure out their own hair styles, let them explore whatever interests them, choose their own way to make a living in life. I never want them to believe I only think of them as a set."

"Is that what your father did?" She sounded hurt for Nic. He loved her so much for caring that he was in a constant state of pain.

"No, not Papa. It was other people and the media who made us feel like monkeys in a zoo."

Her eyes moistened. "I offended you when I told you how much I loved that photo of the three of you. I'm sorry."

"As I told you before, I was surprised Papa showed it to you, but I wasn't offended. My point is, if I have triplets, I'll want them to know I see each of them as an individual. But the last time I checked, the chances of my children being triplets was one in ten thousand pregnancies."

"Wouldn't it be something if you really did have triplets?"

"It might be fun to find out." He couldn't think

about anything but Anelise and having a life with her. "Since we're flying back to Paris in a little while, let's get going now."

Before long he drove them to a café for cassoulet. After the delicious meal, they reached the spot he'd always envisioned for his home. He gave her his vision of everything. They walked around while he watched her expressions. Her eyes shone like stars the whole time. In his gut he knew she loved his ideas too, but it was growing late.

He glanced at his watch. "I'm afraid we've got to hurry."

"Aren't you going to tell your father what happened with the bishop before we leave?"

"Not today. Right now Papa is having to deal with Raimond's illness. They were very close."

"Of course."

"Tomorrow morning I'll fly back here. Raoul and I will spend time talking everything over with him. The news from the bishop will be first thing I'll tell him. Then we'll explain that Claude has heard Jean-Louis was deployed to a new place a few days ago. It'll be a lie because we don't want him to know he was discharged for being seriously ill. Before long Claude will know the location of our brother. We'll reach out to him and learn the truth."

"That's as good an explanation as any," she murmured. "I hope Claude has more information soon. This has to be so hard on all of you. But your good news will make him so happy."

Only one thing could make Nic happier. First, he had to tell her he wanted her for his wife, then pray for the right answer back.

CHAPTER TEN

FOUR O'CLOCK IN the morning and Anelise had never been wider awake. Nic would be leaving at five for the airport. He wouldn't be back to Paris for a few days or even longer. No doubt he and his brother would develop a strategy to deal with Dumotte and try to comfort their father.

She knew Nic depended on her to be in the office and take care of business. His idea that she could run things had to be the most preposterous assumption she'd ever heard. Her mind replayed a part of their conversation.

You take one look at a project and see the merits as well as the flaws. Ever heard of Tom Brady? He looks at the field and knows where he's going to throw the ball before anyone else has even thought about it.

Nic's over-the-top flattery had been ridiculous. But a dark chill had settled over her when he'd said he was working on a plan for his own life. Nothing could have sent her a clearer signal. She needed to make a life for herself as far away from Nic as possible.

The idea that she could go on working for the corporation would be torture beyond comprehension. He'd be living happily in La Racineuse running his research center and building a home. And she? She'd live the rest of her life in the *palais* doing what? Being the head of the hotel division? She'd known pain at Andre's death, but this would represent death on a totally deeper level.

She flung off the covers and packed up her belongings, waiting for Nic to be gone. After showering, she dressed, put her hair back with a clip and went down to the car with her bag and briefcase. The drive to the office was the shortest one in existence.

Within an hour she'd asked for her desk and equipment to be taken back to her former office. Once organized, she sat at Nic's desk and went through the four files that she'd been given to work on. By that time, Helene, Serge and George had reported for work. She phoned the three of them to come into the office for a meeting.

"Thanks for joining me. As you know, Nic has asked me to be on top of things while he's away, which could be for a few days or even a week. But I should tell you now that I'll be leaving the corporation for good. This is my last day."

Shock broke out on their faces.

"My reasons are personal. I've lost my fiancé and can't cope." It was only the truth. "I hope that answers your questions."

They averted their eyes.

"I know how much Nic values the three of you. He's assured me you could all run this office beautifully forever without him. I believe it. I've gone through the cases assigned to me. Since today will be my last, is there one case any of you are working on that needs some legwork done? I'd appreciate being given something that will take me out of the office and keep me busy."

George leaned forward in the chair. "Louis had been looking at a school out in Fontainebleau. Because of flooding, it's up for sale in the classy part of town. He believes it could be converted into an appealing hotel. Of course, a visit to the engineers must be made before any more action is warranted."

"That's exactly what I'd love to do."

George handed her the file. "It's yours."

She looked inside. "I'll make a copy of this to take with me. I think I'll go to the Loizeau Engineering firm first. If I leave now, it will get done sooner. I'll fax you all the information I find. Thank you so much for everything."

"We'll miss you," George spoke for them before they got up. Both Helene and Serge told her they were sorry she was leaving.

She eyed each one of them. "I'll never forget my time here. You've all been wonderful to me."

As soon as they walked out, she made a copy of the file. Once she'd searched for addresses and phone numbers, she made notations and put the copy in her briefcase. After leaving the original on the desk, she picked up her briefcase and left the office through the elevator to the back entrance.

Once she'd reached her car in the parking lot, she

took off for the town of Fontainebleau. No place in France was more beautiful with its forest and the exquisite château that had housed the kings of France.

At the Loizeau Engineering office, the secretary told her to wait until one of the men could talk to her and she offered her coffee. It tasted good since she hadn't eaten breakfast.

Halfway through her drink, an attractive, sandy-haired man came out to the front desk. The secretary said something and he looked over at Anelise. His blue eyes swept over her with male interest as he walked toward her.

"Mademoiselle Lavigny? You're the attorney from Causcelle Hotels—the one engaged to Nicolas Causcelle. I saw you on TV."

"Yes and yes."

"This is amazing! I'm Philippe Boiteux. I thought it was you when I first saw you, but you're wearing your hair back."

"Looks can be deceiving."

He smiled, revealing his dimples. They reminded her of Andre. She hadn't thought of him for what seemed like forever, but she felt no pain. Nic had cured her. "Follow me to my office."

She did his bidding. Once inside, she handed him the assessment done by the seller. "We want another assessment about the flooding at this school and why it happened before we move forward on anything. Does your firm have time to do this for us?"

"I'll do it now."

"That's very kind of you."

"Why don't we drive over to the school."

"Thank you. I'll meet you there."

She found the address on her car's GPS and drove there. The two-story school had a definite charm. Anelise could understand why Louis had been interested. What a shame there'd been a flood.

The engineer's van pulled up next to her and he waved. "I'll go in and investigate the problem. I estimate it will take me two hours."

"Good. I have an errand to run, but I'll be back. Thanks again."

His blue eyes smiled. Nic had constituted her world so completely, she'd forgotten that other men existed. Out of all the millions of them in the world, why had she happened to meet the one who could never be replaced?

Since she wasn't ready to tell her parents anything yet, she needed to find a place to sleep tonight. After driving around for a while, she found what she wanted at the L'Aigle Noir Hotel and registered there. Not until she drove back to the school around six did she realize the fifteenth-century mansion hotel near the Château de Fontainebleau reminded her of Nic's home at La Racineuse.

Philippe Boiteux was waiting for her outside his van when she drove up. "I'm so sorry. I hope I didn't you keep you waiting too long."

"No problem. I just came out."

"What's the verdict?"

"All the pipes need to be replaced. It's a costly job and all the landscaping will have to be redone. If your

client is willing to pay for it, the work can be done."
He handed her his worksheet.

"I can't thank you enough. My client will take a
look at this and make a decision. If it's a go-ahead,
he'll get in touch with you."

"It's been a pleasure to meet you. I'll probably see
you and your fiancé again on TV."

She didn't plan on any journalist filming her with
Nic again. *"Au revoir et merci."*

Right now she wanted to go to the hotel and watch
something ridiculous on TV until she fell into mind-
less asleep. She would turn off her phone. Tomorrow
would be the beginning of the rest of her life.

Nic said good-night to the family and went upstairs.
He needed to hear Anelise's voice and let her know
he was coming back to Paris in the morning. to hell
with it being too soon to ask her to marry him. No
more waiting. One day away from her was too much.

To his chagrin his call went to her voice mail. He
left a message and waited for her to phone him back.
Nothing. That was odd.

He tried texting her, then turned to email. No response.

It had grown late, but he called her parents. Maybe
she'd gone there to sleep. Her mother answered. "Oh,
Nic—"

"Forgive me for disturbing you. I'm trying to find
Anelise. She isn't answering her phone or messages."

"I'm afraid she's not here. Maybe after she got back
to the hotel she fell asleep."

Maybe... "Have you heard from her today?"

"No. She doesn't always call every day."

"I'm probably worried about nothing. I'll keep looking for her. Call me if you hear anything. I'll do the same."

"Of course, Nic."

He rang off and called Guy at the *palais*. He'd be back from vacation by now. "*Eh bien*, Nicolas. How can I help?"

"Have you seen Anelise?"

"*Oui.* She left at seven this morning in her car."

Nic blinked in surprise. She liked to walk to work. "Thanks for the information." He hung up and phoned George Delong.

"Nicolas?"

"I'm sorry to be calling this late, but I've got to talk to Anelise and can't reach her. When did she go home from the office today?"

"Around noon."

"Noon? I'm talking about when she left work for the day."

"That's what I'm telling you. She planned to check out an engineering firm. We need an assessment for that school out in Fontainebleau your father thought of purchasing. The one with the flooding problem."

He grimaced. "But I don't understand why she didn't return to work later."

"I think I do. Since today was her last, she would have no reason. She told us she would fax—"

"What do you mean *last* day?" he broke in on him in a panic.

"Anelise is a professional, Nic. She called us into a meeting and let us know straight out why. We know it's a blow. She's been a real asset, but the poor girl is suffering."

"George—what in blazes are you talking about?"

"You don't need to pretend with me. She told us she just couldn't cope since losing her fiancé. We understood."

The phone slipped from Nic's hand. He felt like a mountain had just buried him alive. "George?" he cried after grabbing it off the floor. "What engineering firm did she consult?" He had to find her!

"Loizeau Engineering, I believe."

"Thank you."

He was frantic, but it was after midnight, and he couldn't fly to Paris until early morning. *Anelise? Where are you? What's going on with you?*

His pilot flew him out the next morning, but there was a delay. Once back in Paris he went home to an empty suite. As soon as Loizeau Engineering answered their phone at one, he called them. The secretary said the man he needed to talk to was on a conference call. Nic had to wait close to an hour before he was put through to a Philippe Boiteux.

"Monsieur Causcelle? The secretary said you were on the line. I'm sorry I couldn't get back to you sooner. Have you already made a decision about the work on that school's pipe system?"

"Not yet." He broke out in a cold sweat. "I understand my fiancée worked with you yesterday. When

was the last time you saw her? This is vitally important."

"She's a lovely woman." Nic's lips thinned. "I finished my investigation at six, then we both went our
separate ways."

"Do you have any idea where she might have
gone?"

"None. What's wrong, monsieur?"

"I'm not sure," he lied. "Thank you very much
for your time."

He felt like walking death as he paced the floor of
the salon. No one had phoned to tell him anything.
There'd been no word from Anelise. Desperate to do
something, he phoned Claude, who didn't call him
back for an hour.

"Thank you for returning my call. As I told you
on the phone, my fiancée is missing and I need help."

"You think this has something to do with Babette
Lafrenière?"

"No. This is personal."

"If you're sure."

"Positive." This had to do with her former fiancé.

"Give me a description of her car and license plate."

"One moment. The license is in her work information on my computer." He rushed in the bedroom
to get it, then got back on the phone with Claude. "I
can never thank you enough."

"I'll get the police right on it."

His eyes closed tightly for a moment. "Like I said,
name your price."

After hearing the click, Nic called her parents

again. Her father answered immediately. "My wife's on the line with us. Any news yet, Nic?" They were worried sick too.

"Did you know that she resigned to the office staff yesterday morning without telling me?"

"What?" Her father sounded shocked. "She would never do that."

"But she did. I can't find her anywhere, and I've got the police working on it. Hugo? Does Anelise have a favorite place where she goes sometimes? You know what I mean."

"Not that I can think of."

"Nic?" his wife chimed in. "Did she tell your staff why she was leaving the corporation?"

"Yes." He'd never been in more agony. "She said she couldn't cope since losing her fiancé."

"That's very interesting. Which fiancé was she talking about, Nic?"

"Andre, of course."

"Fiddlesticks. She confided in me about the night of your public engagement. She said that riding up to the top of the Eiffel Tower with you was the most transforming moment of her life. She claimed she could have stayed there with you forever. Later when you showed up in Orleans at my mother's home, she had those same stars in her eyes and darted off with you so fast we all laughed. What's going on with you two?"

He sucked in his breath. "I'm in love with her."

"Have you told her that?"

"I wanted to ask her to marry me from day one, but I didn't think she would believe me."

"You're not like your father after all," Hugo blurted. "Don't you think it's about time she knew the truth so we can all get some sleep?" Hugo had hit him where it hurt, but Anne laughed.

"You've given me an idea. Bless you. I'll get back to you."

He rang off and raced out to his car. Before long the *Tour Eiffel* came into view. Could it be true she'd been suffering all this time too? Was it possible she'd gone there today to relive the magic of the moment when they'd fallen in love?"

The crowded parking lot aggravated him. He found the first spot available and hurried into the electric elevator. Maybe she was in the restaurant looking out at the view.

Marcel saw him the second he walked in the room and ran over to him. "Ah, you must be looking for your beautiful fiancée. She came in for a while, then left to go to the observation area."

Nic hugged him, so thankful for this news he couldn't find words. In the next breath he hurried out to reach the other level. There was always a crowd of people, but Anelise stood out from everyone else. Her long hair, her bewitching profile and figure robbed him of breath. He drew closer and noticed she still wore the ring.

"Anelise?" She wheeled around and stared at him like he were an apparition. "You need to come home with me now."

"H-how did you know I was here?" she stammered.

"I'll tell you later. Right now the police are looking for your car. I need to let them and your parents know I've found you."

"But—"

"No buts, *mon amour*."

He threw his arm around her shoulders and walked her over to the elevator that would take them below. "You've been one difficult runaway to find. Thank heaven I've come to the end of my search."

"I thought you weren't coming home for a few more days."

They reached his car and he helped her in. "My plans changed. Everything changed the moment I met you."

When he climbed behind the wheel, he messaged her parents and Claude that all was well. He also sent a message to the kitchen to prepare a lavish dinner and bring it to his suite. Finally he messaged Pierre to arrange for someone to pick up her Peugeot and return it to the *palais* parking.

Turning to her, he said, "Your car will be back shortly. All that matters now is that we're together."

"But we're not really together," she cried as Nic drove them home.

"Oh, yes we are! What I don't understand is why you didn't answer my phone calls or messages. And where did you stay last night? I want to hear your explanations once we're in our suite."

Nic's suite, not hers. Arguing with him proved to be impossible. She walked in the salon and sat down on a chair.

He followed and removed his suit jacket, tossing

it on the end of the couch. "I'm waiting for answers, Anelise."

"I stayed at the L'Aigle Noir in Fontainebleau and didn't want to be disturbed."

"Not even by your boss?"

"I was too tired last night to do anything but sleep."

"What if I'd been your husband? Would you have done the same thing to me?"

"Don't be absurd. Haven't you figured it out yet? I've enjoyed being one of the attorneys, but I don't want to be the CEO of anything!"

"I don't want that for you either. I've got something else in mind for both of us."

Her head lifted. "What are you saying?"

"I want to be your husband. A few days ago, I obtained permission to marry you at church without having to wait the usual three weeks. All you have to do is say yes."

Her heart almost collapsed on itself. "Please be serious, Nic. I can't take this any longer."

"Do you think I can? I'm in love with you, Anelise. I want you for my wife." He came closer and cupped her face in his hands. "I realize you think it's too soon for me to tell you how I feel. You're about to tell me I don't know what I'm saying and that I couldn't possibly mean it. Next, you're going to say I never loved Denise, but you'd be wrong.

"I *did* love her for many reasons, but I wasn't in love with her. I didn't know if falling in love was possible for me until I met you. Now I'm aching to marry you as soon as possible. I want you in my bed day and night. I want to have children with you. I want you for my lover and soul mate. But I'm terrified that you could never love me the way you loved Andre. What if—"

Anelise pressed her mouth to his so he couldn't say another word. She stood up and threw her arms around his neck, kissing him with a passion that had been growing inside her from that first day.

Nic picked her up like a bride and lay down on the couch with her. Time lost meaning while they got to know each other in the way lovers do. She couldn't get close enough. No kiss lasted long enough.

"I want to take you to bed right now," he said against her neck. "But I want us to be married first. We might have a set of triplets and I want them to know you and I were legally wed before they came along. But I'm getting ahead of myself since you haven't told me if you'll marry me."

She pressed kisses over his handsome features before finding his mouth again. "I've been showing you how much I want to marry you ever since you asked me to go along with the fake engagement. Thank heaven for Babette, who brought us together.

"Do you honestly think I would have agreed to it if I hadn't already been smitten? The newspaper was right. I fell so hard for you, Nic Causcelle, it was scary. Yes, I'll always love the memory of Andre. He was wonderful, but that was a century ago. You and I are living in this one, and I can't wait to be your wife." More time passed as they devoured each other. Heaven on earth *did* exist.

"Cherie—" he murmured and reached for her left hand, removing the ring. "Do you remember Brigitte asking if I'd let you keep this?"

"I'll never forget that day."

"Well, she's going to find out after I ask this question. Anelise Lavigny—will you do me the honor of marrying me and making me the happiest man in existence?"

"Oh, Nic—*yes, yes!*"

He slid the ring back on and kissed her hand. "It's official now. Let's get married as soon as we can while my father is still well enough to watch the ceremony. Maybe Raimond will be able to watch too. I know your parents would rather give you away here in Paris, but—"

"Don't say another word, darling. My parents knew I was crazy about you from the beginning. I don't want to wait either."

"Your father gave me a grilling when I called them in desperation looking for you. He said I wasn't like my father after all, but he was wrong. I wanted you immediately the way my father did with my mother. But I went about it a different way by getting you to live in my suite with me first. Raoul knew what I was up to. He'd seen us together on TV and wouldn't let me forget it. As for your mother, you'll never know how grateful I am for her. She knew I was in excruciating pain and said something that helped me find you."

"What was it?"

"Apparently you confided in her about the night of

our pretend engagement. Little did you know I wasn't pretending. Not any of it."

"I knew what I felt was real too, Nic. I told Maman you held me in your arms as we ascended the Tour Eiffel. You made me feel safe and cherished. With you I felt we were traveling through this glorious universe together. I admitted I'd found my heart's desire."

"Because of her, I drove there and found you!" Nic kissed her with a hunger that sent them skyrocketing.

"Darling?" she whispered when she could breathe again. "My parents will understand about the ceremony being in La Racineuse. They want to make it easy on your father."

"Why don't we call them tonight with the news and fly to La Racineuse tomorrow? We'll tell my family our plans when we get there and ask the bishop to marry us."

"Let's keep it simple and secret."

"You know my heart so well, it's a miracle."

"I can't wait to go back to La Racineuse. When we stayed in the château, I saw dozens of framed pictures on the walls on the way up to the bedrooms. The pictures of you at different ages and stages delighted me. I have a favorite."

He kept kissing her mouth. "Which one?"

"You had to be seventeen, maybe eighteen, and were driving a tractor. You wore overalls and had a smile as big as the outdoors. With longer curly hair, you were gorgeous. I fell in love with you all over again. Even if I am three years younger, if I'd met you in high school, I would have had a horrible crush on you, and you would have run from me. How many girlfriends followed you around wanting to be with you every minute? Tell me the truth."

Nic laughed, kissing every delectable feature of her face. "Dozens."

"I knew it. Anyone serious?"

"Not until business college, where I had several relationships. But none of them were strong enough to settle into anything permanent. At that time, Jean-Louis broke with father. When our schedule gave us time off from studying, Raoul usually went back to La Racineuse."

"What did *you* do?"

"I did some traveling around Europe and spent a little time in England. I discovered girls everywhere and had some good times. But I couldn't see myself being tied down to one woman. Not until I met you."

"I still can't believe you love me."

"Since the day I saw you walking toward the office, I've dreamed of holding you like this. You didn't know I was behind you."

"That explains why you opened the door to George's office so fast after I went in."

"You hooked me without even knowing it. The happy lilt in your walk, the feminine beauty of you took my breath. You had an aura different from anyone else around you. I wanted to breathe it in, if that makes sense, like I'd been put in a trance."

She kissed his neck. "I have a confession too. When I followed you down the hall to your office, I understood why the press had such a fixation on you.

Talk about a presence—you had it in spades. Looking at you made me feel the way I did when I first saw Michelangelo's *David*. Your essence spoke to me the same way. I have never gotten over meeting you for the first time. To think there are three of you made like that...like gods."

"Anelise."

"So you *do* blush. That's something fun to know about you I'll treasure. I also heard your stomach grumbling. I think our dinner must be waiting."

"You know far too much about me. I love it. I love you." He crushed her to him before they got up and walked to the dining room.

The coq au vin had to be one of the best meals Anelise had eaten in years. Nic poured the wine. She'd had one glass and should have turned down a second. How foolish of her when she rarely drank at all. There was no cure for being in love with Nic, who'd made her forget about other men.

His velvety black eyes wandered over her. "Do you want more of anything?"

"Only you."

"Then let's go in the salon and dance."

Across the table, her azure eyes shimmered. "You have a romantic side to your nature."

"It's one way of making love to you. If you want to know the truth, I'm having trouble keeping my hands off you."

"You're not the only one," she murmured.

He turned on some soft rock music and pulled her into his arms. They danced for a long time, relishing the feel of each other. "Anelise," his voice throbbed. He took her back to the couch, where they got tangled together.

"Nic?" She sounded out of breath. "I keep thinking of the Seine swirling around Paris. It reminds me of the two of us with our arms wrapped around each other. I love you, Nic. So much you'll never know." She buried her face in his shoulder. "Maybe we won't be sleeping together yet, but could we stay like this until we leave for the airport in the morning?"

"You're reading my mind." His hand played with her hair. "*Mon amour?* How would you like to fly to La Racineuse tomorrow by a different mode of transportation?"

"You mean a helicopter?"

"No. I'm thinking of a certain Batmobile."

His response produced a squeal of delight he'd never heard come out of her before. "As it's the spring break, your nephews and nieces will be home. They'll die of joy and love you forever."

"I admit it'll be fun. I'll drive them around the property."

She kissed his lips. "You really do have a secret dream to be a race car driver. I have a secret too. When we whizzed to the *Tour Eiffel*, I found myself wishing we could take off for parts unknown and never come back. At least we've got tomorrow to do that."

"I'll call Raoul and bring him up to date. He'll call the bishop's secretary to make an appointment for us.

Then I'll phone Pierre now so Rudi will bring the car over in the morning."

"Only one half hour with your brother tonight. I want the rest of it with me."

He laughed, then let go of her and got up from the couch. His phone rested on the coffee table. She sat up to watch him. After he hung up, she said, "We'll stop along the way for picnic food."

His eyes gleamed. "Life with you is going to be one continuous adventure."

"Especially if we have triplets. First there was that news anchor who announced the contest about our having triplets and giving the winner a Bugatti. Then you talked about triplets when you showed me the property where you wanted to build your home. I haven't been able to think about anything else since."

"It *is* a possibility. But building our own home is a fact. I'll bring the specs I've had an architect draw up. You can look them over to your heart's content during our drive. Your input is vital. From now on everything we do will be together." He returned to the couch and pulled her on top of him. "For the rest of the night I have to hold you. Maybe by morning I'll believe this is really happening."

CHAPTER ELEVEN

A SEMI-CLOUDY DAY didn't take away from Anelise's happiness. A drive in the Bugatti gave a trip new meaning. She and Nic arrived at the family château the next day in time for lunch. With everyone assembled except Raoul, there couldn't have been a more perfect time to make their announcement. Then they'd go to the church to arrange their marriage with the bishop.

Nic stood up and reached for her hand. "Before I take all you kids for a ride, Anelise and I want you to know we're getting married as soon as possible. When our house is built out at Roselin Woods, we plan to live here in La Racineuse."

"Yay!" the children screeched in delight, then jumped to their feet to hurry outside. Anelise looked up at Nic and they both laughed. That started the adults laughing.

"Go ahead, Nic," she whispered. "Show them the time of their lives."

"I'm marrying an angel." He pressed a kiss to her lips, then hurried out of the dining room.

"I want to watch," Louis declared with a smile. "Let's all go out to the front porch."

Anelise could tell the announcement had breathed new life into Nic's father. Luca pushed him while the rest of them followed. Everyone welcomed her to the family. Their kindness thrilled her heart.

Nic took each child separately, then in groups. He zoomed around and finally let Honore drive it while Nic sat at his side. Because Anelise had never had siblings, she loved being part of this fantastic family. This would be a memorable day in Causcelle history.

"Anelise?" Louis called to her. She moved over next to him. "I've prayed for this day. My son is a different man since the moment he met you. Would that my other two boys could find the happiness that shines in my Nic's eyes. I love you for that."

"I love you too. You raised a remarkable family and saved my father from going to prison."

"So Hugo told you."

"He told me everything. If anyone is a saint, it's you. Nic is going to build that hospital with a research center out of his love for you. If we're blessed to have children and produce a son, we're naming him Louis."

He reached out and took hold of her hand. His eyes danced. "What if you have triplets?"

She chuckled. "As Nic said, it's a possibility. If they're boys, we'll name them Louis, Hugo and Raimond after your beloved brother."

His hand squeezed hers. "He's not long for this world either. His Celine is waiting for him." *Nic's mother was waiting for Louis too.*

While they both wept, the Bugatti roared into view. Honore climbed out of the driver's seat with a huge grin on his face. "He let me drive over to the *grange*. Oncle Raoul couldn't believe it!"

Nic leaned out the open window. His eyes met hers. "Now it's your turn, *mon coeur*."

"Oncle Nic said he wanted *you* to drive it."

She smiled at Honore. "I think I will."

Anelise leaned over to kiss Louis's cheek, then hurried to the car and got in behind the wheel. "I'll take us to the church now." She started the engine and they took off. "The power of this car would make anyone reckless."

"That's why we'll be returning this the second we get back to Paris. After the next turn in the road, pull over to the side."

His good mood had changed all of a sudden. She did his bidding and turned off the car. "What's wrong?"

"I went in the office to see Raoul before he came outside with me. We've hit several snags. The bishop has gone on sabbatical for six months. If we want to be married, Father Didier can do it tomorrow. Otherwise, his calendar is filled for a whole month. But here's the other problem.

"Raoul is trying to contain the tension created by Dumotte. If our marriage takes place at the church and people come, it's going to cause an uproar and Dumotte will go out of control completely."

Anelise was thinking hard. "Will the priest marry us at the château?"

"Yes."

"Tomorrow?"

"Yes. He has an opening at three in the afternoon."

"Will it be okay with Corinne?"

"She'll love it. Everyone will come together and fix food."

"Then I don't see a problem. I talked with your father while you were out joyriding. He knows the end is coming soon for him and Raimond. He's living to see you married before that happens."

Nic reached for her, pressing his forehead against hers. "There's no woman in this world like you. Do you think your parents can handle this?"

"Of course. They know I'm dying to marry you. I'll call them right now."

"Tell them I'll send a car to pick them up in the morning and drive them to the airport. When they arrive, we'll collect them in one of the cars and bring them here."

Anelise nodded and got busy. Her parents were overjoyed and would be ready first thing in the morning. She clicked off. "We need to hurry back to the château and tell Corinne and her husband what we've got planned."

"We won't be able to get away on a honeymoon for a while."

"I feel like I'm on one with you right now."

A wicked smile broke out on his unforgettable face. "That's how much you know about honeymoons. There's another part of the château that hasn't been used for a while. It's away from everyone. We'll spend

our wedding night there and all the other nights when
we're out here until our home is built."

"Nic—" The cry from her heart resounded in the
car. She leaned across to kiss him, then she turned
the key.

Three o'clock the next day couldn't come soon enough
for Nic. The family had gathered in the large salon,
where they were all seated. Corinne had arranged
several sprays of flowers around the room. A painting of Nic's beautiful, dark-haired mother hung over
the fireplace. The priest stood in front of it in his traditional wedding vestments.

That's where Nic wanted to stand with Anelise
to take their vows. Neither of them had time to buy
wedding clothes. He wore his dressiest business suit.
She came into the salon with her father wearing an
ivory *peau-de-soie* two-piece suit her mother must
have brought. The pearl buttons matched the pearls
she'd worn on their way to the jeweler's. He'd given
her a corsage of white roses and he wore one of the
roses in his lapel.

Had it only been a few weeks ago? With the diamond on her finger, the only thing he could give her
was the inscribed gold band he'd been waiting to slide
on her ring finger.

Hugo walked his breathtaking daughter over to Nic
before taking his place next to Anelise's attractive
mother. Nic's father sat next to them in his wheelchair.
Both their fathers looked smart in their best suits.

The priest cleared his throat. He looked around

with a smile. "You have no idea what a lovely sight this is. To see a family like yours, young and old, all joined together to honor a favorite son and the woman he has chosen for eternity, gives me hope for this world.

"The bishop is truly sorry that he had to leave the area and couldn't marry the first Causcelle son. He sends you his blessings and his love to Louis and Raimond for all they've done for the community and France itself. We're aware of Raimond still being in the hospital and pray for him.

"Nic? Anelise? If you'll come closer holding hands, we'll get you united the way you want to be. I'll keep this short and sweet the way that I've been asked to do." He sent Nic a private message.

Father Didier was a good man. Nic grasped her hand and they stepped closer to him. "Nicolas Ronfleur Causcelle, do you take this woman Anelise Mattice Lavigny, to be your lawfully wedded wife? Do you promise to love and cherish her forever, through good and bad, always keeping her in your heart?"

"I do."

"Anelise Mattice Lavigny, do you promise to love and cherish Nicolas Ronfleur Causcelle forever, through good and bad, always keeping him in your heart?"

"I do," she said with a tremor in her voice.

"Then by the power vested in me, I now pronounce you man and wife. You may kiss your bride once you've exchanged rings."

Nic stared into her eyes as he pulled the gold band

out of his pocket and slid it on her finger next to the diamond. Her face glowed before she did something he didn't expect. She reached for his left hand and slid a gold band with a black solitaire diamond on his finger.

"Nicolas? The bride asked me to tell you that you've already lived up to the meaning of the stone that promises to be trustworthy, honest and perfect."

After hearing those words, Nic couldn't think, let alone swallow. Her beautiful face swam before his eyes. He gathered her in his arms and kissed her with his heart and soul, forgetting all else.

Maybe he'd died and gone to heaven with her. That's what it felt like. When he finally came to and lifted his head, he realized they were alone in the salon. Everyone had left quietly and gone into the dining room.

"Oh, Nic   I'm so embarrassed." She hid her face in his shoulder.

"Let's do this right and go upstairs, *mon epouse*."

"Yes, please."

In the next instant he picked up his bride and carried her through the house and up the stairs. While she kissed him, he swept them down the hall to the wing of the château prepared for them. Once inside the suite, he lowered her to the floor and closed the door, pressing her against it.

"When did you get me my ring?" he asked against her lips.

"I called Xan yesterday and told her what I wanted. I asked her to courier it to my parents. She's amazing."

"My ring is amazing. I love it."

"I love mine too."

They began removing their clothes, breathlessly kissing each other at the same time. Nic had never known desire like this. He helped remove her pearl necklace and earrings, putting them on the nearby dresser.

Like before, he picked her up and carried her to the king-size bed, where he followed her down. She kissed his jaw. "I'll love that priest forever for marrying us so fast."

"I'll love *you* forever," he half growled against her tender throat. The age-old ritual began with two people madly in love and finally able to show each other how they felt. Anelise had to be the most exquisite woman on earth inside and out. He couldn't believe he'd been able to stay away from her this long.

By some miracle she loved him and made love to him in ways he didn't know existed. She'd been gifted with an incredibly generous nature. It came out in her loving. Together they soared to impossible heights.

"I adore you," she cried over and over, enveloping him in her embrace. He felt her tears of ecstasy on his skin. They mingled with his own as he rolled on top of her, coming close to devouring her.

Darkness filled the room, but nothing mattered. They'd taken each other on a trip of such sensual pleasure, he knew he'd never be the same again. Again and again throughout the night they brought each other the joy of being man and wife in every possible way.

When the light of morning filtered in through the windows, he lay there looking at the most heavenly creation imaginable. What had he ever done in his life to deserve her? His mind contemplated the years ahead with her, the endless happiness…

"Darling?" She'd opened her eyes and she reached out to stroke his face.

"How long have you been awake?"

He leaned over to kiss her luscious mouth. "Long enough to need to relive our wedding night all over again."

She pulled him closer and wrapped her arms around him. "Not in my entire life did I know I could feel this fulfilled. It's more than happiness. It's joy beyond measure being married to you, knowing we belong to each other. Never let me go."

"Just try to get away from me, *mon tresor.*"

Their excitement knew no bounds in their need to experience the ultimate with each other. Near noon, Nic realized he was human after all and needed to eat.

This time he awakened to see Anelise lying there studying him with a lovestruck expression in her azure eyes.

"I know you're hungry, *mon mari.* So am I. My only concern is facing everyone when we go downstairs to eat."

"We have to deal with it sometime. Let's get in the shower. I've been dreaming of taking one with you. You don't know those nights I pictured you in the shower at the *palais* after you left me desolate."

"Would it shock you if I told you I hoped you'd

come into my bedroom and tell me you couldn't take the separation a moment longer?"

"Now she tells me." He kissed her again.

"I thought you were hungry. If we take a shower together, it could take a couple of hours."

"You're right. Making love hasn't damaged that razor-sharp brain of yours."

"I'll hurry. Don't look at me too hard while I escape," she teased, causing Nic to explode with laughter. Quick as a wink, she slid out of bed and hurried into the bathroom.

Ten minutes later Nic grasped her hand and they went downstairs. She looked at him. "The house seems awfully quiet."

"I noticed."

They walked in the kitchen, where they found Julie drinking juice. "Oh—I'm glad you're up, Oncle Nic."

"Where is everyone?"

"I stayed behind to tell you. The hospital called in the middle of the night. Raimond passed away."

"Oh, no." Anelise put her arm around Nic. Just yesterday Louis had talked to her about his brother's numbered days.

"They all went over this morning."

"*Papa* too?"

"Yes."

"And Anelise's parents?"

She nodded. "There's sandwiches and salad here in the fridge for you from yesterday." She pulled out two covered plates. "If you want coffee, it's ready."

"Thanks, Julie. You're a sweetheart." They both sat down to eat. "Do you want to drive over to the hospital with us in a minute?"

Her face lit up. "Can I?"

"We'll make room for you."

"I'll get my purse. I left it in the other room."

When she ran out, Nic put his arm around Anelise. "We now have a funeral to plan. I'd give anything if we could track down Jean-Louis. He loved Raimond."

"This means Raoul really is in full charge. It's a miracle that we're moving here too. He'll need your support."

"As I said the other day, the family is moving into a rough sea. I need *your* support more than ever, *mon amour*. You just don't know how much."

* * * * *

THE MILLIONAIRE'S ITALIAN INVITATION

ELLIE DARKINS

MILLS & BOON

For all my readers

PROLOGUE

Ally: You're never going to believe what my parents have done now!

Caleb: IDK? Smothered you with love and affection?

Well… Yes. Obviously. But you're going to have to be more specific if you want to win the speedboat.

I already have a speedboat.

What? Really?! Of course you do…

Stop stalling.

Guess!

They… I don't know…made you dinner?

Caleb, that's not smothering. That's normal parenting.

Maybe for people whose parents didn't send them to boarding school and then leave the country...

embarrassed emoji Sorry, sorry. We don't have to play. You already have a speedboat!

It's fine. I was teasing. I want the boat. They...set you up on a date again? Even though you begged them not to after you broke that nice doctor's heart?

I did *not* break his heart!

But was I right?

Sort of... Except it's much worse. Hang on... Need to copy and paste:

Dear Ally, Welcome to the Single No More family! We can't wait to welcome you on board for a trip of a lifetime. A cruise around the beautiful Scilly Isles with other vetted and background-checked singles. Prepare for romantic candlelit dinners, evening strolls around the decks and days relaxing by the pool...

There's more, but you get the idea.

Ally...is this...real? Do they really want you to go?

Yes. I need to get out of it. Any ideas? Also, how's the wedding going?

Excruciating. Rowan and Jonathan are besotted. Adam and Liv are barely keeping their hands to themselves. They glare at me every time I pick up my phone. How early is too early to leave?

You have to stay until they cut the cake. You can do it. I believe in you.

Easy for you to say. Can't believe I have to go to Italy with them in a week. A whole seven days of family time. If you figure out the answer to getting out of awkward family stuff...

Cal?

...

CAL!

...

Cal, are you there?

Hey, Liv confiscated my phone. Have you packed for your cruise yet?

Don't laugh, please? I have to get out of this.

Can't you just tell them you don't want to go?

Tried it. Didn't take. So I did something that you're probably going to be mad about...

What did you do?

I told Mum I had a boyfriend.

You said you'd already tried that?

I did. She didn't believe me. Wanted to know who it was. Because apparently the only person I ever talk about is you. So I told her it was you. My boyfriend. I told her you were my boyfriend...

...

Cal? You still there?

CHAPTER ONE

THIS WAS FINE. He was fine, Ally was fine, and everything between him and Ally was fine.

There was absolutely no reason that he should be freaking out about the fact that her lying to her parents about them dating had somehow snowballed in the space of a week to him standing at the arrivals gate at Bari airport, waiting to meet his best friend in person for the first time. And then trying to convince his own family as well as hers that they were dating for real and didn't need any further interference in their love lives—or lack thereof.

Caleb remembered how inspired he had felt when the solution to both their problems had struck him as he'd read Ally's last message in the middle of the night. She'd needed to convince her parents to stop trying to find her a boyfriend. He could convince his siblings that he was perfectly happy with the life that he was living, and they could stop worrying about him and covertly staring at him between sessions of making out with their new partners in places that were way too public for his liking.

They had gone from subtly criticising the amount of time that he spent staring at a screen to full-on confiscating his devices. Somehow, his protestations that he was both working and talking to his friend hadn't been enough to convince them that he was capable of making his own choices about living his life and that they didn't have to worry about him any more. Perhaps they would be more understanding if they thought that he was sexting…

He'd been facing the prospect of a week of poolside 'family time'—because somehow his brother and new sister-in-law, his sister and her boyfriend, had decided to crash his annual visit to the Italian villa that he had inherited from their grandparents—and if he didn't want them to worry about him he was going to have to occasionally put down his phone and his laptop and spend time with them.

And what better way to convince them that he was *'absolutely fine, thanks'* than by introducing them to the person that he had been spending all his time hanging out with—online—over the last year.

Instead of being dragged away by his family when all he really wanted to do was chat with Ally, he could just…invite Ally along. That way he wouldn't have to justify the time that he wanted to spend talking to her. All that plotting and scheming aside, he'd love for her to come to Italy, for her own sake. For his. Because after all this time putting it off, the thought of actually spending a week with his best friend without a screen between them felt like too much of a treat to pass up.

They'd put this off—the meeting in person thing—

for so long that he'd started to forget that it wasn't the way that friendships normally worked. They lived in the same city. They could have jumped in an Uber and spent time together in the real world any time in the past year.

They'd met on an online role-playing game, started chatting as they'd played. When they'd realised that they'd spent more time chatting than playing, they'd moved their friendship off the platform and for the past few months had spent most of their days messaging one another with something that they thought would make the other laugh. The details of their day. Offloading about their families when it all became too much.

They could have just met for a coffee in London, where they both lived. That would have made so much more sense than doing this here, in a foreign airport, with his whole family waiting for him at the end of their short drive home.

But things had got to the point where they had gone so long with neither of them suggesting a coffee that the thought of doing it had become this big, insurmountable obstacle in their way. Ally's friendship had become so important to him that he didn't want to do anything that might risk her deciding that he really wasn't worth the effort. So rather than tackle that obstacle, he'd let the pressure build up behind it until—*poof*—he was issuing invitations for a week in Italy with his family halfway through his brother's wedding rather than suggesting an Americano in his local coffee shop.

The problem with wanting to get close to Ally was that…well, he knew what happened when someone got close to her—like that doctor who was absolutely not good enough for her. They got shown the door before they could get too comfortable. And he'd seen what happened when people got close to him—his parents had felt so burdened by their children that they'd upped and left them without a backward glance before he was even out of school. And Jonathan had inherited the responsibility for a teenager and had never quite managed to hide how much it had cost him.

If Caleb keeping his friendship with Ally solely online was what kept it alive, he'd been okay with that. But this… If they could do this without Ally getting freaked out and bailing on their friendship, without him feeling as though he was a burden to everyone who cared about him, they could hang out for a week to get their families off their backs, and then they could go back to hanging out online, as they had for the last year.

So why were his palms sweating?

It was just because the aircon in the terminal building was non-existent and Ally's plane was late, so he'd been standing in the heat waiting for her for two hours. Probably his siblings still thought that Ally was going to turn out to be a figment of his imagination and stage another of those 'don't you think you should put down your devices' interventions. It wasn't as if he didn't leave the house—he spent time outdoors, he travelled, he explored London. But he wasn't exactly going to invite his family along when they'd just spend the whole time feeling as though they were responsible for him or something. And these days he preferred to have his phone or his laptop with him so that he could chat to Ally while he was doing it.

It didn't seem to matter how many times that he told his family that he had everything he needed, friends and a social life included, they continued to worry. He wasn't sure how much time a week pretending to date Ally would buy him, but he was willing to take what he could get.

When another stream of people began to pass through the arrivals gate, he watched as couples and families and lone travellers emerged from the corridor without any sign of Ally.

The stream of people petered out and he was resigning himself to waiting even longer when he saw her. She had her eyes on her phone screen, brows drawn together in concentration. She dragged behind her a shiny silver suitcase, and wore a bright orange sundress, almost the same colour as her hair, which had slipped a little to reveal a creamy-white shoulder and the strap of a halter neck bikini. She was going to burn in this heat, he thought. At that moment, she looked up, caught his gaze on her, and a smile spread from her wide mouth, up over rosy apple cheeks to sparkling dark eyes. She stopped in front of him without a shred of uncertainty.

'Ally?' he asked. She replied by wrapping her arms around his neck, squeezing tight and squealing in his ear.

'Caleb! I can't believe it's you.'

'You barely even checked.' He laughed, holding her at arm's length to get a proper look at her. She was…amazing. Bright colours and tumbling curly hair and curves everywhere, so tempting to the eye that he drew his eyes swiftly away and fixed them on her face instead, where he thought they would be safer. He was wrong, because she looked knowingly at him and laughed. 'What if you'd got the wrong guy?'

'Of course it was you. You look… I don't know. Just like you. Have you been waiting long?' she asked. He dodged the question and reached for Ally's suitcase before she snatched it out of reach and pulled it along as they headed for the enormous sliding doors out of the terminal building. 'How long will it take us to drive to your place?' Ally asked as they climbed into the car.

'About half an hour until my family embarrass me completely and you regret ever agreeing to this,' Caleb told her, only half joking.

'Come on, they can't be as bad as mine. So, what have you told them?' she asked as they pulled out of the airport car park and narrowly avoided being swiped by a dinged-up Fiat that seemed to have come out of nowhere.

'About what?' he asked, flicking on his indicator and gritting his teeth as he approached a roundabout. He'd only arrived in Italy yesterday and hadn't quite acclimatised to the local driving yet.

Ally whacked his arm once they were on the road towards the villa.

'So have you told them *anything* about who I am and why I'm here and everything like that?'

He glanced across at her before focusing his eyes safely back on the road.

'I told them that I was bringing someone.'

She rolled her eyes. 'That's it? You didn't tell them that we're friends or how we met or that I lied to my parents and told them we were dating?'

He shrugged again, pulling out to overtake a slower car in front. 'I didn't want to overstep. We haven't really talked about what's going on and I wasn't sure whether the pretending to be your boy-friend was just for your family or mine too.' And even without that complication, he wouldn't know how to explain their friendship to the others in a way that they would understand. It was only occurring to him now—in a way that made him realise how seriously he had had his head in the sand about this—that it would have made much more sense to discuss this before Ally had actually arrived.

He didn't trust that his family would understand that Ally could be his best friend despite the fact that they hadn't met in person before this weekend. If he'd thought about it he would probably have guessed that if he turned up with a woman that they'd not met be-fore, then his family would assume that she was his girlfriend. But perhaps that was why he'd tried so hard *not* to think about it—had he wanted them to jump to that conclusion? What would that mean for his friendship with Ally, his feelings about her?

'Well, I told my parents you were my boyfriend,' Ally observed wryly, her eyes fixed firmly on the landscape ahead of them. 'I probably overstepped for the both of us.'

He risked a glance across at her as he pulled out onto the highway. 'If it helps, my family will probably just assume that we're together,' he told her, trying to keep his voice safely neutral.

'And you're okay with that?' Ally asked.

He took a deep breath. 'I think it will stop them bugging me about whether I have a girlfriend and shouldn't I go out more and is it healthy for me to spend so much of my time working. For some reason they worry about me, and I don't want them to. You'll be doing me a favour if we go along with it. They'd probably just ask more questions if I told them that we're only friends.'

He was aware of her looking at him for a few moments before she spoke again. 'Well, okay. As long as we have our stories straight about this before I meet everyone.'

That surprised a laugh out of Caleb, an uncanny reminder that this was the same woman who made him laugh on a daily basis, only this was the first time that she was around to hear it. 'Ally, we didn't rob a bank. We don't need to *"get our stories straight"*. It's none of their business what we are to each other.'

'Of course it's not, but I don't want to get caught out! I told my family that you were my boyfriend and that you're whisking me away to your holiday home. They're going to want pictures or they'll think I'm making it up. And we can't just say *nothing* to your family. It'll be embarrassing, for one thing, and make them think you're weirder than they already do, for another.'

Caleb snorted another laugh. 'Well, thank you for that vote of confidence. Fine. We'll tell them that you're my girlfriend. They're always telling me that they're worried I spend so much time working or looking at a screen. It never seems to matter how many times I tell them that I don't want them to worry about me. I don't want that happening again, and if it takes a little white lie to make it go away then I'm okay with that.'

Ally gave him a look that was a little too searching to be comfortable. 'I'm not saying that I agree with them,' she said gently. 'And you don't have to lie to your family. I'm happy being your friend, Cal. I just don't want to walk in there unprepared.'

But Caleb shook his head. Because this was the perfect solution. If he turned up with Ally as his girlfriend, there would be no more worrying about him. No more interventions. No more feeling as if his very presence in their lives was a burden that they'd inherited and did not deserve. 'No, this is good. This is a good plan. So, where did we meet?'

'We met playing an online computer game,' Ally said. 'I think that we should stick to the truth whenever we can. Looking like we're overthinking it is going to be the biggest giveaway.'

'And now we're dating.' He looked across at her, suddenly panicked. 'I mean, that's what we'll tell them. I know that we're not.'

'Okay,' Ally said, and he didn't think he could bear to look over at her and try and see what she was thinking. 'Fine. So we met online. Then what?'

'I don't know,' Caleb said, thinking out loud. 'We started talking, decided to meet up as we both lived in London and hit it off. Most of that's true except for the meeting up part.'

'I suppose it sounds plausible enough,' Ally said. 'And then we started dating? How long ago?'

'Six months?' he threw out, trying to remember when chatting to Ally had become something that had become so much a fixture of his day that he couldn't remember what life had been like before.

'Fine,' Ally agreed. 'We've been dating for six months. Which side of the bed do you sleep on?'

Caleb's eyebrows flew up to somewhere near his hairline. 'Ally, we don't have to… I mean, we have a spare room and—'

She shook her head, hoping that the movement would hide the pink she was sure was staining her cheeks. 'I only meant in case someone asks. That's the sort of thing that we should know about each other.'

He reached over and covered her hand with his, feeling the slight shake there that would have given away that she was nervous even if he hadn't already guessed.

'Ally, no one is going to ask us which side of the

bed we sleep on. And if you don't want to share a
bed, or a room, that's fine; we have plenty of space.'

'We're hardly going to be convincing as a couple
if we don't sleep together,' she pointed out.

Caleb shook his head. 'You seem to think that I
care a lot more about my brother and sister figuring
this out than I do about what you want. That couldn't
be further from the truth. I want you to be comfortable here. I want this arrangement to work for you
without you having to do *any*thing that makes you
uncomfortable. If sharing a room is too weird, then
we won't do it. It's that simple.'

'What would you prefer?' Ally asked.

'I'd…prefer that we share. A room, at least. Just
because that way it's easier for us to hang out in there
away from the others. We don't have to share the bed,
if you don't want. I can sleep on the couch.'

'Did it occur to you that it might be fun to hang
out *with* your family?'

He laughed. 'Give it a day and you'll be rethinking that notion. Trust me.'

'What's so terrible about them?' Ally asked, because in all the time that she'd known Caleb, he'd
barely spoken about his family other than that he was
generally just frustrated with them.

'Honestly,' he told her, rubbing at his hair. 'I can't
believe I used to get annoyed with Liv and Jonathan
for fighting. Now Jonathan, my brother, is married to
Liv's best friend—that's Rowan. And then Liv—my
sister—moved in with Adam, who she and Jonathan
work with. Since they all coupled up they're terribly

earnest and smug and settled and won't be happy until I'm making the same life choices as they are. They worry about me constantly and nothing I say or do seems to be able to convince them to stop. It drives me up the wall.'

'I can see why that would be annoying,' Ally said diplomatically. 'What are these life choices they object to?' she asked. 'You look like you're doing okay to me.' She smiled, and he only just resisted the urge to sell his soul to whoever would buy it in order to see that again.

'They seem to think that the only way I can possibly be happy is if I have a partner. I don't think that spending my time with my favourite person will count in their eyes if it's a friend that I met online.'

'In that case isn't spending more time with me going to add to the problem rather than solve it?' she asked.

He kept his eyes on the road, tried to keep his voice neutral. 'Hence the boyfriend charade.'

'Because spending your life talking to me is questionable, but having sex with me is okay?' He could feel his cheeks heat and hoped she would blame it on the sun. Because he really, really couldn't handle her talking about sex right now, when he was only just getting used to the fact that she was an actual real-life person sitting less than a metre away. Someone who he could just reach out and *touch*.

'It's their logic, not mine. I'm not saying that I understand it. Personally, I'm just really pleased that I get to hang out with you for the week.' This time when she looked across at her she was looking at him intently.

'What?' he asked.

'Just checking, but we are just *pretending* to be sleeping together?' she said, and he got the impression that she was weighing her words carefully. It took every ounce of concentration he had to keep the car on the road when his every instinct was to swerve to the verge, get a proper look at her and try and work out whether she was saying that because she wanted... No. No thinking about wanting. Only thinking about driving.

'Of course we're just pretending,' he said, still not daring to look at her.

'Okay, well, no need to be quite so vehement,' Ally said with a thin laugh. 'I'll have you know that some people enjoy having sex with me.'

He wasn't sure that he could blush any harder, but at the same time was sure that with every word that left her mouth he was managing to reach unsurpassed levels of pinkness. 'I don't doubt that,' he said honestly. 'But it is probably the sort of thing that I would ask before you arrived in a different country to hang out with me.'

'Well, yes, I'd have hoped so too,' Ally said with a laugh. 'But it doesn't do any harm to check.'

Thankfully she dropped the subject after that and he managed to keep the car on the road all the way back to the villa, where he clicked the remote to open the gates, and took the opportunity to look at

Ally properly for the first time since they had got in the car.

'Is there anything else we need to cover before we meet people?' Ally asked as the gates of the villa came into view. 'Like are we dating other people?'

He shook his head, stifled a laugh. 'I'm impressed you think I would pull that off in the week that we're here.'

'I meant that if we've been together six months, are there other people we need to explain away.' She shifted in her seat so that she could look at him properly. He put the handbrake on so that he could do the same, because for some reason it felt important to get this right.

'No. I... I've not dated anyone that recently,' he said carefully.

'Okay, well. Me neither. So we don't need to worry about that one.'

A silence lingered, though Caleb couldn't see why. It didn't mean anything that they hadn't been dating anyone recently. That was the whole reason that they were here. And the fact that it coincided with how long they'd been friends? Well, it was just that—coincidence.

It seemed unbelievable to him now that they'd managed to maintain a friendship for more than a year without meeting in person, and yet she was somehow completely familiar. Crazy that she had had that face and that hair and that body and that *glow* all along, and he simply hadn't seen it before. She was bright and warm and just so completely *Ally* that now he'd met her he couldn't imagine her looking any other way.

What he hadn't been prepared for was how he was going to feel when he saw her for the first time. A combination of, *Of course this is her,* and, *She's amazing,* and, *Well, of course I think she's amazing— she's my best friend so that shouldn't be a surprise,* and, *Oh, my God, I really want to kiss her.*

It was only the last one that was a problem, and that made him stall the car as he went to drive through the open gates. Ally raised her eyebrows at him.

'Everything okay?' she asked.

'Yeah, cool, fine, okay,' he gabbled, restarting the car and driving through the gateway into the driveway at the front of the villa. That was bad, the wanting to kiss her, wasn't it? It was just a weird reaction to meeting her in person finally, he told himself, trying to justify the feeling.

It was just the physicality of her that was messing with his brain. It wasn't, like, a crush. He couldn't really want to kiss her, could he? Because wanting to kiss her could lead to wanting other things, and he knew that he couldn't want that. All his own issues aside, he knew what happened to people who wanted Ally too much—she made sure that they didn't have a place in her life. And as much as he might have been blown away by meeting her in person for the first time, he couldn't imagine a future that didn't have her in it. As a friend. Just a friend, because that was the only way that Ally kept people in her life, and he would never ask more of her than she wanted to give.

The only problem with those very sensible reasons why he should not want to kiss her was that he really, really did want to kiss her.

He opened the boot of the car and concentrated on getting Ally's bags out. He would just ignore this feeling, he told himself sternly. There was nothing else to do. He had invited her to stay with him as his friend and he wasn't going to change that. The novelty and strangeness of her actually being here would wear off and they would be who they always were to each other. And what was that?

Well, she was his best friend. She was the person that he wanted to speak to first in the morning. The one he had to text when his family were driving him round the bend, the person he wanted to hang out with more than any other.

Kissing could only ever make that more complicated. He wouldn't burden her with these feelings. Not when that risked pushing her away. They would pass—he was sure of it.

Ally was the best and most uncomplicated part of his life and there was no way that he was going to ask more of their friendship than he already had. It was what he lived in fear of—asking more of people than they wanted to give. Once his parents had farmed him out to boarding school and then left the country entirely, he'd taken the not so subtle hint that he really shouldn't expect too much of other people. It saved him from inevitable disappointment in the long run. And he'd already had more from Ally than he'd expected. He'd been lulled into a false sense of security getting to know her in a space he normally used to cut himself off from people. He should have guessed that meeting her in person would complicate things. He just had to remember that nothing had to change. Nothing had changed—all he had to do was make sure that things stayed that way all week.

'Come on, let me show you around,' he said, putting on a smile that didn't quite feel natural. He could hear the others were by the pool, so he dropped the case by the front door and led Ally towards the corner of the house. The feel of Ally's hand in his drew him up short before they reached it. He had not been prepared for the flush of happiness, anticipation, *desire*, that the simple touch had inspired in him.

She widened her eyes at him in surprise.

'What, is this not okay? I just thought that if we're meeting everyone, we want to make it look like we're...'

Of course. That was why she had done it, because they were playing make-believe. He took a deep breath, fought down the waves of emotions that had just surged out of nowhere and reminded his body that this was all fake. He couldn't read anything into her holding his hand.

'No, it's fine,' he said, giving her another smile that he hoped didn't look too forced. 'I just wasn't expecting it, that's all.' She went to pull her hand away, but he tightened his hand around hers before he lost hold of her.

'Are you really sure you want to go through with the fake boyfriend thing?' she asked. 'Because we could just hang out this week,' she offered, looking at him as if she couldn't trust what he was thinking. 'We don't have to pretend we're something we're not.'

Well, that was enough of a reminder to bring him crashing back to reality. 'No, I'm sure. It's what the others need to hear to stop worrying about me. I just need a minute to get my head around it.'

'Around holding hands?' she asked, her brows drawing together.

'Around all of it,' he said, wondering how he could explain how he was feeling without giving away that he had been feeling way too much ever since he had collected her from the airport. 'I've never faked having a girlfriend around my family before,' he explained, knowing that that wasn't the half of what was going on.

'Maybe we're not the holding hands sort of couple?' she asked tentatively.

'No, I like this,' Caleb said, giving her fingers a squeeze. Realising too late that he was probably giving away too much.

But Ally didn't flinch, she just smiled at him. 'And what about the rest of it?' she asked. 'Do you normally go in for PDAs? Kissing in public?'

Caleb forced himself to take a deep breath, liking the idea of that a little too much. 'Well, I suppose it depends on the kiss,' he said, not able to resist the smile that accompanied his words. He looked her in the eyes for a few moments longer, and then leaned in.

Ally caught the scent of peppermint on his breath

as his lips brushed across her cheekbone so lightly that she could barely feel it.

'That sort of thing would be fine,' he said.

She rolled her eyes. 'Yes, for an elderly relative. I was thinking more along the lines of...'

She paused, considering, and then stretched up on her tiptoes, let her top lip come to meet his, the barest hint of a kiss, a temptation to something more before she thought better of it and pulled away.

'If we're looking for the line, I think we're still a way short of it,' Caleb observed, his voice tight. 'That was barely a kiss at all.'

'Well, I'm sorry to have disappointed you. Maybe we're one of those couples who barely acknowledge each other in public. Or kiss on the cheek like they're in a marriage that has been dying for years.'

Caleb fought down a smile at that, but couldn't hide the way that his hands came to rest on her hips.

Ally shrugged, but still looked at him as if he wasn't making sense. 'Well, just act like you do when you bring a real girlfriend home to meet them,' she suggested. And then asked, 'What?' at the expression on his face.

'I've never brought a girl home before,' he explained. 'No one was serious enough.'

Ally stared at him for a too-revealing moment. 'Okay, well, I'm honoured to be the fake first girlfriend you introduce to your family,' she said carefully, because she hadn't realised how big a deal this was for him. He'd never brought anyone home before. That made this a big deal, right? Even if she was a fake girlfriend, she was a real friend, and it still meant something that he trusted her enough to bring her into his life like this.

She squeezed his hand. Her support was genuine even if their relationship wasn't. 'You sure the hand holding is okay?' she checked, and Caleb wasn't sure that anything had ever made him feel less manly than that check-in.

'Of course I'm sure,' he told her, trying to make himself believe it at the same time. 'I guess we're going to have to do more than that if we're going to make this look convincing.'

'You know, you could do a girl a favour and look less horrified at that thought.'

'I'm not horrified. I promise. Just realising that I hadn't really thought this through. But it's only a week and then everything can go back to normal.'

CHAPTER TWO

AND THEN EVERYTHING could go back to normal, as if he hadn't just looked at her as if he wanted to eat her up, and then the way his face had fallen as if he hated himself for thinking it.

She hadn't been prepared for Caleb in real life. She'd searched online for him once, curious about the man she was spending so much of her life talking to. She hadn't looked at the tabloid coverage of his parents' well-publicised tax irregularities and their subsequent flit to South America. She didn't need to know anything about that that he hadn't chosen to share with her. She had seen that the family business had enjoyed a lot of success recently, the release of a fragrance from their archives having apparently taken the fashion and beauty worlds by storm.

But she hadn't wanted to dig beyond that. She'd simply been curious to put a face to the name that spent so much time in her notifications bar. He was cute. She'd known that from his profile picture on social media. But it turned out there was a world of difference between seeing that face on her phone screen and seeing it in real life, where it came with a whole adorable range of facial expressions that matched his personality so perfectly that she actually had to remind herself that this was the first time she'd properly met him.

They just had to get this first meeting with his family out of the way and then they could hang with a game or a movie or just drink and talk as they did most nights. The only difference would be that she actually got to see the expression on his face when she beat him as she usually did.

He kept a tight hold of her hand as they walked around to the back of the villa, if that was the right word for a place like this. She thought that 'palace' might have been more appropriate. She felt an unaccustomed stab of nerves at the thought of meeting Caleb's family. But there was no need for that, she told herself sternly. For a start, she wasn't prone to people-pleasing. And, more important than that, she wasn't really Caleb's girlfriend so it didn't matter whether they liked her or not, as long as she could get them to stop worrying Caleb or thinking that there was anything wrong with the way that he was living his life and use this holiday to stop her parents trying to force her to have the sort of relationship that they had relied on for so long but she was certain could never make her happy.

She saw how much her parents loved her. How could she miss the way that they watched her, as if they still didn't believe that she had made it so far? Childhood leukaemia had taken the lives of so many of the kids who had become her friends in hospital, it was as if they still couldn't believe that they were the lucky ones who had got to take her home.

She'd seen enough grief and loss in her childhood to know what it would do to her parents to lose her. Why would she let anyone else love her as much as they did? Knowing how much loving her could destroy someone's future, she wasn't going to invite anyone else to do that.

The thought of being the centre of someone's world again like that chilled her. Sure, it might be a nice thing for some people, having the eyes of the person or people who loved you more than anyone in the world looking at you as if they couldn't drink in enough of you. As if they wanted to burn the image of you onto their retinas. But generally, that sort of thing was usually associated with positive experiences. Fixing the image of you in their mind for the sheer pleasure of seeing you. Not because they were taking a mental photograph to cling onto once you'd gone.

Any time anyone had looked at her like that since, she'd been able to feel it again—the fact that no one expected her to be here in a year's time. That every moment with her loved ones was tinged with sadness—they were mourning her before she was even gone. Her not dying hadn't cured that feeling. Couldn't un-taint those memories. The association between love and sadness.

Unfortunately, she couldn't make her parents understand that. Now that she'd made it to adulthood, they wanted her to have all the things that they'd dreamed of for their little girl when they were nursing her through yet another round of chemo. The big wedding, the perfect grandchildren. The idea that Ally might want something different was something they just didn't seem able to accept, no matter how many times she'd explained it to them. If this little white lie would stop them worrying, as well as interfering, that could only be a good thing.

She shook off the mood, remembering that she had a part to play. This week wasn't just for her. It was for Caleb.

She heard his family before she saw them, the relaxed laughs of people on holiday from their troubles with loved ones who were familiar and close and safe. There was an ease to their laughter and voices that was notably absent from the man who now had her fingers in a death grip. It was just starting to dawn on her that she had absolutely no idea what she was getting into here.

She'd focused so much of her energy working out how to escape the unhelpful dynamics of her own family, she hadn't really considered that she was walking straight into someone else's, and that might be just as uncomfortable, albeit in a novel way.

'We'll make this quick,' she promised him, feeling his body tense up the closer that they got to the other. Squeezing his hand as best she could, given that he was close to breaking her fingers. 'I've got you,' she added on instinct, sensing that he needed to hear it.

The strangeness of having known him for a year, and also for less than an hour, kept taking her by surprise. Sometimes he was just Caleb, her best friend who she fired off messages to at all hours of the day without giving it a thought. And sometimes he was the guy who was so much more attractive in real life than she had been expecting, which was going to make this week more confusing than she'd bargained for.

No. There was no need to make a big deal of this, she told herself. They both knew what they were to each other. They'd just agreed it all. They were best friends doing each other a favour. After this week they could just go back to how things were before. They'd both been entirely happy with that. This week was a temporary blip, rather than a fundamental change to their relationship. Friendship. Frelationship?

But this was so not the time to be thinking about this. She had his family to meet and convince that they didn't need to worry about Caleb—or whatever it was that they were doing that made him feel as if he needed a fake girlfriend for a family holiday. And they could also send happy holiday snaps to her family and that would be the end of it.

They rounded the corner of the villa onto an expansive terrace with an infinity pool, and a view out to the lake beyond. There were four people around the pool, in various states of dress and swimwear, all of them sun-kissed and wet-haired. Two women lay back on sun loungers, the tiny one in a bikini, the taller woman in running gear, while the men were chatting and pouring beers at a table between two of the loungers.

'Caleb's here!' the smaller of the two women shouted, and all of a sudden all four sets of eyes were on them, sunglasses being pulled off and both women sitting up on their loungers and interrogating her with their eyes. At least she had the decades of practice of her parents scrutinising her every time that she saw them. They tried to hide what they were doing, of course, but she knew all the same. They were making sure that she was whole, well. That there were no telltale signs on her skin or in her eyes of some invading cells returning to steal their little girl from them after they had fought so hard to keep her.

And she still saw the fear on their faces, that even fifteen years of good health hadn't been able to dispel. That one of these days the overwhelming good luck that had saved her from the clutches of leukaemia would run out and their worst fears would come true.

It was the reason she had a fake boyfriend and not a real one—she was self-aware enough to know that. Because she'd seen what loving her did to a person, and she wasn't going to invite anyone into her life to play the Russian roulette that her parents had been dealing with ever since she had been ill.

But the expressions on Caleb's family's faces were variations on simple, naked curiosity.

'Um, hi?' she said, offering a half-wave, trying to hide her discomfort.

The two women jumped up and came over to say hello and introduce themselves, and she found herself shaking hands with Caleb's brother and sister and their partners, who looked exactly as obsessed with each other as Caleb had said they were, but a whole lot friendlier.

Not that that seemed to be helping with Caleb, who was stiff and awkward by her side. His siblings' polite interest in her seemed to be making him more tense rather than less, and she tried to surreptitiously work out what he needed, the more silent he became. She answered his family's questions as best she could, but neither her heart nor her head were in the game. All she could think about was getting him away from a situation that so clearly made him uncomfortable. She looked up at him, trying to tell him with her eyes that he could pull the plug and get them out of there, but they hadn't had enough time together for her unspoken communication to work. And Caleb wasn't putting himself out of his own misery, so that decided it. She was pulling the plug.

He jumped as she put her arm around his waist, and she hoped that his family hadn't seen.

'I'm sorry to be really rude,' she said, 'but I'm absolutely knackered after my flight. Cal, do you mind if I crash out for a bit?' Her words seemed to jolt Caleb out of his frozen state because his arm came around her shoulder, pulling her closer into his side as he spoke.

'Ally, I'm sorry, I wasn't thinking. Yeah, I'll show you inside. Let's go.'

She had to fight not to show her reaction to Caleb's hand landing on her shoulder. She shouldn't have flinched, she told herself. If they were really together the touch of his hand on her shoulder wouldn't be disconcerting. It would have been the sort of thing that happened so often that she wouldn't even notice it any more. She couldn't imagine it now, with his palm surely burning a bright red print upon her bare shoulder.

Ally concentrated on breathing, because all of a sudden that was apparently something her body no longer did automatically.

He led her to the front door of the villa and held it open for her while she walked inside. He didn't talk as they crossed the living space and he opened a door into a room that had bifold doors with a balcony beyond, a king-size bed, and a low, wooden-framed couch and chairs arranged around a low coffee table.

The steep slope of the hill meant that although they had walked into the villa at ground level, the ground had dropped away, leaving their room with its own balcony that looked out towards the lake and the mountains beyond. An enormous cantilevered parasol provided shade, and the two sun loungers promised privacy.

She breathed a sigh of relief at finally being out of a situation that had made her so tense she wasn't sure her shoulders were ever going to return to their original position.

'That was—'

'Extremely awkward?' Caleb offered, crossing over to the couch and dropping onto it. He leaned forward, his elbows on his thighs, and watched her closely as she sat in an armchair opposite him. 'I'm sorry. I know I froze—I panicked. Normally I'd just say hello and leave but this is your holiday too and I don't want you to have to if that wasn't what you wanted.'

'I was only going to say it was intense,' she amended, 'and I'm here to help *you* out, remember? We can just carry on as you would if I weren't here if you want.'

'Do you think they bought it?' Caleb asked, looking up and meeting her eye.

Ally considered the question. 'I don't see why they wouldn't. I don't think many people meet their brother's new girlfriend and think that they're faking it. They're not looking for lies so they'll just give us the benefit of the doubt if we stumble. I don't think you have anything to worry about. But are *you* still happy with what we agreed? Because I would hate for you to think that you have to go on with this just because you agreed to it before.'

Caleb shook his head, reaching a hand out towards her, before realising that he hadn't had a plan for what to do with it, and letting it fall back onto his knee. 'No. It's fine. I'm not used to spending much time with them. I prefer to do my own thing, especially when I'm here. I don't think I'd know how to be around you in person for the first time anyway—it was always going to be a bit strange—and now we're faking a relationship. I wish we'd had some more time just us, together, before we did this.'

'I guess,' Ally said thoughtfully. 'We have time now though. Do you want to talk about the family thing?'

Caleb sighed. 'Not really, but I've dragged you here. You should at least know what you're dealing with.'

'You didn't drag me,' she said, putting a hand on his knee, just a small reminder that she was on his side. 'I wanted to come. I jumped at the chance, if you remember.'

He shook his head, and she couldn't quite work out why he was disagreeing with that. She'd got on a plane herself, travelled to a different country, just to hang out with him. He could hardly question that she was here of her own volition.

'It suits us all if I do my own thing. When we're in the same house I try and keep out of their way. But it's not like I spend all my time locked away like a moody teenager. Sure, I work a lot. But I go to the gym, I go running, I go sailing, when I can find the time. But it's only when we're all together Jonathan thinks that he has to…be a father to me or something. I don't want him feeling like that so it's better that I keep to myself. And now that they're all coupled up, I'm only in the way.'

'What makes you think that they don't want you around?' Ally asked, her brows pinching together. 'They were practically bouncing with excitement when I got here. I think they would have grilled us all afternoon if I'd not made a strategic exit for us.'

'It's not that they don't want me around. It's that they worry about me when I am. I don't like to make them worry so it's easier if I'm not with them so much.'

'Don't all families worry about each other? I admit

I'm not exactly the authority on worrying about people the normal amount.'

Caleb gave something that might have passed for a smile if it had reached anywhere close to his eyes.

'Yeah, but my brothers and sisters shouldn't have to act like they're my parents. You know my actual parents left when I was still at school, right? Well, Jonathan ended up doing all the parenting after that, and inheriting a teenager isn't exactly what he had planned for his twenties. And ever since Liv started seeing Adam she seems to think that she also needs to start taking responsibility for me or something like that.'

'None of that is your fault though, Caleb. You didn't have a choice in it any more than they did.'

'I know that. But it didn't stop me seeing what a burden I was to them. How much it cost them to care for me. I don't want to do that to them any more than I have to. To anyone, for that matter.'

'Which is why you're bringing home a fake girlfriend rather than a real one,' Ally said, understanding more about him than he was saying out loud.

'Yeah.'

It turned out, he loved watching Ally think. It was as if he could see right through her skull to the whirring cogs beneath, as each individual thought flitted across her features. So much so that when she spoke, he jumped in surprise.

'I've been thinking,' Ally said, after a few minutes. 'Maybe you'd feel more comfortable about being around your family if we were more comfortable around each other.'

Caleb frowned. 'I'm not uncomfortable around you.'

'No, I mean, if we were more comfortable around each other as a couple. I think I need to get used to it—to us—before we go back out there. And I think it would help you too.'

'Okay, I can see where you're coming from,' he said, thinking her words over. 'But we're treading a fine line between our real friendship, and...the thing that we're faking for our families. So I think we should be very specific about what we mean by "comfortable".'

'Well, I just thought, when you put your arm around my shoulder, it was distracting... Just because it was new. Different. I think we want things like that to feel normal, like it would if we were really together.'

'Okay, I get it, I think. So we, what? Practise hugging? That sounds a little weird.'

'Okay then, not practise. Just...acclimatise to it. Is that better? Just so I don't do something that gives us away. We need to take pictures for my family and they'll be poring over them, looking for any sign that this isn't what I told them it was.'

'So, what was it that made you freeze? When I put my arm around your shoulder? I mean, if I do this now—'

He leaned forward and rested his hands on her hips, used them to pull her closer until her front just brushed against his. She looked up and met his eye, and he tried not to think about how much he liked looking at her from this angle. How affected he was just by her being close to him.

'Or, no, it was more like this,' he said quickly, moving her onto the couch by his side, tucking her under his arm. She linked her arms around his waist and looked up.

'So, how do you feel? Still weird?' he asked.

'Not weird,' she said.

'You might want to think about telling your shoulders that,' he mumbled, stroking a hand down them. She took a deep breath and let her shoulders fall. Tried sinking into the hug rather than fighting it. Caleb's body was warm where it was pressed against her side. He let his arms come around her and rested his head on the top of hers, and somehow she could feel that he was smiling.

'This is nice,' Ally said, her voice muffled in his T-shirt.

He mumbled an agreement. 'I can live with this,' he said back.

She pulled away and slipped her hand into his.

'What's this?' he asked as she pushed him down flat onto the couch and tucked her body into the small space next to his, her head lying on his chest. One hand coming to rest on his thigh.

'Not that different,' he observed once they were settled and his body had relaxed.

'So you're not freaking out any more?'

'No,' he said, a little too quickly. 'It's just a hug. Friends hug.'

'Right. So if we're comfortable with this, then what next?' Ally asked.

'Should we try kissing again?' he replied, with an audible gulp. 'Because unless you're going to keep kissing me like a maiden aunt that might need a little work.'

'Right. We just need to get a few out of the way so that we don't look all awkward.'

'Makes sense, so…' Caleb stroked a finger along her jawline and then cupped his hand around her cheek, turning her face up to him.

'Okay,' Ally said, sounding businesslike in a way that Caleb definitely wasn't feeling. 'This is good. This is fine.'

Caleb was about to lean in, and then stopped, held back for a minute. Because they were alone. In his house. Metres from a king-size bed. He had Ally's body pressed up against him and a thousand thoughts flitting through his mind for how that circumstance could play out. They all started with a kiss like this, and he wasn't sure he could trust himself to go through with this without wanting more. 'Caleb,' Ally breathed. 'Do you think you can at least pretend that you're not repulsed by the thought of this and just get on with it?'

'Oh, my God, would you just—?' He clasped his hands to both sides of Ally's face, turned her mouth up to his and kissed her, sure and hard at first, taking her so much by surprise that she didn't even close her eyes. And then his mouth turned gentle, tender, moving against her lips as if he wanted to explore every curve, parting them gently with his own and then teasing her with his tongue. She groaned and opened to him, her body arching into his as she stretched up to reach him better, one hand coming to the back of his neck, the other to tangle into his hair, which fell in soft waves to his jawline. She was aware that her breasts were crushed against his chest and didn't care in the slightest. If he was going to effortlessly ravish her mouth like this, what was the harm?

'I am absolutely the opposite of repulsed. Okay?' he said breathlessly when he finally pulled away, and it took Ally a moment of stunned silence to remember what he was even talking about.

'Okay,' Ally said, a little dazed, touching her fingertips to her mouth. 'Okay,' she repeated. And then she leaned forward and kissed *him*, this time. More gently, more sweetly than Caleb's kiss.

It was inevitable that Caleb should wrap his arms around her waist and hold her tightly against his body as he explored her mouth with his, all the time trying to remember that this wasn't real. It was fake— or had they decided that it wasn't? He wasn't getting anywhere near enough oxygen to really think about it properly. He pulled away, gasping in a deep breath, and saw his own surprise and confusion reflected in her expression. Ally pulled back just as Caleb's hands brushed over her hips. He left them there as she looked up at him, their eyes locked.

'I think we're okay with that one,' Caleb said, still

with a slight tremble in his voice. 'Better than okay. No chance of anyone thinking that we're faking it.'

'We're *really good* at that,' Ally said, a little shakily. 'We probably don't need any more practice.'

'That's a shame,' he said, without thinking.

'Is that your way of telling me you want to kiss me again?'

'No.'

Half of his brain had already closed the shutters and pulled Ally into bed before he remembered they'd agreed that would be a bad idea. So he sat back up and shifted along the couch a little, trying to kid himself that that small amount of space would be enough to get that thought out of his head.

'No, just, that was good. Fine. That was fine. We should probably, you know, go back out with the others…'

'Yeah, yes,' Ally said eventually, shaking her head. 'We should…be around other people. Yes.'

They walked back through the villa, and Caleb gave her a tour. 'This is the bathroom,' he said, his voice clipped as he opened the door from the bedroom into a bathroom with a whirlpool tub and a walk-in shower that he would be turning to ice cold as soon as he had the chance. From there they went through to the open-plan living space with a kitchen in one corner, and low couches around a large, square coffee table. 'That's Jonathan and Rowan's room, Liv and Adam are through there. Dining terrace through the double doors and gym downstairs. I think that's pretty much it,' he said as he opened the double doors to show Ally the dining terrace, which was cooler and shadier than his room at this time of day.

Caleb took a few deep breaths as they walked back out to the pool, his hand still caught in Ally's. He went to force the smile that he usually faked around his family, until he realised that he was already smiling. It had nothing to do with the kiss, he told himself. He was just happy that he was hanging out with his friend, the kissing was entirely incidental to his happiness. Because if it wasn't…that made things so much more complicated, and he needed this to be simple.

He dragged over a couple of loungers to the side of the pool. He pulled his shirt over his head, and when he turned to leave it on the ground next to him he caught the expression on Ally's face. He looked around to make sure that they weren't being watched before he whispered, 'What's wrong?'

But Ally shook her head, her eyes not meeting his.

'Nothing!' she hissed back, before taking a deep breath. 'Nothing,' she repeated more calmly. 'I just didn't know that you, you know, looked like that.'

The corner of his mouth ticked up in an entirely involuntary fashion.

'I told you I go to the gym. A sedentary lifestyle is very bad for your heart.'

She swallowed, dragged her gaze up to his face. 'I'm sorry, I'm just distracted. It's not your fault. I just… I'm distracted.' That quirk of his lip became a full-on smile.

'I think I like having this effect on you,' he said, still smirking.

Ally raised her brows. 'Well, I'm not having you be all smug on me. If I'm distracted then you can be distracted too.' And with that she stood, reached for the hem of her sundress and pulled it over her head.

He audibly gasped at the sight of her: soft stomach, dimpled thighs, breasts barely contained by the deep plunging neckline of her swimsuit. Caleb gulped, pulling on his sunglasses. 'Okay, now I guess things are fair.'

Ally giggled first, and when he looked over she was leaning back on her lounger, soaking up the sun like a kitten who was very pleased with itself.

'Ally! Caleb!' a voice called from behind them. 'We're going to walk into the village, do you want to come?'

Ally looked over at Caleb with her eyebrow raised, but he shook his head.

'Caleb just promised me a swim,' she called back. 'But maybe tomorrow?'

'Sure,' Rowan said, smiling at her. 'We'll come join you in the pool when we get back.'

'You didn't want to go to the village?' Ally asked him when Rowan had gone, because solitude felt as if it was maybe not the best idea after they had discovered that they were mutually speechless at the sight of one another without clothes on and also excellent at kissing.

'I'd really rather not,' Caleb said. 'I think I like your idea better, and we did only just get here.'

'I've got a question,' Ally said, pulling a bottle of sunscreen she'd brought with her out of her bag. 'Why did you come on holiday with them if you dislike spending time with them so much?'

'I didn't,' Caleb complained, lying back with his arm over his face. 'They came on holiday with me.'

'You're going to have to explain the difference,' Ally said, propping up her legs and rubbing sunscreen into her shins.

'I inherited this place from my grandparents after they died a few years ago,' Caleb explained. A glance at him from the corner of her eye revealed his arm still thrown over his face, as if he was worried about catching sight of her.

'Jonathan got the manor in the Cotswolds and Liv got the house in London. Liv sold hers and invested the money in the family business and Liv and Adam's homeless shelter. I wanted to do the same because there's really no point in keeping this place, considering how rarely it gets used, but I wanted to come out here for a week before I handed it over to the estate agent, just to make sure everything was in order. They invited themselves along.'

'So you'd really rather be here alone?' she asked, moving on to cover her arms and her chest with the lotion.

He pulled his arm away and looked at her from the corner of his eye, before pinking in the cheeks and looking away again. 'Not completely alone. I like having you here.'

She smiled, trying not to read too much into that.

He liked having her here as a friend. Just as he had kissed her as a friend, and he had stared at her breasts as a friend…

'So tell me more about the family business. You invested in it too? I read about the launch of the fragrance last year. And now branching out into more beauty lines?' Ally said, desperate for a distraction from her own thoughts. Nothing good could come of that line of thinking. She knew herself too well. The minute she found herself getting too involved, the merest hint that he felt the same way and she would push him away.

'It had a cash-flow problem last year,' Caleb explained. 'Jonathan didn't tell me about it until the whole place was about to go under. I could have helped earlier and saved him all that stress, but he didn't even ask. Now he and Liv, and Rowan and Adam, have turned it around. The fragrance was Liv's baby, and that's how she and Adam met. They've got it all under control, apparently.'

'So you're not involved in the running of the business at all?' Ally asked, and didn't miss the way that he flinched at the question.

'They don't want me to be,' he said, his voice carefully flat.

'Why do you think that?' Ally asked carefully, reaching behind her to try and rub sunscreen under the band of her bikini top.

'Because Jonathan wouldn't even involve me when the company was on the brink of collapse. They feel responsible for me, but they don't come to me when they need help. Why would he want me now that he's got it running smoothly?'

'Because it's a family business, you're an investor and have something valuable to add?'

'I don't need to push him on it. If he wanted me on board he would have asked, he didn't and that's fine.'

'Perhaps he takes the fact that you spend as little time as possible with him as a sign that you don't want to be asked,' Ally suggested, but they stopped talking as they heard voices in the house behind them.

'Do you need help with that?' Caleb asked, gesturing at the sunscreen, and she recognised a change of subject when she heard one.

She held out the bottle, telling herself that this was something completely platonic. Friends did this for each other all the time. She didn't want to burn, and Caleb was just looking out for her. She wasn't thinking already about how Caleb's hands were going to feel on her bare skin, and he wouldn't be thinking about it either. They had both been completely honest with one another about what this was. That they were only interested in friendship and anything else was completely fake.

Of course, it had been harder to remember that when they had been kissing, but it was fine. They had done the sensible thing and put a stop to it. Come out here to the pool. It had all just been so that they could properly play their parts. They weren't doing it because they *wanted to*.

She jumped as cold lotion hit her shoulders. Caleb's hands were brisk at first across her skin, as she sat stiff and upright, picking up first one arm and then the other, held out to her side like nothing more than a scarecrow. But when he reached the back of her neck, where her bikini was tied in a knot, he hesitated. He pulled it carefully down, thumbs sweeping under the fabric, sure and certain once he had made the decision to do it. With his hands pressing into her muscles, learning the shape of her shoulders, her back, Ally let out a low sigh of pleasure without realising what she was doing.

She relaxed into his touch, letting him take her weight, only just stopping herself from giving in to her instincts and leaning back into him, letting her body melt against the length of him. When his hands stopped, it took every ounce of her shaky self-control not to beg him to carry on.

She didn't exhale until her back was covered, and she turned and snatched the suncream from his hand before this could get any worse. At least once he was done she could turn face-down on the sun lounger and close her eyes. Let the sun warm her back and her thoughts wash over her. She couldn't look at Caleb. She needed a break from the heat between them. This was going to be an exceptionally long week if they carried on like this. If they couldn't get through something as innocent as sitting by the pool.

After a couple of hours of lying in the sunshine doing absolutely nothing, she realised that she couldn't do this all week. Too much time with her own thoughts gave her mind too many opportunities to torture her. She didn't need the drama of developing feelings for Caleb. She'd had all the feelings she needed when she was a teenager, between nearly dying, then the emotional fallout of her parents witnessing it. What she'd dreamt of, those months of constant fear and pain and her parents' red-rimmed eyes, was a simple life. Preferably, with no one making her the centre of their universe, and all their future happiness depending on her survival—something ultimately out of her control.

She knew how much pain she'd caused her parents when she was ill. And she didn't want to have the power to cause anyone else pain like that. Love and pain and grief were all tied up together with the people who loved her, and she didn't want to add to that number.

All she'd seen of love was the fact that it could cause indescribable trauma. Why would she want that for herself, or for anyone else? She'd decided a long time ago that falling in love wasn't for her. She'd separated kissing and sex from feelings and enjoyed one without the other. So why was she freaking out now about something as insignificant as a kiss?

Because it wasn't insignificant—that much was plain to her. And, judging by his reaction, it hadn't been insignificant for Caleb either. But what was she going to do about these inconvenient feelings? Ignoring them seemed like the best place to start. They had both agreed that they were faking this relationship and any kissing that happened was simply a part of that. There was nothing to stress about, she told herself—again. She took a deep breath and let it out slowly, and before she could take another, there was a rustle beside her, and then a loud splash, and droplets of water hit her back. She turned and looked over her shoulder, the sun in her eyes, to see Caleb's wet head emerging from the pool.

So she wasn't the only one feeling overheated. She shrieked as Caleb came right to the edge of the pool and shook his hair like a wet dog, splashing her again. But his silliness drove out the troubling thoughts she'd been fending off and he was once more her friend. The person who had been making her laugh since they'd first started talking in the online game they'd both been playing when they'd met.

He threw an inflatable at her, a boyish grin on his face.

'Come for a swim,' he said, propping his arm on the side of the pool. Ally looked at him over her sunglasses.

'And why would I want to do that?' she asked dryly.

'Because it's fun,' he said. 'And cool. Come and play.'

She sat up and narrowed her eyes. 'Play what?' she asked suspiciously.

Ally felt her cheeks heat, and crossed to the pool, sitting beside where Caleb was resting by the edge, letting her toes, her feet, then her calves dip in the water.

'What were you planning?' Ally asked. 'Water polo? Synchronised diving?'

Caleb first grinned and then flicked more droplets of water in her face. 'I just want to hang out. Talk. Be normal.'

She smiled, because that was what she'd wanted for this week too—just a chance to hang out with her friend. So she slipped into the water and glided lazily away from the side, drifting on her back.

'I like being your friend better when I don't have to look at your ugly mug,' she said, and he launched himself at her. She squealed, diving under the water and swimming a length of the pool, until she was forced to surface to take a breath, and when she did, there was Caleb, with his arms ready to wrap around her waist and pull her under, amidst a shout of protest and a rush of bubbles.

'Ugly mug,' he scoffed as they surfaced again, his arms still round her waist.

It's not real. None of this is real, she told herself, concentrating on the fact that she was here to finally hang out in person with her best friend rather than the fact that the feel of his hands on her waist was making her forget that the water was cold. She withdrew herself from his arms and they swam a few lazy lengths side by side before Caleb got out and pulled a couple of lilos into the pool and she clambered onto one of them, then reached out a hand for the cocktail that Caleb had just poured her.

Then he was floating on an inflatable next to her, and she pulled down her white plastic-rimmed sunglasses and shut her eyes, letting the hand not holding her drink trail through the water. She could sense Caleb beside her, and smiled to herself, feeling supremely contented with her life in that moment. She had been overreacting about those kisses. This was totally fine. More than fine. This was an Italian villa and hot sunshine and a cold drink. It was an escape from the pressure her parents unwittingly heaped on her. She would send them photos of her and her gorgeous boyfriend in his dreamy Italian villa and they couldn't possibly set her up on any more doomed singles cruises. She smiled to herself. She would not let her overactive brain ruin this for her.

'Just think, I could have been at singles line dancing right about now if I hadn't let you talk me into this.'

'Not too late to change your mind. I'm sure we can meet the ship in port somewhere.'

She half-heartedly flicked a few spots of water at him. 'Don't even joke about it,' she scolded him. 'My parents are still not convinced you're good enough for their only daughter. They might book me on again for next year just in case.'

'Well, we'll just have to convince them otherwise, won't we?' he said as his family walked around the corner of the villa and onto the terrace. She saw indecision cross his face, but then he pulled up his sunglasses and shouted across to his sister. 'Hey! Liv! Come take a photo of me and Ally!' She heard his sister groan, but Liv dragged herself away from the group and picked up Caleb's phone from the table.

'Fine, but don't do anything gross,' she said as Caleb pulled Ally's inflatable closer to his own. 'Smile, then,' Liv prompted, and Ally suddenly found herself grinning, not sure whether she looked as if she was faking it or not. She was happy. Having fun. All they needed were a few photos that showed her parents that. But Caleb seemed to have something more complicated in mind and was trying to pull her lilo even closer, reaching an arm to go around her shoulders, leaning in as if he was about to kiss her. She reached a hand to his chest, steadying him before he capsized them both, but he obviously misinterpreted her intentions, and leaned in further. At which point his lilo flipped over. He reached out and grabbed Ally in a misguided attempt to save himself, only to drag her down with him. She was laughing as she hit the water, one hand held high to try and save her drink, until she realised that it was already full of pool water.

'I'm so sorry,' he gasped as he broke the surface of the water. 'Are you okay?'

'That was great, Cal, really slick.' Liv cackled as she followed the others back inside, and Ally towed both lilos to the side of the pool.

'Great job,' Ally told him, laughing, pushing hair first out of her face, and then his, pushing a lock from the corner of his eye. 'My parents are definitely going to love you now that you've half drowned their only daughter.'

She pushed herself out of the pool and accepted the towel that Caleb handed her, squeezing water out of her hair and wishing she could do the same with the moulded cups of her bikini top without looking completely indecent.

Caleb came over and scrubbed at her hair with his towel, and she laughed as she looked up at him.

'I'm sorry,' he said earnestly, still dabbing at the

water dripping from her hair onto her shoulders. 'Are you sure you're okay?'

'I'm fine,' she reassured him, sliding her own towel under the strap of her bikini. Caleb's fingers followed the path of her towel, and she looked up at him in surprise. When he reached the edge of her bikini, she held her breath, wondering whether he would venture under the fabric. When she looked up, his desire was written over every feature. His pupils blown wide, his bottom lip caught between his teeth.

There was nothing false about that look. They didn't have an audience. It was just her and Caleb out here. That expression was entirely for her. He was looking at her as if she was the only thing in the universe worth paying attention to. As if he *needed* her. And she couldn't stand it.

'I'm going to go in and dry off,' she said abruptly, wrapping the towel around herself, covering her bikini, the cooling water dripping down her back making her shiver.

For a moment she worried that he was going to follow her inside, and wasn't sure if she was more relieved or disappointed when she was left trying to tease apart the knotted straps of her bikini alone.

CHAPTER THREE

ALLY WAS FREAKING OUT, and he knew that it was his fault. He'd got carried away, hadn't just stepped over a line but thoroughly trampled it, making a mess in the process. What had he been thinking, touching her like that? He had scared her off. Put too much pressure on her, and she had run. He wouldn't be surprised if she came out here with her bags packed and a ticket for the next flight back to London.

He would never forgive himself if he had irreparably harmed their friendship. True, Ally had been the first to fake their relationship, but he was the one who had invited her here. Who had pulled her into his body to practise being close to one another. But that was all it had been. He might have thought that there was something more in it, something beyond the clear parameters that they'd spelled out for one another, but Ally obviously hadn't. He'd gone too far, and now they were going to be awkward and weird with each other. He'd needed too much from her, and that had pushed her away. Every time, he did this. And if he tried to fix things he only managed to make things a hundred times worse, like, for example, trying to kiss her and accidentally capsizing her in the deep end of the pool.

He collapsed on the sun lounger and reached for his phone to see if Liv had taken any pictures that might convince Ally's family that they didn't need to keep meddling with her love life. At least if they had done that she would have got something out of this trip and this friendship he was pretty sure he'd just ruined. He groaned as he swiped through. He looked as if he were actively trying to drown her. Ally looked like she was trying to get as far away from him as possible. His brilliant idea had not been a success.

'That was smoothly done, little brother.'

Liv appeared on the terrace with a couple of beers in hand. He thought about retreating back to his room, but Ally had made clear that she needed space and he wasn't going to go barging in there. He covered his face with his hand, because of course his moment of tragic embarrassment had happened in front of his whole family so that his humiliation was complete. And now he was trapped out here with his sister, who he knew would be merciless about it.

'Liv, be nice,' Rowan scolded her, coming onto the terrace just in time to save him. 'She's lovely, Caleb,' she added. 'We're really happy for you. I'm certain that's what Liv was trying to say.'

Liv snorted beside her, and not even his sweet-as-pie sister-in-law—usually his favourite family member—was going to convince him he wasn't being openly mocked.

'Yeah, well, I think so too,' he said, which wasn't going to count for anything if she was packing her bags even as he spoke. All she'd wanted—perfectly reasonably—was for him to get her out of the hellish-sounding cruise that her parents had booked and he'd spoiled that all because the sight of a water droplet trickling down her skin had been too much for him to resist.

She hadn't asked for emotional complications. This was exactly why he avoided situations like this. The real ones, that was—the fake boyfriend thing didn't actually occur that often. The real boyfriend thing? He'd tried it a few times, but…well.

And that was before he considered who it was he was talking about. This was Ally, who was all but allergic to feelings. He'd been joking about that doctor that her parents had set her up with—but only just. Because he'd got most of the story at the time, and it had sounded an awful lot like as soon as the guy had shown any interest in her, she'd extracted herself from the situation without a backward glance. If she'd thought about the guy since, he couldn't be sure—but she'd never mentioned him again.

He didn't have the full story about her teenage years, or about the difficult relationship with her parents. She'd tell him if she wanted him to know. All he knew was that she bolted at the first sight of complicated emotions—and that his parents had laid the groundwork with what an emotional burden he could be. They'd left the country rather than stick around for his teenage years. The job of seeing him through adolescence had fallen to Jonathan—in school holidays at least—and every line and mark of strain on his older brother's face over the past ten years had shown him what a burden that had been.

He'd thought that doing his own thing and staying out of his family's way was what he should do. But apparently he couldn't even get that right—why else would they have sat him down and asked him whether it was healthy to be spending so much time working, or on his computer? The fact that he'd run his own hugely successful business trading in cryptocurrency since he'd left university hadn't been enough to convince them that he didn't need—or want—their concern. Nor the fact that a huge chunk of that time recently had been spent hanging out with Ally online.

Here he was, with a fake girlfriend, to convince them that he wasn't a kid any more. He wasn't their burden, their responsibility. He wasn't anyone's problem, and that was the way he wanted it to stay. He hated seeing how much loving him had cost the people in his life. Hated the way it hurt when it got too much and they left him. So he knew what he had to do now.

He had to make sure that Ally knew he didn't want a real relationship. If he wanted Ally to stick around, he had to make this simple for her, make her believe that he was no more affected by their kiss than she was. If he let on that he wanted more she would be shutting him out faster than any of the dating-app guys that she'd hooked up with and then left without a backward glance. And he wasn't going to convince her everything was okay by refusing to be in the house with her. He gathered up his things and headed into the villa, thinking that she was probably out of the shower by now.

He knocked quietly at the door—keeping things cool didn't mean walking-in privileges. She was dressed, thank God. Though the whole indifference thing would be easier if she hadn't just pulled on another sundress that wrapped in a deep V across lush breasts and skimmed and flared from generous hips. If he closed his eyes, he could still feel the shape of her in his palms. He flexed his fingers, trying to force the feeling from his muscles. He could just forget…he could act as if he didn't feel anything for her.

'What? Is this not okay?' she asked, looking straight down her cleavage, her hands running over the front of her dress.

'No, it's great,' he said, clearing his throat.

'Then why are you looking at me like that?'

He knew the fact that he was feeling absolutely stunned would scare her off, he knew he had to keep his feelings out of this.

'You look great,' he said again.

Ally looked up and her gaze snagged with his, and he saw her expression heat.

'You're going to have to stop looking at me like that,' she said, half warning, half threat.

Could she see how desperate he was? How far his feelings were getting away from him? How hard he was fighting to keep them under control and how badly he was failing? Desperation was just the sort of feeling that sent Ally running. He had to show her he was in control of this. He had to *be* in control of this.

'I'm sorry,' he said, pulling his eyes away and trying to make the words sound casual.

'A walk, then?' she suggested, and he nodded. The afternoon had cooled a little and he could keep her out of the sun if they stuck to the shade of the olive and lemon groves. The vineyards he'd save for an early morning, when the sun was still low. They could walk the rows of vines, check the fruit, pretend they were the only people on the planet.

He shook his head. That was dangerously close to romantic.

Dangerously close to the sort of sentiment that would have Ally freezing him out of her life, even as a friend, and he couldn't risk that when he had only just met her for real.

'I'll show you around the grounds,' he said, pulling on trainers and crossing to the doors out onto the terrace. They waved at the others as they passed the pool, Caleb shouting that they were going for a walk, his tone making clear that he wasn't extending them an invitation.

'It's so beautiful here,' Ally said as they walked among the olive trees, Caleb sticking to the shade and watching Ally's shoulders for signs of turning pink. He should probably ask if she needed more sunscreen, but they both knew exactly where that would lead, and he didn't trust himself to go there.

'You're really selling this place?' Ally asked, turning to look at him. He leant back against the trunk of a tree, letting it take his weight as he watched Ally wander through the trees. 'Won't you miss it?'

'We hardly use it. And even if we did, it wouldn't be right. Liv and Adam have started a new foundation to support people experiencing homelessness. We all decided that we wanted to keep the house in the Cotswolds. It's been in the family for the longest, Rowan and Jonathan just got married there, and Adam and Liv will have their wedding there in the autumn. I have a little place in London and Liv and Adam have a garden flat near the office. Rowan and Jonathan live in the Cotswolds and commute. I can't see how we can justify keeping this place too when there are people out there without even somewhere safe to sleep.'

'I guess that's true,' Ally said, and dropped to sit cross-legged in the shade of the tree opposite. 'So you helped finance the family business and you're selling this place for Liv's foundation. Wouldn't it be cheaper and easier to just tell your family that you care about them?'

He'd pushed off from the tree and taken half a step towards her before he realised what he was doing. 'I don't know what you're talking about,' he snapped before he could stop himself. 'That's got nothing to do with it. I'm just trying to do the right thing. At this point my investments are making money faster than I can give it away. Why wouldn't I use it to help my family?'

'Of course you want to help your family,' Ally said, looking at him thoughtfully from her seat beneath the tree. 'And if you were capable of having a conversation with them as well as throwing money at the situation, I wouldn't be asking the question.'

He bristled, crossing his arms over his chest. 'I'm perfectly capable of having a conversation with them. I don't know why you'd think I'm not.'

She laughed, but it sounded a little brittle, more than a little forced. 'Um, maybe because all the available evidence proves me right. You've not voluntarily spent a minute with them since we got here. You told me yourself you'd rather they hadn't come.'

'Ally, you've been here for less than a day. What can you possibly know about it?' he said, knowing that it wasn't true. That she knew him better than he was comfortable with. If she hadn't been here in person—if they'd been able to have this conversation safely, with a screen between them—then he wouldn't be taking it like this. He would have thought about what she was saying. Thought about his answer. Replied in a reasoned and sensible fashion. But he couldn't do that when she was here, so very much in the flesh, confusing everything he thought he knew about his feelings for her.

'Don't do that,' Ally snapped in warning. 'Don't pretend our friendship started when you picked me up from the airport. I know you know better than that.'

He stared at her for a moment, wondering whether to quit or double down. But he couldn't do that. He couldn't just throw away their friendship. He imagined what his life would look like without her in it.

Without someone to share his day with, even through a screen. He couldn't bear it.

'Ally, I'm sorry,' he said. 'You know I don't think that. You know how important you were to me long before we got here.'

Her expression softened, and he took another few steps and dropped to sit beside her.

'Then stop acting like I don't know you,' she chided, knocking his shoulder with hers. Taking a deep breath and then letting her head come down to rest on his shoulder. 'I don't like it when you pretend you're someone other than the Caleb that I know I know.'

'I know that you know me. But I don't see how you can know about my relationship with my family. I've barely spoken to you about them,' he explained.

'And you think that doesn't say anything about how you feel about them? I've seen you all together and how much they obviously care about you, and then I see you lying to them about us, and it makes me wonder why you don't just talk to them.'

'Like you do with your parents?' he shot back, keeping his face as innocent as he could, knowing that his deflection was as good as starting a fight.

'We weren't talking about me,' Ally pointed out, her voice terse.

Which meant that he was on the right track. That he could lead this discussion away from his own failings. 'Well, maybe we should have been. You've never given me the full story on why we're lying to them anyway,' he said.

'If I'm honest with you, will you return the favour?' Ally asked, and he hesitated. Because that would be fair, wouldn't it? But opening up to Ally, being vulnerable with her, that wasn't going to do anything but burden her with things that she couldn't fix. Talking to her wasn't going to change the fact that responsibility for looking after him had been dumped on Jonathan without him asking for it. He couldn't undo the years that Jonathan had lost worrying about him, trying to keep the business afloat without his help because he didn't want Caleb drawn into the mess. And if he couldn't stop Jonathan fretting, he could at least stop anyone else feeling as though they had to worry about him too.

'I don't really understand why you're so keen to talk about my family,' he said carefully. 'But, sure. Show me yours and I'll show you mine.'

Ally sighed, leaned back and closed her eyes. She wanted to distance herself from him—and, fine. He could understand that. He should have expected that. 'Well, you know I was sick as a kid?' she asked, and he murmured a yes. Because she'd mentioned it, in passing, before. Glancing words, never enough detail for him to build a real picture of what she had gone through.

'You've mentioned it, but not the details,' he prompted her.

'Well. It's not fun to talk about,' she said, eyes still closed, an arm thrown over them now. 'It was bad. I had leukaemia and they were pretty certain that I wasn't going to make it. I was close, too close, to not making it. By the time I got the bone marrow transplant that I needed, no one actually thought that I could come back from how sick I was. My parents were already grieving for me, I think, even before I was gone.'

'I'm sorry,' he said, reaching for her hand and giving it a squeeze. He couldn't help it. She wanted space, and that was fine, but he didn't want her to think that she was alone. She opened her eyes, turned her head towards him and smiled before pulling her hand back.

'Don't be sorry,' she said with a smile he was sure she'd performed hundreds of times. 'I'm fine now. I made it! I hardly ever think of it—it isn't really what this is about.'

'Can you explain what it is, then? Because not to be...you know, all self-involved, but... How do I come into this?'

She laughed, and he wondered again how he'd been her friend for so long without hearing that sound. He valued what their friendship had been before they had met in person. It hadn't been any less real just because it had happened online. But now that he'd done this, he wasn't sure that he'd be able to go back to being satisfied with emojis. Without hearing her laugh again.

'What's that look for?' Ally asked, suddenly looking suspicious, narrowing her eyes at him.

'Nothing bad. Just enjoying you being here,' he admitted.

There was no way she could cover her blush on that skin, sunshine glow or not.

'Aren't you supposed to be interrogating me about my tragic childhood?' she reminded him.

Caleb nodded lazily. 'I can if you want, but the option to just…offer up information is there too, you know. If you wanted this to be more like a regular conversation. I want to listen.'

'Okay, fine.' Ally gave way with a sigh. 'Where were we? I nearly died, my mum and dad were devoted to me. Gave up their own lives to be with me. Spent every day in the hospital with me. I was the centre of their universe, making memories. You get the picture. And every time they looked at me like I had sunbeams shining from every orifice, I knew that they were thinking about when I wouldn't be there any more. It wasn't about me, not really. It was about shoring themselves up for when I was dead.'

'That sounds…impossibly hard,' Caleb said, trying to imagine it.

'It sounds so ungrateful,' Ally said, shaking her head. 'I should just be glad that I survived it. That they survived it. And, honestly, I am. But every time someone looks at me like that, like I'm the centre of their world and their whole lifetime of happiness depends on me just existing—I can't. And they're desperate for me to fall in love and have children of my own. To have all the things that they thought that I would have lost by dying too young. But why would I want that? Why would I want anyone else to love me when I see what loving me did to my parents?

Why would I want to love someone when I've seen how much it can hurt? It's too much pressure and it's too much pain. No, thank you. I think I like things how they are.'

'I'm sorry, Ally. That sounds like it would be a lot for anyone to bear.'

'I know that it's just because they love me! And I should be grateful for that! And they just want what's best for me! But honestly the crushing pressure of having to be happy as well as alive because they're waiting, watching for me to fulfil all this potential that I was never even meant to have. I genuinely don't know what to do with all this *hope* that they have invested in me. I just want to be loved a normal amount,' she said finally.

He nodded, thinking through her words. 'I think I can understand that.'

'But isn't that what you've got with your family?'

'Loving me a normal amount? No. I don't think I have. If we were a normal family they'd barely have to think of me. I'd just be the annoying little brother who usually showed up late to stuff. But Jonathan ended up having to parent me and that pretty much ruined his twenties, and I can't undo that.'

'Is that how he sees it? Have you asked him?'

'I don't need to; I was there. I saw it all first-hand. But we were talking about you. I'm sorry that your parents don't listen to you. That they don't respect your choices.'

'Your turn,' Ally said, shaking her head as if she could shake her thoughts away. 'Why are we faking this for *your* family? Why not just date someone for real?'

He sighed into his forearm. 'Because "I don't want to" is good enough for you but not for me?'

She frowned and pulled his arm away, fixing him with a look that was too hard to look away from. 'That's not all I said and you know it.'

'Okay, fine. I don't like to date,' he said. 'It's hard to see how you can love someone without it turning into a situation where you end up causing them more hassle than it's worth.'

He had to look away from the understanding expression on Ally's face. So both of them were going to resist this pull between them. Well, good. That was a good thing, because if this was dependent on him holding himself back, he wasn't sure that it was going to work.

'So you have an end date to save you from the disaster that falling for me would be,' Caleb said, trying to laugh.

'You're not a burden,' Ally said, looking deadly seriously at him. 'Your siblings don't just worry about you. They love you,' Ally added, as if that were in question. 'They want you to be in their lives.'

'Of course they do,' Caleb said, shaking his head. 'I know that. The problem is that I don't *want* them to. Not when I know what it costs. I hate that loving me means that I can hurt people. I don't want to do that to anyone else. I know that you understand this, Ally, so I don't know why you're trying to convince me to change.'

She half smiled, one corner of her mouth turning up. 'So does that mean we're not talking about our feelings any more?'

'I think you should be honest with me about how you felt before you walked away from me earlier, after getting out of the pool. If we're not honest with each other, things could get confusing. You need to tell me if I overstepped, or… I don't know. I just think we should talk about it.'

Ally pushed the heels of her hands into her eyes. She didn't have to ask what he was talking about.

'I think… I don't know. It was more confusing than I was expecting, having you touch me like that. I thought that we would be able to compartmentalise what was fake and what was real, but it wasn't that easy. I mean, a friend who you kiss is more than a friend, right? And you were looking at me like you wanted me and… It's hard that one part of that is the most real thing I have in my life, and the other is completely fake. It's hard to learn two ways to be around each other and remember to do the right one at the right time, but we'll get there. I know we will.'

He sat with her words. He could see her thinking, still turning them over and trying to find a solution for them. 'I understand,' he said carefully. 'And I feel the same way, but I don't think that just because it's difficult we have to call the whole thing off. It's okay for us to admit that it's hard, and to keep trying. We can practise a little at a time. Take things slow.'

She looked up at him. 'So you're saying that I'm freaking out over nothing and that if we just talk about our feelings everything would be much simpler? I don't know, that sounds too easy.'

Caleb laughed. 'It's got to be worth a try. And I didn't say that you freaked out over nothing. Just that maybe if we talked more, there would be no need to freak out in the first place.'

'And we both know how we feel about relationships,' Ally added. 'So we both know there's no danger of either of us wanting more than the other does, even if the lines get blurred at times.'

'Right,' Caleb tried, reaching for Ally's hand, turning it over and pretending to inspect the palm. He ran the pad of a finger across the creases before lacing their fingers together. 'So we keep practising holding hands until it feels completely natural. And neither of us is going to think that it's a big deal, or if we do then we'll talk about it and it won't be a problem. And if we touch in a more than friendly way, even when no one's around, it's just because it's sometimes hard to keep things straight. It doesn't have to mean anything. Once this week is over we'll just go back to normal and everything will be fine.'

'Exactly,' Ally said, looking down at their joined hands. 'And neither of us is going to freak out about the way that I looked at you earlier, because it didn't mean anything and it's not going to lead anywhere we don't want it to.'

'This week we're hanging out and having fun. Next week we go back to avoiding human company.'

Ally pressed a kiss to his knuckles. 'And all this

time I've been telling my mother the perfect man doesn't exist.'

She stood and pulled him up. The sun was lower than when they'd entered the grove, the shadows a lot longer. When they reached the villa, the furniture around the pool had been tidied into neat clusters. Empty glasses and bottles cleared away.

The delicious smells of garlic, butter and lemon were emerging from the kitchen, where Adam and Liv seemed to be squabbling over a frying pan on the stove. Ally couldn't help but smile at their easy intimacy. She might not want it for herself, but that didn't mean she didn't recognise real love when it was right in her face. And she saw what she was sure Caleb didn't or wouldn't—that they were all delighted that Caleb was there with them. She had no interest in changing Caleb's mind about romantic relationships—but she wasn't sure that she would be able to leave this alone. She couldn't leave him believing that his family would be happier without him in their lives. She knew that she wouldn't be happier without him. As a friend. It was important to keep reminding herself of that.

She'd assumed that Caleb would be dragging her off to their room, but he pulled up a seat at the dinner table and poured himself a glass of wine. Perhaps he made an exception when food was involved.

Or perhaps he was thinking over what she'd said and was making an effort.

Dinner passed without incident, though without a lot of conversation from Caleb, and it was only as Liv produced some local limoncello, in a bottle without a label, that Ally remembered when this meal was over they would be sharing a room—perhaps they should have talked about sleeping arrangements before they'd started on the wine. She glanced across the table at Caleb, wondering if he was thinking about it too. Probably not, because they were just friends sharing a bed, nothing more dramatic than that. She really didn't need to blow this out of proportion.

She passed on the second round of limoncello though, because lowering her inhibitions didn't seem like the best idea. The combination of pasta, red wine and limoncello was making her eyelids heavy, but it wasn't until Caleb's hand on her shoulder made her jolt that she realised that she'd been drifting off even while she was still sitting up.

'You look shattered,' he said gently, standing behind her with his hands settled comfortably on her shoulders. 'Ready for bed?'

She didn't have enough brainwaves still awake and functioning to form words. Instead she let out a tired little sigh. When she looked up at Caleb, his face was warm and affectionate. He reached a hand down to help her up. 'Come on, sleepy head.' He towed her out of her chair with a less than flattering little grunt. Everyone called goodnight as he steered her down the hallway with his hands on her hips and then reached past her to open the bedroom door.

'Why didn't you tell me you were so tired?' he asked, kicking the door closed behind them and leading her over to the bed. He'd turned the air con up earlier, and somehow it was now arctic in here. Ally shivered and goosebumps prickled on her arms.

He pushed her into the bathroom, along with the oversized T-shirt she slept in, grabbed hastily from her bag, and shut the door.

They were just friends, Caleb reminded himself. Friends who were in a fake relationship that had required that they practise kissing earlier, meaning that now he couldn't pretend he didn't know how good it felt to have his hands, his mouth on her.

He smiled indulgently as the door to the bathroom opened and Ally leaned against the frame. Her T-shirt stretched over generous breasts, skimmed her tummy, and ended above soft dimpled thighs. She was utterly delicious. Or, at least, that was what he would have been thinking if he really had been her boyfriend, rather than just a friend that she'd decided to fake feelings for.

But as he met her eyes and she leaned against the doorframe, he realised that she was already half asleep. He turned back the sheets on the bed and grabbed a blanket from the wardrobe.

'You get in the bed,' he told her as she crossed her arms over her chest and rubbed her upper arms. 'Sorry about the air con. I've turned it down so it'll warm up in here soon. I'll sleep on the couch.'

After he was done in the bathroom, he came back into the bedroom and found Ally still awake despite her exhaustion. The shape of her body was visible through the sheet and thin blanket, lying on her side, hugging her knees.

'I'm sorry it's so cold,' he said again earnestly, brushing a hand over her cheek before he could stop himself. 'You're freezing!' he announced, and felt ridiculous—because of course she already knew that.

'Get in,' she said, wrapping her arms tighter around herself. 'Please?' she mumbled, shivering. 'Just until I warm up?'

He hesitated, but it really was freezing in here, and he couldn't leave her literally shivering and asking for his help. So he grabbed more blankets from the wardrobe, climbed in the other side of the bed and wrapped his arms around her waist, pulling her close.

His arms learned the shape of her as he tucked her head under his chin and inhaled the scent of her—chlorine and sunscreen and limoncello. It was a friendly gesture to keep her warm, he repeated to himself as her shivering stopped and skin smoothed under his hands. 'Better?' he asked, and heard a gentle snore as his answer.

Just a friend. Just a friend, he told himself as he started to pull himself away. He had told her that he would sleep on the couch, and he wasn't going to share a bed with her under false pretences.

He tried to ease himself away, to give them both a little space. He wasn't sure that Ally had meant for them to sleep like this. She'd just temporarily needed him for his body heat and the last thing he wanted to do was take advantage. He reached behind him to turn off the lamp. Probably for the best, he thought, letting out a long breath that ruffled the hairs on the top of her head. But as he went to get out of bed,

Ally just snuggled back harder, her softly rounded bottom rubbing against him in a way that was decidedly more than friendly and was not at all going to help him sleep.

'Ally?' he whispered, in case she'd woken and he'd just not realised. But she didn't reply, just wrapped her arms more tightly around his and made any chance of moving impossible. He took a deep breath and willed sleep to come, or for Ally to wake up, or for his erection to subside. One way or another, this was going to be a long night.

CHAPTER FOUR

ALLY WAS WARM. Her memory returned in bits and pieces. She was warm because she was in Italy, she was in Italy because of Caleb. And the hardness pressing against her back was because… Oh. She glanced down and saw her arms wrapped tightly around his, caging his forearms across her stomach. She released them suddenly, looking at her hands as if they didn't belong to her. Disloyal things. Well, she hadn't asked them to pull Caleb close and hold him there. They'd taken the initiative on that. This was so mortifying. Except…from what she could feel behind her, Caleb didn't seem to be complaining. That didn't mean anything. It was just a physiological thing. When Caleb woke up he was going to be as embarrassed about this as she was.

'Mmm…' She heard gentle waking sounds from behind her and held her breath wondering how she could extract herself in the seconds, probably, before Caleb woke up and realised what they'd done in the night. How she'd tucked herself into him and pressed back against his body. Wrapped her arms around his so he couldn't get away even if he'd wanted to. She listened to his breathing change, and then felt the tension through his body as he came to wakefulness and realised how they were lying.

'Morning?' she whispered into the dark, closing her eyes with embarrassment even though she couldn't see him.

'Hey, good morning. Oh…um…sorry,' Caleb offered from somewhere behind her, his arms suddenly springing from around her waist. 'God, sorry, Ally. I'll…' She turned over so that she could see him, putting the space they needed between them to be able to hold a conversation without dying from embarrassment. 'I'm sorry,' Caleb said again, and Ally lifted a hand to his cheek.

'Hey, it's all right. Nothing to apologise for,' she said, trying to add some lightness to her voice. 'It's just morning, and I'd made myself pretty comfortable and…now I'm rambling.'

Caleb laughed, a quiet little huff of air that she wouldn't have been able to hear if she'd not been sharing a pillow with him. She pulled her hand away from his face, tucking it safely under her cheek where it couldn't be tempted to stray and make trouble.

'You were cold,' he explained. 'Do you remember? Because of the air con. And I tried to move once you were asleep, but—'

'I aggressively spooned you? I'm sorry, I should have warned you that I do that sometimes. I would have, but I didn't expect to wipe out like that.'

'Let's just forget about it,' Caleb suggested. And

sure, yes, perhaps it could just be as easy as that. 'What do you want to do today?' he asked, and Ally took that to mean that simply being half naked in bed together all day wasn't one of the options on offer.

'Do you really have a speedboat?' she asked hopefully.

'I really have a speedboat,' he confirmed.

'Want to show it to me?' Ally asked, in a way that she hoped wasn't too suggestive.

'I suppose it's too late now to try and protect my modesty,' Caleb admitted with a groan. 'Sure, I'll show you my speedboat. Want to pack a picnic? Make a day of it?'

She narrowed her eyes at him. 'So that you don't have to spend time with your siblings?'

He tapped the end of her nose with his fingertip. 'Because once you're out in the middle of that lake you aren't ever going to want to come back. I'm not going to let you starve.'

'Fine,' Ally agreed.

'Fine.'

'Good.'

'Good.'

Ally paused. 'You haven't got up.'

'Nor have you,' Caleb replied.

No, she hadn't, because she was in bed with a nice guy. But a speedboat was a speedboat.

'You, um. You should go first,' Caleb said, his cheeks turning pink. 'While I shut my eyes and count slowly to ten.'

'Right. Right!' Ally said, her voice a high-pitched

squeal. She edged away from him across the bed, the sheet clutched to her even though she was perfectly well covered by her T-shirt. 'I'll…um…just…go.'

She jumped from the bed, ripping the Band-Aid off, knowing that letting herself linger wasn't going to lead to sensible decision-making.

Caleb grazed through the fridge, looking for delicacies to add to the cooler he was packing to take out on the boat with them. It was moments like this that reminded him there were vast swathes of the friendship landscape that were missing. He had spent more hours than he could count talking to Ally, knew her taste, how she liked to be kissed, the shape of her hips. But he didn't know if she liked olives. Whether he should pack ice-cold lemonade or beer or prosecco.

He rubbed at the back of his neck as he stared into the fridge, wondering what it meant that he could know her so well in some ways, and not at all in others. In the end, he packed the cool box indiscriminately. He might not know what she liked, but there was one sure way to find out. That was what this week could be—getting to know one another. And in the daytime, that could mean learning what she liked in a picnic. At night? He shivered. He couldn't even let himself think about what he might learn in the six nights that they had left together.

'How long have you been staring into the fridge? You've got goosebumps,' Ally said, appearing behind him.

Better that she thought they were a result of the

cold, rather than the direction his thoughts had just taken. 'Ooh, olives,' she said, reaching past him to snag a jar from the top shelf. 'Yum. You weren't leaving these behind, were you?' she asked and added them to the cooler.

It could be as easy as that, then. The more time they spent together, the more this friendship would feel like something solid and real. Perhaps by the end of the week it would feel just…normal to be around her. This weirdly expectant feeling in his gut would disappear and being around her would feel less like something he should be afraid of.

The worst part was, he couldn't talk about it to the one person every instinct he had desperately wanted to talk to. Her.

'Are you sure you're okay?' Ally asked, and he realised that he hadn't answered her question.

'I'm fine,' he said, plastering on a smile to hide his confusion. 'Just thinking if there's anything else we need. Have you got sunscreen? A hat?'

'Yes, Mother.' She slapped a hat on top of her strawberry-blonde waves, and he realised he hadn't properly looked at her since she'd walked into the kitchen. She was wearing a navy-and-white-striped vest top, which revealed the red halter strap of her bathing suit beneath. And shorts. Short shorts. Cut-off denims that revealed an expanse of soft, pale, dimpled thigh that made him want to drop to his knees and worship them.

He drew his gaze away with what little self-control he had left and pulled his sunglasses down from the top of his head for good measure. Deep breaths. Seriously deep breaths.

He was aware of the questioning look that Ally was sending in his direction, and that the fact that the sight of her thighs made it all but impossible to breathe meant that…

'What can I carry?' Ally asked, but he picked up the cooler in one hand and the bag of towels in the other. Ally rolled her eyes at him.

'I'm not going to argue about the cooler because I've seen your muscles and you are absolutely the best person for the job. But I can carry a bag of towels. Hand them over.'

He passed her the bag with a grudging expression. 'I'm trying to be a good boyfriend.'

That startled a laugh out of her, and she pressed a quick kiss to his cheek.

'You are being an excellent boyfriend. Stop worrying.'

Caleb kept sneaking looks at her as they walked across the terrace, and then down the steps to the dock where the boat was moored.

Ally stopped in her tracks. 'You know, a less generous woman might worry that you were over-compensating for something,' she said when the boat came into view.

He bumped her shoulder with his.

'Hey, I've got nothing to prove.'

She smirked. 'Yes, well. I think I found that out for myself this morning.'

He felt heat rising in his cheeks at the memories that brought back and couldn't quite meet her eye.

'But this is pretty fancy,' Ally said as Caleb climbed aboard and then reached out a hand to steady her as she stepped over the gunwale and onto the deck.

Caleb shrugged. 'It's a toy and I can barely justify it even to myself. I bought it when my grandparents were still alive, but I've hardly been here the last couple of years so it doesn't get used much.'

'Cal, come on. You're allowed to do nice things for yourself. And if your nice thing is a speedboat to impress all the girls, then all the better for me.'

'Girl,' he corrected, because that seemed like an important distinction to make. 'I've not brought anyone else here.'

This time it was Ally's turn to blush. No, it was probably just the sun.

'Sunscreen,' he said, holding out a hand.

'You've not going to give me a tour before you ask to feel me up?'

He shook his head, laughing. 'I didn't know that talking about our feelings was going to be quite so direct. I'm not trying to feel you up, as you so elegantly put it. Your nose is pink already and I don't want your shoulders going the same way.'

'You know, you're very bossy when you're taking care of me,' she accused, passing him the sunscreen from her bag and turning her back, sweeping her mass of hair over one shoulder.

'Be quiet and move your straps,' he told her, pulling her closer. She might not be able to see him, but

she could hear the smile in his voice. Ally rolled
her eyes as she pulled the straps of her vest off her
shoulders. He was mercifully quick, leaving her half
wishing that he'd taken better advantage of the situation. And then his hands were off her skin and she
shouldn't be as affected by that as she truly was.

She'd imagined that maybe his hands would linger.
That maybe he'd be looking for excuses to touch her
because that was what she wanted, deep down, even
if she couldn't tell him that. It was simpler if he just
gave it to her without her having to admit what she
wanted. Because telling him that would mean having
to work out for herself first what she really wanted,
and she wasn't sure she could look at herself in the
mirror and admit to herself that she wanted his hands
on her. Wanted him as her best friend, and—yes, if
he had been anyone else, perhaps she would have
given him an access-all-areas pass to her body. But
she couldn't do that with him. He was too precious to
her to risk losing. To risk needing to push him away
because she'd started to care too much.

Admitting to herself that she cared at all scared
her. Acknowledging that there was a chance that she
could want more from him would be too much. Her
best friend. What would it be like if he were her lover
too? She didn't doubt that it would be good. But she
also didn't doubt how much she would get hurt if it
all fell apart. The sex wouldn't be a problem. But
the wanting could. Falling for him would be a huge
problem—for both of them. She knew first-hand how
much it could hurt, how terrifying it could be to love

someone. Right now, her feelings for Caleb were manageable. Safe. She didn't want that to change. She absolutely wasn't going to *ask* him to change that.

So she took a seat at the back of the boat, and watched Caleb steer them away from the dock and out towards the centre of the lake. She should really have her eyes on the landscape, she told herself. It wasn't as if she were going to find herself in a speedboat on a private Italian lake every week. But she supposed that Caleb had put a lot of work into those arms and someone should be admiring the results of all his hard work.

She let her eyes drift from muscular arms to shoulders, down Caleb's broad back, where it narrowed to waist and hips. Which was, of course, exactly when he looked over his shoulder and caught her ogling.

He grinned at her, flicked a switch next to the steering wheel and then came to sprawl by her on the seat. 'Neat toy,' she said, not wanting his attention on the way she had just been staring at him.

'I think so. And, er, the view.'

She directed her gaze very pointedly to the mountains in the distance.

'Not too bad,' she pronounced, and Caleb laughed.

'So, do you want to swim? Or I can show you what the boat can really do or...'

'Or?' Ally asked, wondering how distressed—or how tempted—she would be if he suggested something that could possibly ruin their friendship for ever.

'We could try taking some photos again for your parents?'

'Photos?' she asked, her comprehension still lagging by a few seconds.

Caleb frowned at her. 'Yes. Magical pictures you take with your phone and can send to other phones. Like the ones you planned to send to your parents to make it clear that they don't need to rebook you on your singles cruise.'

'Oh, those types of photos,' she said with a nervous smile, burying any thoughts of other sorts of photos that they could be taking out here, in the Italian sunshine, with no one around to see. The sort that she would never, *ever*, send to her parents. 'As long as you promise not to try and drown me again.'

'You're never going to let me live that down, are you?' Caleb groaned, covering his face with a hand.

'I'm not planning on it,' Ally confirmed. 'So,' she said, shuffling closer to Caleb and pulling her phone out of her shorts pocket. 'Cute couple selfies?'

She glanced up at him, but looked away when their eyes met, afraid of what it would mean if she let herself gaze into his eyes, as she was tempted to do, and pulled her sunglasses down onto her face. She rested her head on his shoulder and held her phone out for a selfie, firing off a couple of shots. Caleb reached an arm around her shoulder, pulling her into him as he took the phone from her hand. 'Longer arms,' he explained, smiling and kissing the top of her head as he took another few pictures.

This was all just for show, Ally reminded herself, not letting herself get carried away with thinking about his body pressing against hers, the warmth of his cheek on the top of her head. How easy it would be to close her eyes, relax and simply enjoy being close to him. She couldn't do that. She knew how much she could get hurt, or—worse—she could hurt Caleb, and she wasn't prepared to do that.

So when Caleb handed the phone back, she scrolled through the gallery as an objective observer. Not at all moved by the sight of them looking happy and affectionate in their photos.

'What do you think?' Caleb asked.

'Fine. They're fine.'

'I think we look like friends,' Caleb said, frowning a little.

She snorted. 'We are friends.'

'I'm just not sure that your mum will buy us being a couple. I think we could try a bit harder to be convincing, if you wanted to.'

If she wanted to? Did *he* want to? She had her suspicions about what 'trying harder' might look like, and it wasn't the sort of thing that she usually did with her friends.

'Like what?' she asked.

'Like you could take your shirt off, for a start.'

She raised her eyebrows. 'Once again, it's hard not to think that you might have an ulterior motive.' God knew she was not going to turn down the chance to see him shirtless again. *Looking* was safe enough, surely. Looking wasn't touching.

'Just take your shirt off,' he said, and she should have hated the bossy tone in his voice, but instead she found herself reaching for the hem of her top.

She stopped herself a fraction of a second before she complied unthinkingly.

'I will if you will,' she challenged.

Well, that backfired, she mused as he whipped his shirt off and managed to take a picture of her still drooling before she could pull herself together.

'That's not going to prove anything to my mum,' she reasoned. 'You're not even in the shot.'

'No, but I'm going to keep it anyway,' he said, smiling as he sent it to himself.

'Right, get down here,' Caleb said, lying back and stretching himself out on the deck of the boat. She lay down tentatively beside him, but he scooped her closer with an arm around her waist until she was lying half on top of him. His arm moved higher, until his hand met the nape of her neck, his fingers threaded through her hair and tilted her face up. He nudged her nose with his.

'This might be a bit more convincing,' he suggested, his mouth so close that his lips brushed against hers as he spoke.

She pulled together every ounce of self-control she could muster to avoid kissing the smug expression off his face. 'And if we were here, on your boat, like this, why exactly would we be taking pictures to send home to my parents?' she managed to say, praising herself as she did it for her ability to string a sentence together while distracted in the most complete possible way.

She was distantly aware of the presence of her phone while Caleb stroked strands of hair out of her face. And then of Caleb shifting them slightly, his nose crashing against hers.

'Wh—?'

'Light's better at this angle,' he said, and she couldn't believe he had the capacity to be thinking of lighting and camera angles when she was doing her best just to remember to keep her heart beating and breath going in and out of her lungs.

He rolled and the boat rocked as he landed on top of her, any chance of breathing lost completely as his hair fell into her eyes and filtered out the sunshine, isolating them in their own world. She wrapped one foot around his calf before she could think about what she was doing, and both of them froze.

'I really don't think we should be sending photos of this to my parents,' she managed to say in a shaky voice, before realising that Caleb had already dropped the camera. This wasn't for show, then. This was just the two of them, bodies as close as two people could be.

'So we should probably stop this now,' Caleb said, without any suggestion that he was going to move.

'Definitely,' she agreed.

She held her breath as he lay half on top of her for another second. And then another more. And then she remembered, this wasn't some cute guy that she had just met. This was *Caleb*. Her Caleb, and she had promised herself that she wasn't going to risk losing him over a kiss or a fling.

So she wriggled away before she could do anything stupid, the boat rocking slightly in the wake of her movement. She closed her eyes against the sun, listening to Caleb's breathing, and wondering whether she had just spoiled things.

'That was pretty convincing, then.'

'Do not send those photos to my mother,' Ally managed to say while she tried to get her breathing under control.

'Definitely not,' Caleb agreed. 'I'll delete them.'

'No!' Ally almost shouted. 'I mean, just… Fine, yes, delete them. If that's what you want.' Caleb just handed her the phone back.

Great, something else for her list of things not to think about, she thought as she slid the phone into her pocket.

'We should do something less… NSFW,' she suggested, looking desperately for safe ground.

'I brought a pack of cards,' Caleb replied, still not properly looking at her.

'Yes. That,' Ally said with a sigh of relief, reaching into the cooler and pulling out two cans of lemonade. She cracked the first and handed it to Caleb.

They played a few hands of poker, using olives to place stakes, until the game took a back seat to simply reclining on the seats, feeling the sun on their faces and the gentle rock of the boat on the water.

The boat gave a gentle lurch, and Ally opened her eyes to see what had caused it, only to groan and snap them closed when she remembered that Caleb still had no shirt on.

'Next time we are going on holiday somewhere

cold,' she declared, throwing her arm over her face for added drama.

Caleb laughed. Then, 'Next time?' he asked tentatively.

'I mean, just a holiday. Maybe. I think I'd miss your face if I never saw it again. I'm looking forward to things being normal again, but maybe once a year we can hang out like this. But with less nudity,' she suggested, with a pointed look at his bare torso.

'I hear Scandinavia is nice in the winter,' he offered.

She thought about it. 'No hot springs.'

'Deal.'

She just sat and looked at him, wondered how long she could get away with that. Before she shook her head and brought herself back to real life. 'You need sunscreen, too,' Ally said, looking critically over the skin he had on show. She held out her hand for the sunscreen, telling herself that this didn't mean anything. Being careful about sun protection was just a responsible thing to do. And Caleb's back was so broad there was no way that he could reach it all by himself.

She started with his shoulders, tucking his body between her knees as she smoothed the lotion over his shoulders, sliding her hands up to the nape of his neck and learning the shape of his muscles, the give and the slide of his skin.

As her hands moved, the tension leached from his muscles until he was languid and heavy, and she could just imagine him sinking back against her until she had no choice but to give up on the pretence of sun protection, let her arms wrap gently around him and rest her chin on the top of his head. But the longer that she thought about it, the less she could be sure that their friendship would survive it. So she flipped the lid back on the sunscreen with an audible click, making Caleb look back at her over his shoulder.

When his eyes met hers, it was as if a hook grabbed her somewhere behind her sternum and pulled. It must have been her axis that shifted. Her centre of gravity that moved. She knew on an intellectual level that it couldn't be the whole planet or the universal laws of physics that had altered when his eyes met hers. When she noticed for the first time the flecks of green in with the brown and golds, but that didn't mean that it didn't feel that way. She smoothed her thumbs over his cheekbones, telling herself that it was just because she still had the sunscreen on her hands that this was purely practical. Not because she wanted it so much that she physically could not keep her hands off him.

And then when he groaned, she felt it on every plane of her existence and on several that she was sure had yet to be discovered. He shifted around so that he could look properly at her, and one hand cupped her cheek, leaving her in no doubt what was coming next. He was going to kiss her, and she was desperate for him to do it. Which was why she couldn't let this happen. Not when she couldn't be sure that her usual defence mechanisms wouldn't snap into place.

The last thing that she wanted was to freeze him out, but she knew herself well enough to realise she didn't do it by choice. She got scared and she lashed out. Caleb didn't deserve that, especially not now she had more of an idea of how he'd been hurt by his parents leaving him. By all that his family had been through since. He had trusted her with that and she wasn't going to repay that trust by letting her own relationship issues get in the way of a friendship that was so important to her. They could fool around later once she had this wobble, or whatever it was, under control.

She shifted to put some space between them, and, as she had known that he would, he instantly took the hint and moved away. 'Shall we make a start on this picnic?'

Ally smiled, relieved and grateful to have a friend who understood her so well, with just an undercurrent of discomfort about what it meant if she was already having feelings about wanting to kiss him and not wanting to lose him. Walking away from the danger wasn't an option this time. She had to deal with them in a way that wouldn't mean closing off Caleb from her life. She would just have to compartmentalise, she told herself. The Caleb she loved as a friend in one box. The Caleb she had kissed and whose body she couldn't keep her eyes off in another.

Eating a picnic equalled Friend Caleb, which meant easy banter and not staring at his chest. She put on her sunglasses and sat up, but didn't breathe right until Caleb took pity on her and pulled on his shirt.

Caleb spread a blanket on the floor between them, and they both pulled items out of the cooler, passing cheeses and artichoke hearts and stuffed olives between them. And if their hands brushed as they both reached for the *taralli* crackers, or Caleb's tongue flickered against her finger when she insisted that he try the sun-blush tomato that had just changed her entire world, well, that was fine. She would simply file those feelings away in the 'Hot Caleb' box and carry on her increasingly perfect afternoon with Friend Caleb.

When they were sleepy and full from an excess of antipasti and Sicilian lemonade, they stretched out on the blanket in comfortable silence, and Ally had to actively resist the urge to let her fingers play across the hair on Caleb's stomach and trace it down to the waistband of his shorts. To let her fingers dip into the valleys between his abs, under his pectorals, and then measure his biceps by squeezing her hands around them. The sleepier she got, the harder it was to keep the contents of those two Caleb boxes strictly separated. She forced herself upright, resting on her elbows.

'Bored?' Caleb asked beside her, turning to his side and propping his head up with one hand.

'Not bored, but thinking that it would be a shame to come all this way to see your speedboat and not see it doing any actual speeding.'

He grinned. 'I think I could be talked into showing you that.'

They packed away the picnic and stowed their bags then Caleb sat at the wheel while Ally perched on a seat behind him. She was leaning forwards, elbows on knees, in her eagerness, which did something so unholy to her cleavage that he had to look away before he did something that would capsize the boat.

He fixed his eyes on the water ahead of him and opened up the throttle, letting the tension in his body ease as he watched the speed climb and climb. Not letting off the throttle, he leaned on the wheel, turning them in a wide, graceful circle, keeping them on the edge of control. And when he slowed down to a steady cruise, Ally's eyes were bright and a huge grin had spread across her face. A few drops of water glistened on her hair.

'Do you want a turn?'

'Oh, my God, can I? You trust me?'

He laughed off the question, refusing to read more into it than he was sure that she had intended.

'Of course I do. Come, sit here.' He shifted so that she could sit between his thighs. Considering that their relationship was supposed to be entirely fake, and there was no one else on the boat to see them right now, there was rather more physical contact than he had been expecting.

'I'll show you the ropes,' he said, forcing himself to think about anything other than Ally scrambling into his lap, pushing his thighs wider apart, settling her hands over his on the wheel. To try not to notice the way that his forearms brushed against the sides of her breasts, that if he leaned forward and looked down he'd be able to see… He looked up at the sky and squeezed his eyes shut as a matter of urgency, trying to shift back in his seat without touching any more of Ally's sinfully tempting skin.

It took more than a few long moments before he trusted himself to speak.

'Ready?' he asked, and pushed her hand on the throttle to pick up speed. Ally squealed as he guided her hands on the wheel, taking them in a series of sharp turns that had spray catching their faces and hair. She looked back over her shoulder and met his eye, and she had droplets of water on her eyelashes, little jewels glinting in the sunshine. Her cheeks were pink, her smile lines deep, and he wanted to capture the sight in oils and pastels and watercolours. He wanted her smile and her flushed cheeks and her wide eyes immortalised on the walls of his house, so that he would see her like this wherever he looked.

That was not how he was meant to feel about his best friend. That was so much more complicated than liking hanging out with someone. Or wanting to make them laugh. Or even wanting to sleep with them.

He wiped a sheen of lake water from Ally's cheekbone with his thumb. 'I'm having second thoughts about selling the boat, if this is the expression it puts on your face.'

'Can you have it shipped home?' Ally asked, still grinning and glowing in equal measure. 'I can see us tearing up and down the Thames in it.'

It was on the tip of his tongue to remind her that after this week they'd agreed to go back to keeping a screen between them. If she hadn't noticed her slip, and her intention to keep him in her life, then he wasn't going to be the one to remind her.

'I'll absolutely think about it,' he told her, attempting in vain to hide his smile for fear of tipping her off.

The rest of the afternoon passed in a haze of sunshine, stretching out on the loungers, passing cold drinks to one another, picking at the remains of their picnic, swapping titbits of gossip and not allowing their conversation to drift anywhere that might lead to a serious discussion of exactly what they were to each other.

Despite the compelling urge he seemed unable to bury to pick at the conversation they'd had in the olive grove the day before. She was so convinced that falling for someone would only lead to trouble. And, well, he could hardly take her to task on it when he was no more keen to have someone fall for him than she was to fall.

But there was still a part of him that made him want to change her mind. Made him want to ask her to give him a chance. To take a risk. But then he remembered what happened to the people who decided they cared for him, and that he had told himself that he had every much as good a reason to resist whatever was happening here as she did. They neither of them wanted to be more than friends. Nothing that had happened here, and nothing that had happened in his bed this morning, changed that. It was all part of the pretence they were playing on their families, that was all.

'What are you thinking so hard about over there?'

Ally asked without opening her eyes, which made him wonder how she could possibly know that he'd been thinking about anything at all.

'Nothing,' he lied, turning onto his side and propping his head on one hand. 'Just wondering if we ought to head back.'

'We've run out of food so I won't argue.'

'We'll probably have to deal with the others.'

Ally let out something halfway between a laugh and a sigh. 'You say that like it's an elaborate form of torture.' She rolled to her side, propped up her head, and he had no choice but to notice that she was mirroring his body language. He wouldn't let himself read anything into that. He. Would. Not. 'Dinner was fun last night.'

'I just find them hard work,' he said, deliberately not making eye contact.

'Do you think maybe you find yourself being hard work around them?' Ally asked.

'I have no idea what that means.'

'It means, whenever I've seen you with them, you put more effort into holding yourself apart from them than being involved. Perhaps if you just…relaxed and allowed it to happen, allowed them to be close to you, you wouldn't find it so hard just being with them.'

Caleb bristled, because all that was a little closer to the truth than was entirely comfortable. 'I don't do that,' he said.

'I think you do,' Ally argued. 'I think when you're faced with the choice to be a part of their lives or not, you choose not.'

'I'm on holiday with them, aren't I? Doesn't that count as being a part of their lives?'

'They invited *themselves*. And you brought a fake girlfriend to act as a buffer,' she pointed out, somewhat unfairly. 'And now we're hiding from them in the middle of a lake.'

Well, when she put it like that, it made him sound completely unreasonable. 'We aren't hiding,' Caleb protested, searching for any high ground in this argument. 'We're hanging out. Spending quality time together. It's different.'

'Then why do you look so forlorn at the idea of going back to the house?'

'I was just looking out for you!' he said, his voice raised. 'Rowan will try and make you play tennis, or Liv and Adam will want you to take sides in one of their arguments. Jonathan will start talking about balance sheets!'

Ally crossed her arms, pulled off her sunglasses so she could look him properly in the eye. 'And I'm telling you I don't need you to look out for me! I'd *like* to get to know your family. I would have done it already if you hadn't kept dragging us away from them at every opportunity!'

Caleb shook his head. She was being so stubborn about this and she didn't understand. This wasn't her family, and she'd only been here a day. 'We all had dinner together last night,' he pointed out, determined not to sound sulky.

'You were the first to leave the table!'

'Only because you fell asleep!'

'I was not asleep! And even if I had been, it wasn't like you were devastated to have your evening cut short. You were looking for any excuse to leave from the moment that we sat down!' There were frown lines on her forehead that *he* had put there, and he wanted to kick himself. This was meant to be a fun trip out, and instead they were fighting about his relationship with his family. He hated that he did this. And he didn't know what he was meant to do to stop it—it didn't matter who he was close to, it always ended up like this. With an argument, and him hating that it was happening.

'Fine, okay, I didn't want to be there,' he conceded at last. What was the point in arguing when Ally could see right through his lies anyway? 'You were the only thing that made it remotely bearable. But I couldn't wait until we were on our own again and I could have you all to myself. Are you happy now?'

It was true. From the minute that he'd sat down at the table last night, he'd wanted nothing more than for dinner to be over. But for once that hadn't had anything to do with his family and had had everything to do with getting Ally on her own. With not having to share her or her attention or see her smiling at his family. He knew he was selfish, and that it made him sound unreasonable, but he only had this week with her and he wanted all that for himself.

She said nothing for a beat, and he wondered how badly he'd screwed up. Had he freaked her out completely? Was she going to walk away?

'Why did you want that?' she asked slowly, carefully. 'What would you do with me if you had me all to yourself?'

He drew in a deep breath, let it out slowly, trying to keep his racing heart under control. 'Because I like being with you, Ally,' he said. She deserved his honesty. He might be a screw-up, but he could at least give her the truth about that. 'Because I never stop thinking about you. Because I held you in my arms all last night and…' He trailed off, not trusting himself to finish that sentence.

Her eyes widened in surprise, and then narrowed, drifting down to focus on his lips as if she couldn't help herself. 'And?' she prompted, taking both of their lives into her hands with that one word.

'And I don't know what to do with that,' he admitted. 'I don't know what to do with the fact that I can't stop thinking about kissing you, even though the only times we've kissed it wasn't even real. Wasn't meant to be real. I don't know what to do with these feelings I'm having for you, Ally.'

Her body stiffened immediately, and she drew her knees up to wrap her arms around them. He'd gone too far, he realised instantly, and reached a hand out to reassure her, but she flinched away. 'Ally, I'm sorry. I didn't mean to say that. Pretend that I didn't say that.' But he could see the damage he was doing already. Something had closed off behind her eyes and she'd drawn herself inwards, protecting herself. Protecting herself from him.

'No, it's fine. It's nothing,' she said, but he knew that she was lying. 'It's just confusing because we've been faking being together. You don't have real feelings for me, Caleb.'

How could he argue with her when he could see full well that it was only believing those words that was stopping her running for it? That and the fact that they were in the middle of a lake. He knew that what she wanted, needed, right now was space. He was convinced that if they weren't currently on a boat in the middle of a lake, she would have walked away already. And it was his fault that she couldn't.

'I'll take us back now,' Caleb said, and Ally faked a smile that didn't convince him in the slightest. Because she could tell him that his feelings weren't real, but he knew that wasn't true. And if Ally had believed it then she wouldn't be so freaked out right now.

'Yeah. I think that's probably a good idea,' she said, not meeting his eyes.

The speed of the boat meant that the silent, awkward journey back was at least mercifully short. He had made a mistake bringing Ally here, to Italy, and now she knew it as well as he did. He had no doubt that she would already be making plans to get away from him. He knew her usual reactions when things got emotional, and it wasn't to stick around and talk about it.

This was a disaster, Ally thought to herself. Why had Caleb decided that the right place to be honest about his feelings for once was in the middle of a lake, where the universal laws of physics made it impossible for her to run away? At least Caleb was wasting no time getting them back to the shore. He was gunning the boat every bit as fast as he had when he had been showing off to her what his toy could do.

Why had he told her that he had feelings for her? Of course she had suspected it… She hadn't missed the crazy chemistry of their practice kiss, nor the way that they had woken wrapped around one another this morning. But she had thought that they were both going to ignore it. That was the sensible thing to do, the right thing to do that wouldn't ruin their friendship. That wouldn't make her push him away because she was scared of how big her feelings for him might grow. How much they could hurt each other if they allowed that to happen.

What was the point of having a fake boyfriend if you ended up in the same arguments that you would with a real one?

Why couldn't everything just stay the same? Sure, Caleb had become more important to her than just about anyone else over the last year. And that had seemed fine, before, when they didn't see each other in person. Because how much could somebody hurt her, or how much could she hurt somebody else, if they didn't know each other in real life?

And then the fact that they *were* good friends, that was meant to stop something like this happening. They were meant to skip the flirtation stage, had gone straight into deep devoted friendship. Attraction wasn't meant to rear its head when they'd already been platonic friends for so long.

Even when they'd realised that that was what was going on, why couldn't he just ignore it as they had been doing until now? Why drag it out into the open where they had to look at it and be scared of it, forcing her to try and protect herself?

She would have to leave. She could get a taxi to the airport, and…well, even if there wasn't a flight that day, there had to be one the next. She could sleep on a bench at the airport for a night if she had to. It was no big deal. All she had to do was get herself away from Caleb to a safe distance, where she couldn't hurt anyone, or get hurt herself.

Caleb steered them alongside the jetty, tied the boat securely and disembarked. He held out his hand to help her do the same. And, oh, but it was inconvenient that it was so much harder to pretend that she was halfway home already when her hand was in his, so present and so very real. And then came the moment when he should have let her hand drop, if all he'd been doing was steadying her back onto dry ground, but he…didn't. She watched the moment when he should have done it come and go, and looked up at him, wondering what he was thinking.

'Ally, I'm really sorry. We're friends. I don't want that to change. If you want me to, I can find you a flight home because I know that must be what you're thinking about. So just give me an hour and I'll get everything sorted.'

His words stopped her thoughts in their tracks. It was exactly what she had expected to want. But now that she was here, with the keys to doing a runner in her lap, it didn't seem so appealing. He'd known that she'd want to leave. To run. And he was, what? Just okay with that? She couldn't see how if she left now they'd be able to pick up their online friendship as if this couple of days had never happened. So walking out on this argument meant walking out on all of it. The fake dating charade. The scarily real-feeling kiss. And their extremely real, extremely-important-part-of-her life friendship. Was she really willing to lose all of that because Caleb had admitted that he was, what, confused about his feelings for her? Perhaps she was overreacting. They had created a confusing scenario, after all. It made sense that some of the things that they were faking would leak into their real lives. But that didn't mean that it *was* real. Things could just go back to normal if they carried on behaving as if they already were.

'Do...do you want me to leave?' she asked. Because maybe that would save her from trying to work out what she wanted, if his words had been a demand rather than an offer. 'No,' he said, hand in his hair again. 'No, I don't want you to leave. I just thought... I overstepped and I know you don't like to stick around when things get...intense like that. I don't want to be something that stands in the way of what you want. You deserve that, Ally.'

She took a few deep breaths, until she couldn't hear her heartbeat pounding in her ears. 'I... Thank you. I appreciate you saying that. But I want to stay. If that's okay with you.' She didn't want to examine her reaction to the grin that appeared on his face at her words. If she did that she'd have to acknowledge the cool, empty space that had been opening up in her chest as they'd headed back to shore. And then how his words had triggered the whoosh of it refilling with something warm and glowing and threatening to fill her up. 'I like hanging out with you, and I know you didn't mean what you said, so we can just carry on hanging out like you never even said it. Okay?'

'Okay,' Caleb said, his voice carefully uninflected. 'Okay,' he said again, with a little more warmth.

He didn't let go of her hand, and she didn't pull it back. The net result being that they found themselves walking along the jetty hand in hand, both of them seeming to do their best not to mention how close their friendship had just come to tearing apart, but instead of that happening, somehow they were literally hanging onto one another. They slowed, the closer they got to the villa. The closer they got to spending time with his siblings, which was what had started their argument in the first place. If he wanted to hang out just the two of them, then fine. It wasn't her job to fix whatever was going on with him and his family. She had no intention of further rocking the boat—even if only figuratively speaking—now that they had recovered from what had happened out on the water.

As they reached the terrace, she could hear familiar voices, and guessed that the others were all by the pool, and that they'd be invited to join them. She would absolutely not read anything into whether Caleb would have changed his mind as a result of their…argument. She absolutely did not want him to change. Not least because of something that she had said. But she would like him to be happy. And she could see quite clearly that the gulf between Caleb and his family hurt him. The way that he held a part of himself back—the best part, the part that really cared—when he was with them. He was scared to lose them. That much seemed pretty clear to her. But if pointing that out resulted in them fighting, she wouldn't point it out again. It wasn't worth losing him over. No more than it was worth him turning her searching questions back on her.

Caleb's fingers tensed as they reached the terrace, and she was about to reassure him that they could go and be on their own if he wanted. But then with a tug on their linked hands he pulled away, all but towing her towards the pool.

'Caleb!' Rowan called as soon as they came into view. 'Come and play tennis. Your sister won't get off her butt and we need a fourth for doubles.'

He glanced across at Ally with a look that was pure 'I told you so' and she gave him a careful smile and squeezed his fingers in a reassuring sort of way. 'Are you going to play?' she asked.

He wanted to say no. But it was just a game of tennis, and if it pleased Ally to see him do it… He liked pleasing Ally, and it didn't cost him anything. 'Will you be okay by yourself?' he asked.

She leaned in and, after just a fraction of a second's hesitation, kissed him on the cheek. 'I'll be fine. Go and have fun.'

CHAPTER FIVE

WHAT ON EARTH did she think she was doing? Ally had to ask herself.

Caleb had given her the perfect opportunity to run headlong in the opposite direction from whatever it was that they had been circling around here, and she'd just...not taken it? It wasn't even that she'd been passive in not leaving—she had made an *active* decision to stay, even after she'd been handed the chance of a prompt flight home.

But she'd stayed—because she wanted to.

Because she was scared of what it would mean for her and Caleb's friendship if she walked away from him now.

She went to sit beside Liv on one of the sun loungers and adjusted the angle slightly—just so that the sun wouldn't be in her eyes, she told herself. Nothing at all to do with the fact that it gave her a better view of the tennis courts where Caleb and Rowan were knocking a tennis ball between them, and Ally smiled, relieved to see him trying when an hour ago he had been so tense that she wouldn't have been surprised to see him shatter in front of her. The others had gone quiet when he'd walked over to the tennis court, as if they couldn't quite believe that he'd accepted their invitation. But their surprised expressions had soon turned into grins of pleasure as they'd started to play, and Caleb had begun to ease up a little.

She couldn't make herself think about what he'd admitted to her on the boat about his feelings. But she couldn't avoid thinking about the fact that she was still here. He had offered her a way out, knowing that her instinct would be to shut him out. He had understood what she had needed without her having to say it, and had offered it to her even though it would have hurt him. But here she still was.

Perhaps the fact that she'd chosen to stay would go some way towards convincing him that he was the sort of guy who was worth sticking around for. If he decided he wanted to date someone—not her, obviously—for real one day. It was totally up to him if he wanted to choose that or not. But she couldn't leave him out in the world thinking that he was someone who she could walk away from without a backward glance. He deserved to know—to believe—that he was worth more than that. It was just her job as a friend to keep showing him that, again and again if need be.

His friend.

A friend would take an interest in how his tennis match was going, she told her herself, as her eyes followed the ripples in the muscles of his arm as he easily returned the ball across the court.

'He's one of those annoying people who are just good at stuff, isn't he?' she huffed in Liv's direction.

Liv lifted her sunglasses and shot her a sideways glance. 'Well, until a couple of days ago I wouldn't have said so. But then you come along and it turns out he's been keeping all kinds of secrets all along.'

'I didn't realise I was a secret,' Ally confessed.

'We didn't realise my brother was such a dark horse,' Liv said with a wry smile.

Should she be upset that Caleb apparently hadn't said a word about her to his family? Ally wondered. Not once, in the year since they had first met online. It would probably be more of a worry if she hadn't seen for herself how actively he avoided even the company of his siblings, never mind talking with them about someone who was important to him. Even with everything that she was unsure about, the fact that she was important to him—there somehow wasn't any doubt in her mind about that—even if his sister hadn't known that she'd existed two days ago wasn't enough to change her belief.

'Don't let him push you away,' Liv said, looking serious for the first time since Ally had met her. 'We've all been trying to get through to him. It's the reason we invited ourselves here in the first place. But he doesn't listen to us when we tell him we want him around. Apparently he pays more attention to you. I'm glad he's got you,' Liv added, letting her sunglasses fall back down. 'He seems happier.'

Ally let out a long breath, slotting puzzle pieces together and trying to work out how they added up to a Caleb. 'Yeah, I'm not sure that he'd agree with that right now.'

Liv scoffed. 'What? Did you have a fight? Every

couple fights sometimes. Me and Adam haven't properly started our day until we're three arguments deep. Caleb'll try to push you away—I'm warning you. If you care about him, don't let him do it, okay?'

If Ally had had any doubts about whether staying was the right thing to do, as she looked back at the doubles match, they fled. If she couldn't stay for herself, she could do it to make sure that Caleb knew that he was exactly the kind of person that people around him wanted in their life.

That when he cut people off, he wasn't protecting them, he was hurting them. The thought gave her a stab of guilt, thinking of all the perfectly nice men that she'd shut out of her own life over the years. How many of them had been hurt when she'd laid down her rigid boundaries?

But just because Caleb was guilty of flawed thinking didn't mean that she was as well. After all, the only person she was trying to protect was herself. And, yes, she was aware of how selfish that sounded, but she'd spent a large portion of her life with every choice and action taken out of her control. Why shouldn't she be selfish, now that she actually had choices about what happened in her life rather than having it dictated to her by her doctors and her parents? Just because she questioned whether Caleb was hurting himself with his choices didn't mean that she was doing the same.

She tried to concentrate her mind on the tennis match to try and quiet the sense that she wasn't being entirely honest with herself. Caleb had once again sacrificed his shirt to the heat of the afternoon, which led her to believe that this temperature, whatever it happened to be, was her ideal weather. The beads of sweat that were trickling down his spine were only further evidence of this, whatever she'd said on the boat about going somewhere cold next time.

Caleb glanced over just as she was wondering how creepy she was to be practically salivating over his sweat. She at least had her sunglasses down to hide the flame emojis that she was certain were flickering in her pupils at that moment, though she was sure from the smug grin that appeared on his face that her general appreciation for the scene had been apparent enough. How was she meant to survive five more days of him looking at her like that without her emotions doing something stupid in Caleb's direction? Five days were frightening enough. The nights were another question entirely… They couldn't count on her practically falling asleep at the table again to ensure that they made sensible decisions after they retired to their bedroom for the night.

She hadn't been good in her adult life at denying herself the things that she wanted. Why not, when she had missed out on so much earlier in her life? But she was also used to having ultimate control over the consequences of her choices, and she knew in that moment—without a doubt—that wouldn't be the case here.

If she slept with Caleb, well, if she did more than sleep with him, she would no longer have control over their relationship. She couldn't—wouldn't—hurt Caleb by shutting him out, but if she wasn't willing to do that, then how would she be able to stop herself getting hurt? She sat up abruptly when she realised that the sporty types had finished their game while she had been performing mental gymnastics. Caleb came over and collapsed at the end of her lounger.

'Remind me never to do anything competitive with Rowan ever again,' he gasped, his hand over his eyes to shield them from the sun.

'Aw, poor baby,' she said, remembering that, whatever had happened between them on the boat, she was meant to be playing the part of the adoring girlfriend. She combed her hands through his damp hair, trying not to think too hard about how much of this easy intimacy was their real friendship, and how much was the fake relationship that she was going to lose at the end of this week. She pulled her hand away at the thought, but Caleb caught her wrist and brought it back until it was tangled tightly in his hair again. 'That feels nice,' he muttered as she pressed her fingers into his scalp.

She reached for her glass of water and nudged him with her knee until he opened one eye and looked up at her. She let a couple of drops of condensation snake down the side of the glass, linger on the rim at the bottom, and then drop onto his overheated skin. Caleb pushed himself up onto his elbows and looked at the glass of water as if he had just trekked across a desert.

'I would do terrible, terrible things for a sip of that water,' he told her, his voice low and rough. 'You can name your price.'

Ally raised one eyebrow and smiled as she considered what she would ask for. A kiss was the obvious answer in a situation like this, but she was already entitled to those as his fake girlfriend. She wasn't going to waste it.

'You can have it on credit,' she said, smiling wryly as she handed him the glass. 'I'll set my price later.'

'I don't know—what if I don't like the price?' Caleb asked, regarding her suspiciously.

She shrugged—that was so not her problem. 'I don't know...' she repeated sardonically. 'I suppose it depends on how badly you want the water.'

He sat up and gave her a meaningful look, not even breaking eye contact as he took one long gulp of the water after another until the glass was empty. Ally raised her eyebrows, refusing to smile, to rise to his provocation. She liked this playful Caleb, wondered how she could keep him for longer. 'I thought it was a favour for a sip,' she observed as he collapsed back beside her thighs. 'You drank the whole glass.'

He smirked, closing his eyes. 'You don't scare me.'

She laughed, giving up the pretence of being serious. 'You *should* be afraid,' she told him. 'Don't think I won't make you pay up.'

That only broadened his smirk into a smile. 'I can't wait.'

Her whole body warmed at the thought of the favours she could call in later that night. For a moment, her brain short-circuited, overwhelmed by the possibilities unravelling before her. The only option her brain didn't consider was the one that they'd planned from the start: a chaste night with no sex.

She looked down at Caleb and wished she could

read his mind. He had said that he had wanted her all to himself the night before. Did he still feel that way? What might have happened if she hadn't sparked out on him the moment that her head had hit the pillow?

And they hadn't discussed sleeping arrangements for tonight. He *had* held her all of last night, and she had let him. Could she risk letting him do that again? Risk letting him do more than that?

'Jonathan's going to light the pizza oven!' Rowan called from somewhere behind them. Ally let a small smile catch the corner of her lip and nudged at Caleb's side with her knee again, inspiration striking. 'Hey. Get up, I'm cashing in a favour.'

She saw the flash of heat in his face before she caught him with a hand on his chest.

'Go help your brother,' she said before he could get any ideas, and his smile instantly dropped.

'You have carte blanche to ask me for anything. *Anything*,' he reminded her with a meaningful stare. 'And you're choosing to ask me to hang out with my brother?'

Ally took a deep breath, committing to this, despite the clear temptation that he was offering. Some things were more important. She had to make him see how much he was cared for. Loved. Even if it made him angry with her. He was worth it. His happiness was worth it.

'You agreed to anything and this is what I choose,' she told him firmly. 'If you manage to look like you're enjoying it I'll knock two credits off your account.'

He gave her a stern, hard look, and the degree to which he was fighting this only made her trust her instincts even more. After all, she wasn't forcing him. This was just a game. A way to nudge him towards something he needed. A way for him to take something he wanted without admitting it—to himself or to anyone else.

He gave her a final scowl as he got up, but she felt something warm and glowing in her chest as she looked over her shoulder and saw Caleb in stilted conversation with Jonathan. It wasn't happy families. Not yet, but it was a start. And at dinner, she had to hide a smile as she watched him get drawn into conversations with his brother, his sister, with Rowan and Adam too. Could see the surprise and pleasure in their faces. When she finished her glass of wine and decided she couldn't possibly manage another slice of pizza, she could see the fatigue and strain on Caleb's face.

'I'm ready to turn in,' she said softly, leaning into him.

He let out a long breath. 'Yeah, me too,' he said, his body relaxing in front of her eyes. He slipped his hand into hers as they wished everyone goodnight, and she squeezed it tightly as they walked across the terrace, reminding herself all the time that this was just for show.

How long did she have to decide what she wanted? she wondered, as they headed to the door of their room. Did it even matter? She had shot Caleb down earlier when he'd tried to talk about his feelings. Maybe she was out of chances to work out what she wanted this friendship to be. She caught her breath as she looked up and met Caleb's eye. He was looking at her as if he wanted to devour her—could she cash in her credits in order to make that happen? How many sips of water had been in that glass? How many favours could she claim?

Caleb reached for her other hand and pulled her close.

'Thank you,' he said, stepping in closer so that the front of her body was brushing up against him. It was just a hug, she told herself. Friends hugged all the time. This didn't mean anything more than his hand on hers had done.

'I thought you'd be angry with me for meddling,' she admitted, tipping her face up more to him.

'Oh, I'm angry. That was a mean trick. I intend to get my revenge.'

He caught her chin with his thumb and finger, holding it still so that she couldn't look away from the intensity of how he was looking at her.

'What sort of revenge did you have in mind?' she asked, barely risking a breath. Because this was more than friendly, and there was no one else here, so it couldn't be for show. No, the way that Caleb was looking at her right now was for no one else but her.

'I could be creative. Really make you suffer.'

A quirk at the corner of his mouth gave away that he wasn't entirely serious, but if playing along meant that he would keep looking at her like that, would keep his hand on her cheek in the way that was making her skin sing, she would go along with it.

'What if I said that I was very, very sorry?' she asked, catching one side of her lower lip between her teeth. Caleb pulled on her lip with the gentlest of pressure, and then leaned in to press his mouth to where she had bitten.

When he leaned back, she felt her head swim, held tighter with the hand still trapped in Caleb's, and leaned more into his chest to steady herself.

'That would be a start,' Caleb said, turning her head so that he could kiss the other side of her face. He had kissed her. Caleb had kissed her. And there wasn't any way that they could pretend that this was about anything other than the fact that they liked each other. They had liked each other for such a long time, and now they were here, both of them, together, and his skin on hers made her body sing, and she didn't know if she was too scared to want this or to lose it.

Caleb pulled her gently backwards by the hand, right across the room until the bed was at the back of his knees, and he sat back, leaving her standing in front of him, tucked between his thighs.

'Not going to fall asleep on me tonight?' Caleb asked, but she knew that he was asking more than that.

'Not feeling very sleepy all of a sudden,' she admitted, and she was rewarded with a huge, unguarded grin as Caleb's arms came around her and pulled her even closer. It was nice having him look up at her for a change. Especially when he was looking at her like *this*, as if he adored her.

She should want to run from that. Should be worrying about what it meant that he had those sorts of feelings for her. But really, all she wanted was to bask in it. It had been so long since she had been the centre of someone's world for a *good* reason. Since someone was treasuring their time with her for the pure joy of her being there, rather than stacking up memories in case she didn't make it through the next week, or month, or year.

She leaned down to kiss him, keeping it light. Not wanting to rush. This wasn't anything they hadn't done before. This couldn't scare her. She was quite happy just looking down at Caleb in the lamp light casting a soft glow in the room. To learn the pattern of the freckles appearing on his cheekbones. The soft curl at his hairline where strands had escaped the elastic that kept his hair off his face. To touch his lower lip with her thumb, learning the creases, and the dip in the centre that made it look so soft and plump. She kissed him there, and then the corner of his mouth. The curve in his top lip. The place where soft skin met the scrape of stubble on his cheek.

His eyes had closed, his head tipped back, letting her take the lead. Making no demands, refusing to rush her.

She traced the long line of his jaw. Scraped gently over his Adam's apple with her fingernail. Down into the open V of his shirt until she reached the first button and flicked it open.

He took over from there, swiftly undoing buttons until his shirt lay open, and she was able to follow his fingers with her mouth, until standing was impossible even if her legs had been able to hold her up, and it made much more sense to kneel between his thighs. His eyes didn't leave hers for a second. Not as she pushed the shirt off his shoulders or reached for his belt buckle. His hands threaded through her hair as he pulled her up to meet his mouth in a hard, demanding kiss. His other arm clamped around her waist, holding her firmly against his bare chest. And then he was lifting her up, and over and around until somehow they were both flat on the bed, his arm still making clear that he wasn't letting her go, his mouth making clear she could take absolutely anything she wanted from him.

If this was his idea of a punishment, she didn't have much incentive to behave herself.

'Are you sure?' he asked, minutes, hours, days later, as she pulled him into the cradle of her thighs. 'You want this?'

The words slipped out, too honest, too revealing, but she nodded as she moaned, as she pulled him into her body. 'I want you,' she said, her words ending on a gasp as he filled her, as he rested his forehead against hers, his eyes closing as if it was all too much. She kissed his eyelids, first one side, then the other.

'Caleb, sweetheart…' The word just slipped out, she couldn't help it.

He groaned, opened his eyes, finally looked at her.

'This is…' he said, his eyes rolling, his words trailing off as he started to move inside her. 'I didn't think that it would… I couldn't imagine…' His head dropped to hers again. She ran her hands gently up his back, from the dimples at the bottom of his spine until her hand was cupped around the nape of his neck. She wanted to tell him that it was okay. That she hadn't imagined it would be like this either. But when she opened her mouth to tell him all that, all that came out was a little cry, and his mouth found hers, swallowing the sounds.

And she knew that he understood. Knew from the urgency she saw when she met his gaze. From the staccato rhythm of his body against hers. From the way that he threaded his fingers through hers and gripped her hand hard that they wouldn't be able to forget this. That whatever lies they had told themselves and each other in the safe light of day—this couldn't be undone. They couldn't pretend that this hadn't happened and go back to how they had been before.

She buried her face in his throat, tasting the salt of his sweat, drinking in the smell of woodsmoke from the tips of his hair. 'It's okay,' she whispered, not sure whether the words were meant for him or for herself. 'I've got you,' she said, when he shook in her arms. And then there were no more words. She didn't need them. Not when she could open her eyes and see everything that he felt for her in his features, when she could show him everything that she felt for him with her hands and her mouth and her body.

And after, when his heavy weight still pinned her to the mattress, and she stroked her hands through his hair, she knew that this had changed everything. And when they woke up in the morning, they were going to have to choose what this was. Who they were to each other. They couldn't carry on pretending any more that this week was something that they could play at and then go back to normal.

* * *

Ally woke up slowly, light filtering past the blinds, memories filtering through her sleepy fog. And when she remembered what they had done, she squeezed her eyes shut. Perhaps if she just refused to remember what it had been like to make love to Caleb, she could pretend that it hadn't happened. That they hadn't irrevocably changed the nature of their friendship, the only one she had that meant anything to her.

But she'd obviously been thinking loud enough to wake Caleb, and she felt him moving behind her. She pulled the sheets up to under her chin and turned over.

'Morning,' she said, forcing a smile that she was sure looked more like a grimace. He looked at her warily. Was this broken already? Was he going to make her talk about what they both felt last night and admit that she—?

'Shall we go sightseeing today?' he asked, and she could have kissed him for the reprieve if that wouldn't have been the worst idea she could possibly have come up with. Maybe they could just pretend that everything was normal. She'd been sure, with a sense of doomed certainty, when she'd gone to sleep last night that they'd ruined their friendship with no way back. But perhaps she'd been overreacting. It was probably the wine and the hormones and, well, the sex, that had made her feel that way. Perhaps, with sunshine to wash all that away, it would turn out that it had been very nice, but perfectly ordinary sex, and they could carry on just as before.

'I'd like that,' she said, playing along with the whole *normality* thing. 'Where were you thinking?'

'The nearest town's about twenty kilometres away. It's quite small but there are some Roman ruins. About a dozen churches. A few nice restaurants. It's not Rome or Venice, but…'

'No, that sounds lovely,' Ally said, venturing a real smile. Letting out her first proper breath since she had woken up and letting some of the tension go from her body.

Maybe she *had* just imagined it. Invented a whole drama when there was no need. It had probably just been a relief for both of them after a long dry spell and she'd misinterpreted it as some life-changing experience. Caleb was obviously not giving it a second thought. Thank God.

She was about to get up and get dressed when she remembered that she was wearing absolutely nothing under this sheet and, fake girlfriend or not, a girl sometimes needed a little privacy. She sat, clutching the sheet to her, and gave Caleb a meaningful look. 'If you don't mind?' she said pointedly, and he turned away as she slipped from the bed and pulled a robe from the wardrobe.

'I'm decent,' she told him, tying the belt at her waist and making sure it wasn't gaping too inappropriately at her cleavage. 'I'm going to jump in the shower,' she told him. Doing her best not to look him in the eye.

'I'll, um, start breakfast,' Caleb offered, and she darted into the bathroom before either of them could say anything that wasn't utterly mundane.

* * *

Caleb drove them into the centre of the town, through several terrifying junctions that explained why she hadn't seen a single undented car since she had left the airport. She felt as if she hadn't breathed out since they'd entered the city limits until Caleb pulled into a parking space and shut off the engine.

'Promise me I never have to drive here,' she begged, turning to Caleb with wide eyes. He laughed, and she watched him carefully to see if his good humour reached his eyes. He'd been concentrating on the road all the way here, she told herself, and she was glad of it. There was no way that she'd have wanted to do that drive with him distracted. But even now that they were stationary, when she looked over at him there was something…guarded in his expression.

Well, she wasn't going to ask him about it. It was good that he was on his guard. She was too. They both needed to be after what had happened the night before. Guarded was safe. Guarded meant not doing something stupid just because they'd got carried away.

'I promise you never have to drive here,' Caleb said, opening his door as far as it would go in the tiny space and contorting himself out of the car. Ally did the same on her side and grabbed her bag from the boot, pulling on a wide-brimmed straw hat for good measure.

Right, because it wasn't as if she would be coming back.

'What do you want to see first?' Caleb asked as they followed the signs to the centre of the town.

'Roman ruins?' Ally suggested. 'If they're out-

doors we should make the most of the cool morning.'
Because they'd neither of them wanted to linger in
the vicinity of a bed, so they had been up and out of
the house before any of the others had even stirred.

'Ruins, coffee, churches, lunch?' Caleb suggested,
and Ally nodded.

'Perfetto.'

They strolled through the town until they reached
the ruins, which had been excavated in one corner of
the main piazza. She spent a while reading the information boards, aware of Caleb doing the same in her pe-
ripheral vision. Was she never going to be able to look
at him directly again? she wondered. They'd pretended
that nothing had happened when they'd first woken
up, but the longer the morning went on, the more she
realised that they were both pretending. She couldn't
put her finger on what was giving them away, only
that the ease of conversation that they usually had was
gone, replaced by something more stilted and awkward.
Whereas before they'd been easy looking at each other,
now it was all sideways glances and quickly looking
away when one or the other of them got caught at it.

It would be fine, again, after this week, she promised herself. This wouldn't last for ever. Once they
were back home, she wouldn't have to see him, smell
him, remember how his skin felt against hers. How he
had trembled in her arms last night. How she'd come
apart in his. If they could just avoid looking at each
other for the next few days, perhaps they could still
rescue this. Because however awkward this morning
after might be, it wasn't worth losing their friendship

over. It was clearer than ever that that wasn't something that she was going to be able to let go—she couldn't imagine her life without him in it, at least in some way.

She glanced across, relieved to find that he wasn't doing the same this time.

'Shall we go and explore?' she asked, and for a moment she thought Caleb was going to reach for her hand as he agreed. But he snatched it back at the last moment, and she took herself out of reach just to be sure. She jumped down into the amphitheatre, walking the sweeping arcs of the seating, trying to absorb the knowledge that they had been built nearly two thousand years ago, and were still in use today. She couldn't make her brain compute those sorts of time spans, and when it grew tired of trying she sat down, pressed her palms into the stone and tried absorbing some of their magic.

'It's hard to get your head around,' Caleb said, coming and sitting beside her, his posture a mirror of his own. His fingers close enough that she could brush her little finger against his without even having to think about it. But she resisted, because she was honestly scared of what would happen if she didn't. If she let herself have that, that tiny brush of skin on skin, where would she draw the next line, and how long would it take her to slink across it?

Caleb looked down at their hands, too, and pulled his away.

CHAPTER SIX

SHE WAS ACTING as if everything was fine—but Caleb knew that nothing could be further from the truth. Last night had changed everything, Ally had seen how he really felt and that had terrified her. He'd seen it in her eyes yesterday afternoon, and again this morning when she'd woken up and panicked. And the only way forward that he could see that would stop her from running was to pretend that everything was fine. That something in him hadn't changed for ever last night.

He'd had plenty of sex before, and it hadn't been anything like that. It hadn't stripped him down and left him utterly vulnerable, utterly revealed. And Ally had seen it. He knew that she had, because why else would she panic? He had shown her everything, and she wanted to run away from him. He knew her too well to think otherwise. He'd known this happened when other people had got too close to her.

So he was going to lie and pretend that it hadn't meant anything. Because anything else was unfair on Ally. It was burdening her with his feelings—ones that she had made absolutely clear that she didn't want to be responsible for. And he absolutely, definitely wasn't going to talk about what they'd done.

'They still put on performances here,' he said, remembering something that he'd read on the information board.

'Maybe next time—' Ally started, before stopping herself. Because, no… Of course there wasn't going to be a next time. 'You're selling the villa, so I guess you won't be coming back here either.'

Or perhaps her every waking thought wasn't about him, after all, Caleb told himself wryly. 'Yeah. I guess not. I wish I'd thought about it in advance. I could have booked something.'

The silence stretched awkwardly between them, and Caleb wondered whether a friendship like theirs had ever recovered from ill-advised sex before, or whether this was it for them now.

'Come on, you promised me coffee,' Ally said, standing abruptly and heading for the café across the piazza. She snagged one of the tables right on the edge of the piazza and had ordered coffees in beginner's Italian from the waiter by the time that he reached her.

'Quick work,' he said with a smile, and a head tilt towards the waiter. 'I didn't know that you spoke Italian.'

'I've been listening to podcasts,' she said with a shrug. 'I've barely had a chance to practise.'

'I'm sorry,' Caleb said, feeling suddenly guilty.

'I've not been a good host, have I? We've barely left the villa.'

But she smiled at him indulgently, and he tried to remind himself that he didn't get to keep that expression. That nothing this week was real. Because if he had been a different person, with a different history, he would have loved her looking at him like that. But he couldn't quite shake the knowledge that with a look like that came the potential for him to totally mess it up. For loving him to become a burden that she wasn't prepared to bear. She deserved better than that. Had survived to live whatever life she chose, not being stuck with him because he'd let his feelings for her run out of control.

'When the villa comes with a pool and an olive grove and a speedboat, I don't think there's really anything to apologise for,' Ally pointed out with another smile. 'Anyway, I didn't come here for any of that. Or to speak Italian to waiters, for that matter. I came here to spend time with you.'

And it hit him right in the chest when she said something like that. So easily expressed, that she wanted to spend time with him. But that wouldn't last—and when that pleasure in being together turned into a feeling of obligation, he didn't want to have to see it.

'I think you're here because you wanted to get out of that singles cruise,' he reminded her with a wry smile, deflecting.

She nodded, but her expression had fallen. 'And to get out of the singles cruise. Speaking of...' She pulled her phone out of her bag. 'We're meant to be sending photos to my parents, remember? So far the only ones we have either look like you're trying to drown me or aren't exactly suitable to share with family members.'

Caleb forced himself to smile as they snapped a couple of selfies, but the results looked as strained as he had felt taking them. How could they be *this* awkward after how close they had been the night before?

Well, that was a question with a simple answer. Because neither of them could afford to show what they were really feeling today. If he let Ally see how much last night had meant to him, she would be out of here faster than he could call her back. If there was even the slightest chance that she was feeling the same way about him then he knew that his instincts would be telling him to do the same. So here they were. Pretending that it hadn't mattered. That it was just something that they'd done to blow off steam, for fun. Rather than it being something that he suspected had changed the path of their friendship for ever.

But if they could just survive this week. Put some space and a screen between them so that there would be no temptation to do anything like it again, maybe they could get back to where they had been before she had arrived here.

Was that what he wanted?

'What are you thinking about?' Ally asked, after she had taken a sip of her coffee and let out a sigh that was a little too reminiscent of the night before to be decent in public.

'Nothing,' he lied. And then wished he'd come up with anything—*anything*—to say, because then perhaps there'd be even the tiniest chance that she wouldn't just assume that he was thinking about the night before.

She smiled at him, but she wasn't fooling him.

'Let's have dinner here tonight,' he said out of no-where, and he wasn't sure if it was an olive branch, an apology, or a hope for the future. But once he'd said the words he couldn't take them back. He just knew that he had to do something different. It seemed im-possible that the night before would change nothing. *Could* change anything.

'Here?' Ally said, over the rim of her coffee cup.

He tried to keep his expression neutral, shrugging slightly. 'Doesn't have to be *here* here. Just, let's eat in the town tonight, rather than with my family.'

Ally looked at him, and he knew she was trying to calculate the implications of what he was suggesting. He held up his hands in a show of innocence. 'We don't have to, but—'

'No, I'd like that,' she said quickly, as if she was afraid that she was going to change her mind.

'Are we going to talk about last night?' he asked suddenly. Once the words were out of his mouth, he would have done anything to pull them back, but short of inventing time travel there was nothing to be done now but ride it out. To watch her facial expressions and try and work out what she was feeling.

'Do *you* want to talk about it?' Ally asked, her expression so guarded that he couldn't tell whether that was an invitation or a 'back the hell off'.

'I don't know. It just feels strange that we're not,' he admitted. 'We're both carrying on as if nothing happened. As if nothing has changed.'

She leaned forward and rested her elbows on the edge of the table, cupping her chin in her hand. 'Has something changed?'

'You don't think it has?' he asked.

She shook her head. 'I didn't say that. I just want to know what you were going to say…'

'…before you tell me what you're thinking. That hardly seems fair.' She'd sat back now, arms crossed over her chest. Putting space between them.

'Well, short of us both speaking at exactly the same time, one of us has to go first,' she pointed out.

Caleb took a breath. She was right. One of them had to do this, and unless he wanted to continue to spend this week trying to guess what she was feeling rather than talk about it, he had to show that he was willing to do this, too, and talk. 'Okay, fine,' he said. 'I'll go first. Last night was…nice.'

Ally choked on her coffee, which was fair, he supposed, given the weakness of his words. Saying 'nice' was worse than saying nothing at all. He tried again. 'It wasn't what I was expecting it to be. It was… more.'

She seemed to have recovered her composure enough to swallow her coffee, and he supposed that was something to be grateful for. Even if this conversation wasn't exactly going to plan.

'More…in what way?' she asked. He hadn't counted on this conversation being entirely one way. Was terrified that any minute she was going to decide that he'd said too much and decide to leave. But surely she wouldn't be asking if she didn't want to know how he felt?

'I don't know. I thought it would be…nice, like I said. That it would be something that we'd just done because we were here and we like one another and I think you're beautiful. I didn't expect to get so… emotional about it.'

'Nor did I,' Ally admitted.

Caleb looked up and met her eye in surprise, because the last thing that he'd been expecting from her was that sort of honesty. Why wasn't she packing her bags and putting space between them? He knew that the last thing that she'd wanted out of this week was the sort of romantic entanglement that she'd been specifically avoiding for years. What did it mean that she was willing to talk about this now?

'It was like everything about us,' Ally continued. 'It felt like you understood me in a way that no one has before. And adding sex into the mix…it was a lot. Overwhelming.'

She leaned in towards him again, and that little bit of proximity made it easier for him to breathe somehow. 'And maybe that's why you pretended it didn't happen?' he asked.

'I didn't do that!' Ally protested.

Caleb raised his eyebrows in challenge, and she softened a little, as if thinking over what she'd just said.

'Okay! Yes, I tried to be normal,' she admitted. 'I didn't want it to spoil things.'

'It will only spoil things if we let it,' he said gently, hoping that if they both believed that they could make it true. 'We can talk about it if that feels right. If we want to.'

'What is there to say about it?' Ally asked with a slight note of desperation in her voice.

'Well, did you like it?' Caleb asked.

Ally laughed, and he felt it in his chest. 'What sort of question is that?' she asked. 'I mean, if you don't know the answer to that then there's no help for us. Of course I liked it. What I didn't like was waking up this morning knowing that things had changed between us. I don't like having to try and guess what you're thinking—I'm not used to that. I've never had to think about what I was saying to you before. I always just said exactly what I was thinking. I don't like things not feeling natural between us. I don't like worrying what this means for us.'

He reached for her hand, which might have been crossing a line, but it was a chance he was willing to take if it helped with the doubt that he could see written on her face. He'd say anything to smooth the lines on her forehead that showed how unhappy she was. 'You know that you're important to me. Last night hasn't changed that, even if it doesn't happen again.'

She pulled her hand back and he instantly regretted his words.

'You don't want it to happen again?' she said in carefully measured tones.

Caleb closed his eyes, rested his head in his hands. 'I know you, Ally. Don't forget that. I know what happens when someone tries to get close. You don't like having relationships and I'm not here to try and talk you into one, not if it means losing you.'

'Okay.' She nodded. 'You're right. It was…it was lovely. But I don't want a relationship, and letting it happen again would just complicate things even more.'

Caleb shook his head, because this conversation wasn't going the way that he wanted, but anything he said to try and fix it seemed to make it worse. They were friends who had discovered that something really good happened when they slept together. And he didn't want that to mean that anything changed between them. Perhaps if she hadn't made it clear that at the first sign of anything resembling feelings she was going to freak out and leave, then he might have had something different to say this morning. But she had got up and pretended that it had never happened and so he'd moderated his feelings, kept things safe, and somehow still hurt her.

CHAPTER SEVEN

GOD, THIS WAS exactly why she didn't do this, Ally thought as they finished their coffees in silence. Because she had a pretty good idea of what Caleb was feeling this morning. Probably something pretty similar to what she herself was feeling. And that could only be bad news. Because what she was feeling was that last night had been like nothing she'd ever experienced before. Something that had filled her with joy and hope and expectation. And every single one of those feelings made her want to run.

Caleb had looked at her last night as if no one else in the universe had existed. And she hadn't even hated it—had been too far out of it at the time for it to trigger her flight response. There wasn't a fight option, or even freeze, for her. It had always been flight—she'd spent her adult life running from making these sorts of connections. But she couldn't run away from Caleb. If she was going to, she would have done it yesterday after the argument on the boat, when he'd offered to book her a flight. But she'd stayed because she knew that it was what he needed, what he deserved. And then his sister had told her that he would try and push her away, tried to push everyone away, and that it was hurting him.

So she'd put his feelings first, doubled down on her decision to stay, and it had only made everything worse.

'What was next on our plan?' she asked, their coffee long finished, ten minutes of avoiding eye contact not magically fixing the cracks in their friendship.

'Churches,' Caleb said, glancing at her, letting his gaze slide away as soon as she looked back.

'Plural?'

He nodded. 'Yeah. There's a dozen, I think. There's a trail and everything.'

She raised her eyebrows at him. 'You like churches?'

'I don't know. I like these ones, and you'll get to see the most beautiful parts of the town.'

'Show me,' she said, risking a small smile at him as she stood up and swung her bag over her shoulder.

They walked across the square to what Caleb had told her was the first church on the trail, an imposing baroque building with a large circular window high above the door. She stood at the base of the walls and looked directly up, shading her eyes from the sun and its blinding reflection on the near-white stone. She wasn't sure how long she would have stayed there, marvelling over the intricate carvings, the details around the windows, the towering height of the columns, if Caleb hadn't interrupted her.

'Come on,' he said, taking hold of her hand and leading the way up the wide shallow steps to an enormous doorway. Ally wandered into the church, pulling a cardigan over her shoulders and rubbing her arms at the abrupt change in temperature. And then her eyes caught on the beautifully decorated columns flanking the aisle, and her gaze was guided upwards, to a window bright with light above an altar blazing with candles. She stopped, overwhelmed by the sight, the scale. Candles hanging in chandeliers between each column and flowers festooning the ends of the pews nearest the altar.

She turned to look behind her, at the enormous rose window above the door where they had walked in, and caught her breath, the sight of it stopping her in her tracks.

Light flooded through its concentric circles, creating a starburst effect that fixed her feet to the floor and had her feeling her heart beating hard in her chest. She could feel Caleb behind her and swayed into him. His arm came around her waist and she didn't push him away. Didn't say a word. Instead she soaked in his presence in the same way that she did the light from this window. Overwhelmed by something so much larger than herself that she could barely understand it.

Caleb let his chin come down to rest on her head, and she point-blank refused to read anything into it when his other arm came round her waist as well. This was just something nice. Something that she could enjoy for its niceness, and she wasn't going to ruin it by doing something as stupid as *thinking* about it. When they eventually pulled themselves away from the window, they made their way around the church, looking at the paintings of the stations of the cross, lighting candles at the altars and in the chapels. Stopping in front of the altar to look back again up at the window. As entranced by its light as they had been the first time that they'd seen it.

Stepping back into the sunshine outside felt like re-entering the world after falling through a fissure into an alternate universe. The sun was hotter than it had been when they'd gone inside, and Ally pulled off her cardigan, and dropped her sunglasses over her eyes. 'Good luck following that,' she said with a smile at Caleb, who was just behind her, doing something with his phone.

He pulled her back to him with a hand on her hip and held out his phone in front of them both, taking a selfie with the church in the background.

Ally was looking up at him, her expression soft and affectionate, still slightly dazed from the other-worldliness of their walk around the church.

'If we send that to my mother she'll be expecting me to come home engaged,' Ally said softly, unguardedly, unable to look away from the picture. Caleb had captured something between them that she couldn't quite put her finger on, but that made her nervous and excited in equal measure.

Caleb shrugged and posted it to the group chat that she'd set up with her mother for this purpose and kissed her softly on the cheek. 'We'll worry about that when we get home,' he said easily, and his mention of home made her think of something quite different from the life she had left, where home was her alone in a flat, with Caleb on the other end of her messaging app.

Something about being in the quiet and stillness of the church had made them soft with each other. Smoothed over the fractiousness that had threatened to derail their coffee, and when, as they followed the map to the next church on the trail, their hands brushed together, they reached for each other, rather than flinching away. After everything that they had said to each other since they had arrived in Italy, especially everything they had said to one another that morning, neither of them should have reached for the other. Threaded their fingers through the other's, clasped onto their hands as an anchor in all the uncertainties swirling about them.

Remarkably, the next church was more beautiful than the first, and the one after that more beautiful still. By the time that they were ready to stop for lunch, they'd seen every historical church within walking distance. Lit dozens of candles and managed a few more selfies to send back to her parents—hopefully enough to convince them that Caleb had taken her very much off the market, if not quite up the aisle yet.

And Caleb's arm around her shoulder had come to feel as comfortable a presence as he had been in her life for this last year. Doing that should have made things more complicated, but that didn't matter because she couldn't help herself. Was equally sure that if Caleb had been physically capable of stopping himself he would have done so.

All there was left to do was trust that they would find their way through this. That the foundations that they had built over the last year—the urgent texts and the pointless ones, the long, middle-of-the-night conversations and their quick over-a-coffee catch-ups—would help them find their way. It wasn't as if there was anyone other than Caleb that she could talk to about something like this. He had been her best friend for months. Understood her better than anyone. She'd explained what she'd been through with her family, what she was still going through with them. He knew about her dates and that she'd pushed away perfectly lovely men, and was still here, taking a risk on her, knowing that it would be hard. That there was a risk that she would hurt him too.

She squeezed closer into his side, not really thinking about it, just grateful to still have her friend, despite their mutual efforts to complicate things. He glanced across at her, and for the first time since last night, she didn't look away. Just imagined what things would be like for them if they could be so uncomplicated. That she could look at him just because she liked him. And he could look back at her, as he was now, as if she was everything to him.

That was normally her trigger to grab her bag and run. Instead, she took a deep breath, tried to make the decision to stay. Not to start screening his calls or blocking his number. She wasn't proud of how she usually acted when her commitment issues came a-calling—she just did what she had to do to protect herself. But she wouldn't do that to Caleb, he deserved so much better than that. So that meant hanging onto his hand as if it were a lifeline, even though he was the one who scared her, and trying to find a way to overcome her fears.

Caleb looked away then, and she had to wonder if he knew how challenging she had found that moment, but he didn't let go of her, not until they were at the restaurant, being shown to a table by the terrace, just shady enough to be comfortable in the lunchtime heat.

'So, Liv mentioned something yesterday,' Ally said, figuring that talking about *someone's* emotions was a good a start as any, even if it wasn't her own. 'She said that you'd try and push me away if I got too close and that I shouldn't let you. Just, you know, in case you were wondering about how much they all want you around.' Caleb opened his mouth to speak, but she cut him off quickly. 'She didn't mean it as a criticism,' she said, heading him off. 'She was just worried.'

'Oh, my God, why do sisters have to be so *annoying*?' Caleb said, resting his arm around her shoulder and pulling a menu towards him. Ally tipped her head up so that she could look him in the eye.

'Hey, no, I didn't tell you to make you mad. Please don't tell her I said anything. I just want you to know how much they care. That if you choose to let them in, they'll all be there for you. And not because it's an obligation or because your parents left or because they feel that they have to. But because they *love* you, and they want to see more of you. If you, you know, needed someone to talk to, I'm sure Liv would be, you know, up for that.'

'You say that like it's easy,' Caleb said with a resigned sigh, his hands tracing circles on her upper arm. 'Like I can undo the way that I've felt my whole adult life. All the damage that's already been done.'

She shook her head. 'I'm not suggesting you time travel. Or that you're not entitled to feel the way that you feel. You can't change the past. But you have a choice to make about what you want your future to look like, and if that future featured seeing a lot more of your family I think they'd be really happy about that.'

He sat with her words for a few minutes, and she wished she could guess what he was thinking. Until he spoke, and she wished that they'd stayed sitting in silence instead.

'You know the same applies to you, don't you?' he said, dropping his eyes and finally meeting her gaze head-on. His hands drifting further round her back until she was fully in the circle of his arm. 'I know that you've avoided letting people close since you were sick. That you're scared that you might hurt them by getting sick again. Or, I don't know, that you would get hurt if you had to go through what your parents did. Your folks have put a lot of pressure on you to want the same things that they want for you. But if you wanted to talk to them about it, and you wanted someone there to support you… Then we could do that.' He took a deep breath, obviously choosing his words with care. 'If you wanted things to be different in the future, with the people who care about you, they could be.'

She narrowed her eyes at him, trying to work out if he meant what she thought that he might.

'With people who care about me,' she repeated carefully. 'Are we still talking about my family here, or are we talking about us?'

His hand stilled abruptly enough that she was worried that she had got completely the wrong idea, and he had only been talking about her relationship with her parents.

'I'm talking about your family,' he said slowly. 'But I'm talking about us as well, that's if… You said yourself that this is normally when you get freaked out and leave. I really don't want that to happen. So if you want things to be different, with me, then I want to try that too.'

'Different like being together? Properly?' she asked before she could think better of the question, preoccupied with wondering how this had turned around so that they were talking about her. She wasn't sure how that had happened, or how Caleb had got such a good insight into her worst fears that sometimes it felt as if he were reading her mind. Voicing her most insidious fears. That was the only reason that she could ask him that—even hint at the possibility of them having a relationship in future. Because the way they were going, he'd be able to guess without her saying a word anyway.

Caleb gulped—with nerves, she guessed, at the

bluntness of her question, the implications of which were only just beginning to sink in. She fought the urge to take the question back, too curious to know what his answer would be. To explain that she wasn't suggesting that they changed things right now, only that she wanted to know how he felt about it. And part of her wanted to see his reaction. Whether he was taking a chance on this, or whether he was going to follow his instincts and run.

'Yeah, like being together. With me. Is that…are you going to panic if we talk about this?'

She nodded, and then shook her head, and then nodded again, which was as good a representation of her feelings as anything she could manage with words right now.

She reached for his hand, and the moment her fingers were laced with his, she found the courage to be honest. 'I'm trying really, really hard not to run. But what if I do? What if, even if after this week and us both trying to mend things with our families, and you meeting my parents…? What if, even after all that, I still want to bail at the first thought of…falling for you?'

Caleb took a deep breath, because the scenario she'd just outlined was a real possibility. He had to face that. After everything that they had talked about. Everything they had shared. Everything that they had *done* together, if Ally didn't want this, if the emotional baggage that she brought to the friendship was too much to overcome—or even if she decided she didn't *want* to overcome it—he would still be her friend. He would still want her in his life. He couldn't imagine what his days would look like if she had no place in them.

'You don't owe me the things that will make me happy any more than you owe your parents the things they want for you,' he told her. 'You get to decide for yourself what your future looks like, and I'll support you either way. Even if things get hard, I'll still be here for you. Having you in my life means more to me than anything else.'

'But that's terrifying,' she admitted, gripping his hand to try and stop her own shaking. 'That I mean so much to you that you can promise me that. What if I get sick again? What if I die and you get hurt?' she asked.

He thought about it, properly, because he owed her that. 'The thing is,' he said carefully, not wanting to spook her, 'if that *did* happen, I would be devastated anyway. Whatever else happens between us. And I'm not saying that to try and hurt you, or pressure you. But you can't hold yourself responsible for how other people might feel if they lose you.'

'And if I lose you?' she asked, her voice slightly desperate. 'I've seen what grief does to a person. I don't want that to happen to me either.'

'You've seen what *love* does to a person,' he suggested gently. 'I can't tell you not to love me. All I know is that for me it's not a choice. I love you, and whether we're together or not isn't going to change that for me.'

She shook her head, clearly despairing. 'So I'm

going to hurt you either way, that's what you're telling me.'

'I'm telling you that I love you, Ally,' he said, reaching out and tipping up her face so that she couldn't avoid looking at him any longer. 'And I'm telling you that what you or I decide happens next between us isn't going to change that. If I thought that cutting me out of your life would make you happy, I'd help you do it. But I don't think that that's how it works.'

'We're both so screwed up,' Ally said, resting her head in her hands. 'We'd never be able to make this work.'

'All I know is that I haven't wanted to try with anyone else,' Caleb admitted, because what more did he have to lose now? 'I want you in my life, and if you thought, even for a minute, that you would be willing to give a relationship a try, I would... I don't know. Fight tigers, or other gladiatorial feats of bravery for that relationship to be with me.'

She shook her head, trying to sort through her thoughts to get them in order so that she could share them with him. 'The thought of you with anyone else...it's unbearable,' she admitted. 'And...' She swallowed, took a deep breath. 'No, it's not fair of me to say something like that. You're my best friend and I'll support you no matter what. If you decide to keep on as you are. If you meet someone else...' She trailed off, not able to finish the thought, never mind the sentence.

'I... I can't do this, Caleb,' Ally admitted, struggling

to control her breathing. 'I don't know what to do with the fact that you want all of these things and I want them too.' She pulled her hand away from him and looked at it as if it belonged to someone else. 'I'm trying so hard not to push you away right now because I know how much that would hurt you, and I'm trying so hard not to kiss you because I have never felt like this about anyone before and don't know if I can promise you the things that you deserve. I never *ever* want to hurt you, Caleb.'

'Then don't hurt me,' Caleb suggested, reaching for her hand again, as if it were just that easy.

'I'm not. I'm not going to hurt you,' she said, deciding on the spot that she wasn't going to just react. She'd spent her whole adult life doing that. Running towards the things that she wanted, and then away again the second that they scared her. For once, she was going to take a minute. Ask for the space and time that she needed to make a real choice.

'I need some time,' she said gently, watching Caleb's face carefully for his reaction. There was no hiding his disappointment, but she couldn't be sorry for it, because rushing her choice was sure to hurt him. She was either going to run because she was scared or rush into something because she was scared of losing him, and neither of those things were giving Caleb what he deserved.

She took a deep breath to calm her nerves. 'Caleb, I'm sorry, I know it's not a yes. But it's not a no either. I want to think about this, properly, before I decide if I can take this risk. Can I sleep on it? Alone?'

She could see from his face that he'd already decided that she was rejecting him, and she ached to tell him that he was wrong, but if she did that, and then decided she couldn't hope for more than friendship with him? That would be worse. She squeezed his hand.

'You're right, we should think about it,' Caleb said at last, after a silence that had stretched too long. 'Our friendship is too valuable for us to rush into something.'

The shadows were stretching out as they made their way home. Their linked hands swung between them, somehow having become the default rather than the exception over the course of the day.

The traffic was quieter leaving the town, and with the less life-threatening experience Ally allowed her eyes to close as she contemplated the changes that had taken place since they had left the villa that morning. They hadn't made any commitments—other than to think, and to try—but somehow that decision, that commitment to herself, felt more meaningful than any she'd tried to make to another person over the years.

CHAPTER EIGHT

CALEB WOKE, ALONE, and groaned aloud. How had his body expected Ally to be there? They had only spent a few nights together, but already his arms felt empty without her.

'Space' had meant Ally sleeping in one of the spare bedrooms, and he couldn't help but think that this was it for them. Even with everything that Ally had said about wanting to take her time to make the right choice, and even with everything he had said agreeing that she was right—he didn't need time. His bed felt wrong without her in it. His body felt wrong when he wasn't touching her.

He would go back to being her friend, if that was what she wanted, because he felt too much for her to lose her from his life for ever. But there was no question about what he wanted—he wanted Ally, any and every way that he could have her. He wanted to love her as a friend and an accomplice, as a lover and as a partner. But he couldn't tell her any of that without spooking her more than she already was.

He was asking more of her than anyone she'd stuck

by in a long time. She had her reasons for not wanting a relationship—and it wasn't his place to decide what was right for her. The only hope that he could cling to was that she was still here. Yes, she'd decided that 'space' meant separate beds. It would hardly have qualified if it hadn't.

But she hadn't ghosted him, hadn't told him that it was never going to happen, as he knew that she had with others when she'd got scared. Instead, she was… talking about what they were to each other. Asking for what she needed. Still trying to take tiny little baby steps towards what this might be if they both decided that they could lay their traumas to rest.

He tried to mentally prepare himself for the conversations that they would have to have if they were going to make this work. The effort that he was going to have to make with his family if he wanted to find out whether Ally was right, and he'd been wrong about his relationship with them all this time.

But what if she was right? What if his family hadn't resented needing to take care of him all this time? What if they really did want to spend time with him? If he had got that wrong…what else was he mistaken about? How much of his identity had he built on that false assumption, and what was going to be left if he decided that he had to unpick it all? Was he the same person if he realised that he'd been wrong about something so fundamental all his life?

He just hoped that he would still have Ally in his life while he tried to figure it out. That realising he could be open to someone having feelings for him didn't scare her off. Whatever realisations he'd come to about himself, he'd have to be careful about how much he showed her. Just because he was rethinking things didn't mean that she was too.

He heard noise coming from the kitchen and figured someone was up making coffee. Was it Ally? He eased himself out of the bed, slightly buzzed from nerves—what would he say to her?

'You're up,' Liv said, sounding surprised as she poured water into the coffee pot, and he deflated. 'Do you want coffee?' she asked. 'I don't think anyone else is up. Does Ally want a cup?'

'I think she's still asleep, but, yeah, I'll have one,' he said.

'Cool, come sit while it's brewing,' she said, and he hesitated for only a moment before dropping into one of the chairs by the table.

'Ally said you talked about me a couple of days ago,' he said, figuring this was one of those conversations that you just had to dive into.

Liv raised an eyebrow at him. 'Yeah, I did. Oh, God, you're not telling me this because you've gone and done something stupid like break up with her, are you?'

He huffed out a laugh. 'Thanks for the vote of confidence. But no, we've not broken up.' That much was true, though he'd be hard pressed to describe what they *were*.

'She said you'd all like it if I hung out with you more,' Caleb said, the words spoken so fast he wasn't even sure that they were intelligible.

But they must have been because Liv punched him in the arm in the way only a sister could get away with. 'Duh. We've been literally saying that to your face for a year. But when your *girlfriend* says it, you listen?'

He was about to retort when a door opened behind them and Jonathan appeared in the doorway to his and Rowan's room. 'Is there any reason you two can't squabble at a more decent hour?' he asked, rubbing at his forehead. 'Or a more reasonable volume?'

Caleb went to stand, but Liv grabbed his forearm, forcing him down into his seat. 'He's teasing,' she told Caleb with intense eye contact. 'He only sounds serious because that stick up his backside doesn't dislodge until after eight o'clock. Jonathan, Caleb is talking about his feelings. Come and sit down.'

Caleb sighed. A year ago, Liv and Jonathan couldn't be within ten feet of each other without a fight breaking out. It was one of the reasons it had been so much easier to spend time alone than with the two of them. But somehow things had got worse as their relationship had healed, and he had been the one left out as they had started to spend more time together. Jonathan did as he was told, ruffling Liv's hair affectionately on the way, and Caleb felt a pang of something like affection and something he realised was a little like jealousy.

How had they managed to sort their lives out? he wanted to know. He knew that his brother couldn't have been unaffected by their parents leaving them. And he'd had so many more responsibilities to shoulder. He should be more affected by it than anyone. And Liv—she had been closer to their parents than her brothers, and yet here she was seemingly settled and happy. She and Adam shouldn't work. From what Caleb had seen of their relationship, they spent more time arguing than not. But he couldn't deny from the way that they looked at each other that they were completely besotted. And he *knew* that Liv had had things tough. That she'd pushed people away after being abandoned. So what was the trick? he wondered. How did you get past that?

All of a sudden he felt that for the last year he'd been a spectator at a dance that he didn't understand, but now he was starting to recognise the patterns. Somehow his siblings—survivors of the same trauma as him—had come out of it unscathed, and he was the only one left floundering. Except, he knew that wasn't true. They had wounds as well, but they'd allowed theirs to heal, whereas he was still here, crouching over his protectively, not letting it see sunlight or fresh air. Not even giving himself a chance to recover.

He supposed that the sensible thing to do would be to ask Liv or Jonathan how they had managed what looked impossible from his perspective. But in order to do that he'd have to have the sort of relationship where he could talk to the people who knew him best about the pain he had lived in for so long without really feeling it—and he had ensured that that relationship could never grow as it should.

'So what's going on?' Jonathan asked, once Liv

had left to retrieve the coffee, and returned with three steaming cups. 'Are we having a family meeting?'

'We're having a family meeting,' Liv agreed, and Caleb only just managed to suppress his groan. 'I'm telling Caleb that, yes, we actually meant it when we've all been trying for the past year to get him to spend more time with us.'

Jonathan nodded approvingly and pulled one of the cups of coffee towards himself. He gave Caleb what he'd once called his Disapproving Parent look. 'Of course we want you to spend more time with us,' he agreed. 'How could you doubt that?'

All of a sudden, with Jonathan looking so sincere, and Liv watching them intently, her chin resting on her hand, Caleb wasn't sure why he doubted what they were saying. Did it really make sense that they would be saying the exact opposite of what they were thinking? If he removed his emotional baggage from the picture and just took them at their word, then... he'd been wrong all this time? But he had to be sure. If they were going to make him talk about his feelings, he could at least make sure that he would leave this conversation without any doubts.

'I believe you want to see me,' Caleb said, taking his first sip of scalding-hot coffee. Tiptoeing through his words with just as much care. 'I know that you all care about me—'

'Good,' Liv interjected, punching his arm, almost making him spill his coffee. Jonathan sighed, and Caleb took a breath, soldiering on.

'But I also know that part of the reason you care

about me is because you think you have to. Mum and Dad left, and you were left in charge, Jonathan, and then our grandparents died, and we were all each other had. And I know you both think that you have to keep an eye on me because I'm the youngest. I just don't want you both feeling responsible for me. I'm an adult. This isn't—I'm not—something that you have to be burdened with indefinitely. Mum and Dad didn't consider taking care of us a life-long commitment, so I don't see why you should have to either.' He finished speaking and kept his eyes on his coffee, not able to risk seeing what his brother and sister thought of what he had said. It had all come out in a rush, gaining momentum so swiftly that he wouldn't have been able to stop if he'd wanted to.

Jonathan slowly, carefully, replaced his coffee cup on the table. 'Is that what you think, Caleb? That we want to spend time with you because we feel *responsible* for you? That you're some sort of obligation that we've been stuck with all this time?'

Caleb risked a glance up. 'Well, isn't it?' he asked, in all honesty not sure of the answer.

'No!' Liv and Jonathan cried in unison. Oh. That was...compelling. Convincing. They weren't faking their shock at his words.

'Of course you're not an *obligation*,' Liv carried on, sounding horrified. 'We want to spend time with you because we *love* you and you're *fun* and you make us *laugh*. We've all been screwed up but somehow me and Jonathan have landed two pretty amazing people who have made us happy and like hanging out with us and we just want to share that with you.'

'And if I don't want to be with someone? What if I'm always just the spare wheel, tagging along with his grown-up, married siblings?'

'That's not what Liv meant,' Jonathan said, taking his life into his hands by speaking for his sister, Caleb thought. 'Listen, Caleb—what Mum and Dad did to us…it messed us all up. How could it not? But that doesn't mean we have to stay that way. For me, it was meeting Rowan that made me see that, but it doesn't mean you have to want or have the same things that we do. We—all of us—want you in our lives. And if you also want to share that life with a partner, that's great, anyone you love is a part of our family whether they like it or not. And if you don't, we'll take you just the way you are.'

Caleb sat in silence while Jonathan's words sank in. 'I don't know what to say,' Caleb admitted eventually. 'You guys felt like this too? But it gets better?'

'It honestly does,' Liv said, topping up all of their cups. 'I know that Jonathan and Ro are gross, but letting go of what Mum and Dad did to us… It's honestly pretty great. And I got a hot beefcake of a boyfriend out of it, so there's that.'

'Hot beefcake fiancé,' Adam corrected her, appearing in the doorway. 'Is this a Kinley-only breakfast or can I have some of that coffee?'

'In a few months half of my coffee will be legally yours anyway,' Liv conceded, taking a last sip before passing him the rest of her cup. 'Adam, come tell Caleb you want to hang out with him.'

'Caleb, I want to hang out with you,' Adam said obediently, pulling out a chair and sitting beside Liv. 'What's going on?' he added, quirking a brow at Caleb. 'Am I marrying Caleb instead now?'

'Is this another one of Liv's interventions?' Rowan asked, appearing behind Jonathan and bending down to wrap her arms around him. 'Has it worked this time?'

'Looks like it might have,' Jonathan said, turning to kiss her. 'He's still here, so it's already going better than the last one.'

'You okay, Cal? They going easy on you?' Rowan asked, flashing him an understanding smile.

'Yeah, I think I am okay,' he admitted, and then scraped the legs of his chair back when he spotted Ally, still in her robe, in the doorway.

'Hey,' Caleb said, looking sleep-ruffled and pink across the bridge of his nose, sitting at the table surrounded by his family. She'd missed him last night. Had used every shred of her self-control to insist to herself that she needed to take the space that she'd asked for to think and decide on her future. But if her taking some space had led him back to her family, she couldn't be sorry for it.

'Morning,' she replied with a hesitant smile. 'Did I sleep in?' she asked, taking in the coffee cups and the whole family gathered around the table.

'Impromptu family meeting,' Liv informed her

and pulled her down to the table with a hand on her arm. 'You got through to him,' she announced gleefully. 'I knew you would.'

Ally smiled back, looking over at Caleb. She wanted to reach for him, but didn't know if she could. Didn't know if she still had touching privileges after asking for space the night before.

'I didn't do anything,' Ally said, looking around her warily, her eyes snagging on Caleb's. 'You guys all love him; he was bound to work it out eventually. He's smarter than you give him credit for.'

Liv grinned, not disagreeing. 'All the same. Thank you. We like you—we're not going to let you go now, you do realise that. We sort of have a once-in-never-out rule these days. You should ask Rowan and Adam.'

'What was that?' Adam asked, breaking away from a conversation with Jonathan and coming to sit on the arm of Liv's chair and giving her something that could have been a kiss on the temple or a headlock, it was hard for a casual observer to tell.

'Nothing,' Liv protested immediately, and loudly. 'We were just telling Ally that we like her very much and we have every intention of keeping her.'

'Liv, drop it,' Caleb said, and Ally could hear the warning in his voice. Because he didn't want his sister pressuring her into a commitment? Or because he'd decided himself that this wasn't going to work and was planning on breaking up with her as soon as he found a convenient moment? Or perhaps it was just because she had asked for space and she was reading something in his words that hadn't been there.

'Well, I've enjoyed meeting you all too,' she said. 'I'd love to see you all again.' That was non-committal enough, she reasoned. She and Caleb would be friends in the future, if nothing more. She couldn't imagine that she would never meet them again.

'Well, you'll be at the wedding, of course,' Liv said, as if that were something that had been arranged long ago.

'Um…wedding?' Ally asked.

'Mine and Adam's,' Liv said slowly, her brows drawn together. 'At the Cotswolds house, in the autumn. Don't tell me Caleb hasn't invited you, because then I would have to hurt him.'

'Liv—' Caleb said, but his sister waved him away.

'We're not making a big song and dance of it. Just close family. But we'd love you there. Wouldn't we, Adam?'

Adam looked surprised to have been consulted, but agreed with his fiancée anyway.

'Thank you, that's a real honour,' she said politely. 'Then of course I'll be there.' She forced a smile, hoping they couldn't see the strain. Even as Caleb's best friend, she'd want to be there for him at the wedding. The only real question was whether he would want her there after they'd talked about what they were going to be to each other.

'Liv, give her a break,' Caleb said with a smile that she noticed didn't quite reach his eyes. He reached for her hand and squeezed tight, and she relaxed slightly under its pressure. Whatever happened, she and Caleb would deal with it together, one way or another—she had to trust in that. She might be terrified of what came next, but at least she had her best friend with her while she did it.

'So, are you two going to be following us up the aisle?' Liv asked, and Ally froze.

'Right, that's it,' Adam said, pulling Liv off her chair and wrapping his arms around her waist, taking her off her feet. Liv squealed, only half in dismay. 'I'm sorry about my fiancée,' Adam said. 'Please ignore her completely, she's a terrible person.'

At this, Liv was so distracted in arguing with Adam that she quite forgot about interrogating Ally. Rowan and Jonathan had drifted off for a walk, talking in low tones as they took the steps from the terrace down to the shore of the lake.

And then the whole kitchen had emptied out, and Ally was left looking at Caleb, who was still sitting at the table, looking slightly shell-shocked. She gave his hand a gentle squeeze, pulling him back into the moment, and he made himself smile at her.

'Ally, I'm sorry. That was—'

'Are you okay?' she asked. 'Things okay with your family?'

'They're fine,' he said, aware that she had just dodged his question. 'Better than fine. I think we might actually be working some stuff out,' he admitted.

'I'm so pleased for you. Honestly, I know how much you mean to them, and they're so great. I mean, your sister just proposed on your behalf and everything.'

Caleb groaned, dropping his face into his hands. 'Ally, I'm so sorry she said that. I'll talk to her, honestly. I know you need space and the last thing you want is that sort of pressure.'

'It's fine,' Ally said. 'She doesn't know how things really are between us.' And, somehow, her words only added to the extreme awkwardness of the moment. 'And nor do we, yet.'

'No. I already told you, you can take as much space and as much time as you need. The only thing I'd ask is…' He hesitated, not knowing if he was doing the right thing. 'If you've decided that this isn't what you want, just tell me. Get it over with. I know that it will hurt, because even though I've tried so hard I don't think I know how to not fall in love with you. And if I'm going to have to try and get over you, I'd rather know now.'

'But you can't really be in love with me—it's only been a couple of days,' she said, surprise forcing the words out of her.

Caleb gave a strangled little laugh, hoping that it would cover how close his heart was to breaking.

'Ally,' he said gently. 'I know what I feel. It was already too late for me by the time your plane landed. It's been going on for months. You know it has. And I'm not saying this to pressure you. I'll still love you as a friend. But you deserve all the facts before you make a decision.'

'I'm still worried that I'll hurt you,' Ally said quietly, leaning in and resting her forehead on his chest, hiding her face from him. 'That you're going to pin all your hopes on me being…everything to you, and one day I won't be here. It nearly broke me, seeing how much pain love can cause. You don't deserve any more pain after everything that you've been through.'

Caleb brushed her hair back from her face, tipped it up so that she was looking him in the eye. 'You know, if it's what's on offer, I'll go back to texting, and looking forward to my phone buzzing and knowing that it's you. And I'll still want to tell you about the good stuff that happens in my day or to call you and moan when it's a bad one. And I never want to do anything that might risk me losing that. But…' He took a breath, and she hoped that it was for courage. Because they were so, so close to them both having what they wanted. All they had to do was each keep being brave, just a little at a time. 'I've seen what we might be if we trusted ourselves to have more,' Caleb went on. 'And now that I know what we could be, I don't want to let go of that. I will, if you need me to, but what I *want* is for you to be the centre of my world.'

He leaned in, risked brushing a kiss against her lips, and let out a groan when she leaned into it.

'You're the reason that knowing my family loves me doesn't make me want to lock myself in a cellar and never come out,' he told her when they broke apart. 'I had fun with them, Ally. Actual fun, and that was all because of you. I'm not asking you to love me back. I'm just asking you not to shut me out just because I love you.'

Ally tucked her head beneath his chin again. 'I'm not going to shut you out. I'm not going to walk away. I can't,' she promised him.

He kissed the top of her head and breathed out a sigh of relief. 'Thank God, Ally.' He squeezed his arms tight around her and kissed her again. 'Because I don't know how I would cope if I had to let you go.'

Their agreement not to lose one another had been so fragile that it still felt too risky to loosen his arms, to move his chin from where it rested on the top of her head, without losing the fragile equilibrium that they had just found.

He'd spent the night away from her, giving her the space she needed. But now he held on tight for fear of losing her for ever. Her arms were tight around him too, as if she knew too how precarious was the situation in which they found themselves.

Ally stirred in his arms, and he looked down at the top of her head, waiting for the moment when she would look up and meet his eyes and they would have to decide what to do next.

He loved her, but that didn't make anything certain between them. If anything, they were on shakier ground than they had been before. Even if she felt the same way, that didn't mean that she would want to commit to him.

But she hadn't run yet.

He breathed in the scent of her hair, committing it to memory. Perhaps this was just the calm before the storm, and any minute she'd be spoiling for a fight, looking for an excuse to leave.

She stood up suddenly, knocking over coffee cups. 'I'm panicking again,' she said, just as he was about to ask her what was going on.

'Okay?' Caleb replied, standing up more slowly. He wasn't quite sure what to say to that. Was he meant to hold her hand while she broke his heart? Well, at this point he probably would. He wasn't sure that he'd had much pride to begin with, and whatever he'd started with he'd sacrificed when he'd told her he loved her knowing that there was no way she would be saying it back to him.

'I'm… I don't know what I am. Help me, Caleb! I should be walking out of here but I don't want to, but I don't know how to stay either. Please. Help me. Help me stay.'

He stared at her a few moments. Because this was it. This was where they made this work or accepted that they never would. This was where he decided how much he was going to put on the line. 'I'm not going to talk you into it,' he told her firmly. Much as he might want to, this would never work if she had to be persuaded. She had to at least want to try this if it were to have any hope of lasting.

'I don't need to be talked into it,' she told him, leaning into him slightly before catching herself and putting space back between them. 'I *want* to be here, Cal. I *want* to stay. But I'm working against the best part of fifteen years of habit, here. *Please.* Don't let me mess this up. Don't let me lose you.'

He took a breath, thought quickly. She was asking him, begging him, to make this work. That wasn't the act of someone who wanted to run away, it was someone who wanted to be here, but had never done this before. Well, it wasn't as if he knew how to do this either. But maybe that was for the best. Maybe a clueless pair muddling through, trying to work it out together, was exactly what this situation needed. There was only one way that they were going to find that out.

He reset the cups on the table and mopped up the coffee. 'Right. We are not going to screw this up. I want this to work. You want this to work, so we will sit at this table with a cup of coffee each and talk about it like adults.' He marvelled that he sounded as if he knew what he was talking about. Because he didn't. He was very much making this up as he went along in the blind hope that somehow they would find the answer. All he wanted to do—all he could do— was keep taking the decisions that kept Ally in his life. He couldn't allow himself to do anything else.

'But what if I—?' He knew what she was about to say, and it drew a smile from him. Because he knew what she was most scared of, and it wasn't him. It wasn't this relationship. It was herself. It was her need to run that scared her, and at least he could reassure her about that.

'I will sit between you and the door and I will tackle you to the ground if it looks like you're going to make a run for it,' he promised her, chancing half a smile when she returned it.

'That sounds like too much fun to be a threat,' Ally said, half under her breath.

'For God's sake go and put some clothes on,' he suggested with a tortured look as her robe gaped open.

Caleb heated a tray of pastries while he waited for a new pot of coffee to brew. There was nothing more that he could do other than trust that Ally was showering and dressing just now rather than escaping out of a window. He stood staring at the stove, still no idea how they were going to rescue this. Whether it was even possible.

'So. Tell me how we do this,' Ally said, when she came back in.

He stared at her for a minute before shaking himself out of the spell that the sight of her always seemed to cause. 'You say that like I've actually done this before,' he pointed out.

'So you're as clueless as me,' Ally replied with a sigh that told him she still wasn't convinced that this wasn't hopeless.

'I think that's been long established.'

'Fine. So we're both clueless. But let's not allow that to stop us just yet.' Ally reached past him to take the pastries from the oven and tipped them into a basket.

'I think we've mastered step one. Not running away,' Caleb said hopefully.

'Don't speak too soon. You might jinx it.'

'You still want to go?' he asked, suddenly dejected, but Ally shook her head.

'No, I don't want to. I'm not saying that the *urge* isn't still there, it's like muscle memory, you know. But I'm not giving in to it. That seems like a first step to me.'

He reached for her hand, pulled her to him and wrapped one arm around her waist as he pulled the percolator off the stove.

He pressed a kiss to her lips. 'It's more than a first step. It's everything, Ally. Because now that you've told me that it's what you want, we're doing this together. And I'm not going to let you fail. What do you think about that?'

'You won't let me leave?' she asked.

'Well, not in a kidnapping sort of way,' Caleb said with a grimace. 'You can go any time that you want— *if* that's what you want. But you already told me that it's not. If you tell me to make you stay I'm going to do anything in my power to try and persuade you.'

'Anything...?' Ally asked with a finger trailing down his chest.

'Don't try distracting me with sex,' Caleb warned, catching her by the wrist. 'Because I promise you it will work, and we'll only find ourselves trying to have this same conversation in an hour or two. Putting it off isn't going to make it any easier.'

'Fine,' Ally said, pulling her hand back. 'If not running is step one, what's step two, if it's not sex?'

Caleb thought about it. About what he wanted after they left here. About what he wanted in their real life, rather than the fake one that they had made here.

'It's making a plan for when we get home,' he said.

'It's agreeing that we aren't going to let things go back to what they were. That I'm going to take you for dinner, Saturday night. Stay over. Eat a lazy brunch with you Sunday morning.'

'And then what? Lunch with my parents?' Ally said with enough doubt in her voice to make it sound like a threat.

Caleb forced a smile. 'Why? Because you think they'll still need convincing you're off the market?'

'No, because… Because if you're really my boyfriend, Caleb, that's what people do, isn't it?'

If he was her boyfriend? So she really was thinking about this. Committing to this. She had thought about what they were going to be to one another when they weren't here any more and the word she had come up with was 'boyfriend'. It was more than he'd ever been able to hope for. He pressed a kiss to her temple.

'Yeah, I think that's what people do. So you mean it. We're really going to do this? You're my girlfriend now. For real.' He knew it sounded juvenile, but he wasn't going to risk not being clear about this.

'If you can stop me bolting,' Ally replied, in a voice that was still too brittle to assuage his doubts.

He took both her hands in his and pulled her to him, pinning their hands between their chests. 'Please, don't talk like that,' he entreated her in a soft voice. 'Don't pretend that you don't have a choice in this. I need you to make the choice, Ally. I need you to choose *me*. Even if you're scared of it. Even if you're worried that you're going to fail. I can't spend the rest of my life—' He stopped for a moment when he realised what he had said, until he was sure that he had meant it. 'I can't spend the rest of my life worrying that I'm not going to be enough to keep you here, with me. I need to know that it's what you're choosing. I know you're half joking. That you're talking like this because it scares you to commit. Because it's easier to think of me not letting you go than you choosing to always be here. To be the centre of my world and not let that be too much for you.'

'I'm choosing you,' Ally said quietly. 'I'm choosing this. Us. I still don't know about being the centre of your world, but I want you at the centre of mine. I want to prove to you every day what a pleasure it is to love you.' She stretched up on her tiptoes and pressed a kiss to his lips. 'Because it is, Cal. It's a pleasure and a privilege to love you, and anyone who feels differently is an idiot. I'm sorry that I find this so hard. I'm sorry that the things that have happened to me have made it so hard for me to show you how much I like you. How much I love you.'

'You don't have to apologise, Ally. Don't be sorry for who you are, or your past. I wouldn't want you any different from who you are. I love you.'

'I love you too,' she said, punctuated with kisses, the coffee forgotten beside them.

'My God, can't I get a cup of coffee around here without seeing something that makes me want to stick needles in my eyes?' Liv announced from somewhere behind them, and Ally broke away with a guilty smile.

'Sorry,' she said, feeling herself blush as she held out the coffee pot to Liv as a peace offering before fixing her gaze firmly back on Caleb as colour flushed his face too.

'Never mind,' Liv said, and Ally could practically hear her rolling her eyes. 'Am I pouring coffee for you two love birds or are you going to let me drink the whole pot?'

Ally could tell from the goofy grin on Caleb's face how disgustingly happy she herself must look. But there was nothing she could do about it. Her face was aching with the force of her own smile, and there was not an inch of her body that did not scream to be pressed against Caleb. From the way that his arm was still clenched tight around her middle she didn't even need to guess that he felt the same. It was perfectly obvious.

Liv shouted to the others that breakfast was finally ready, snatching the basket of pastries and dumping them on the table.

'I guess we're having breakfast with my family, then,' Caleb said, through barely gritted teeth.

'Suck it up, little brother,' Liv said, planting a kiss on his cheek and giving Ally a one-armed hug before half jogging from the room to shout to the rest of the family that she was about to eat all their breakfasts.

Ally slid both her arms around Caleb's waist and tipped her head back to look up at him. 'You almost sound like you're going to enjoy it,' she accused with a smile.

'Well, falling in love with you must have turned

me soft,' he said, leaning down to kiss her, and not bothering to break away when wolf whistles broke out behind them.

Ally finally pulled back, still half embarrassed to be caught snogging by his family, despite the googly eyes that the two other couples had been making at one another all week.

It must be the surfeit of oxytocin and all the other intoxicating love hormones that was making her grin, she told herself. That had her smiling and reaching for Caleb's hand when a week ago every rational instinct would have made her run. But, she realised, as Jonathan liberated the coffee pot from Liv and poured her a cup, and Rowan passed her the last pastry in the basket while Adam stuck another tray in the oven, and Caleb... Caleb wrapped his arm around her shoulder, pulled her into his side and pressed a kiss to the side of her head, leaning his forehead against her temple for a moment, just to soak her in. She realised that there was nowhere else in the world that she wanted to be.

CHAPTER NINE

'Hey, have you seen my T-shirt?' Caleb asked, walking into their bedroom with just a towel wrapped around his waist.

Ally let herself look, unhurried, unapologetic. Even after three days to get used to the idea that Caleb was her boyfriend now—her real boyfriend, with no fakery involved—she couldn't quite believe that she just got to *look* at him whenever she wanted. She could just *show* him whatever she was feeling, and it didn't cause anyone to break down. It was just... fine. Better than fine. It was perfect.

'You know, the blue one with the...the thing on the front?' Caleb went on, and she registered what he was saying just a second too late.

She sidestepped quickly to block his view of her suitcase, open on the bed while they packed, but from the triumphant look on his face she was too late. He walked towards her slowly, clearly trying to hide the smile that was turning up the corners of his mouth.

It was just a little souvenir of their trip, she'd told herself as she'd tossed it on the pile of clothes that she was packing. The past days had felt like a dream, with her and Caleb finally admitting how much they wanted each other and doing everything that she had been fantasising about since she'd met him. Since before that.

But what if it was something about being here that had made everything fall into place? And what if that went missing somewhere between this villa and London. What if they got back, and everything they had worked so hard for just didn't…translate?

At least this way she would have something to remind her of how good it had been, in case her brain tried to trick her into believing it had been something less than, well…perfect.

'Ally,' he said seriously. 'Let me see in your suitcase.'

'Absolutely not,' she replied, trying to reach behind her to flip the lid closed, blocking his view with her body, subtly deepening her cleavage with some clever upper arm action to try and distract him.

He rested his hands on her hips, staring straight down at her breasts. She allowed herself a moment of victory, before he said, 'You wouldn't be trying to distract me because you don't want me to see that you have stolen my T-shirt, would you?'

'Why on earth would I need to steal your T-shirt?' she asked, with such bravado and innocence it made absolutely clear that she was lying.

'I don't know,' Caleb said, pulling her closer so that he could look over her shoulder. 'Perhaps you've got used to having me around, and you're going to miss me once we're not staying in the same place every night at the end of this week.' He pulled back to look her in the eye, obviously satisfied that it was, in fact, his blue T-shirt with the thing on the front that was sticking out of the zip of her case. Dammit. 'Perhaps you're hanging onto my T-shirt so that you can keep it under your pillow and sniff it before you go to sleep,' he suggested with a smug grin.

She snorted and deliberately wrinkled her nose, making his lips quirk again. 'That's gross,' she told him.

'It's exactly the sort of behaviour that someone who loved their boyfriend would indulge in,' he suggested.

She tilted her head. 'Is this your way of telling me that you've stolen something of mine to take home and sni— You know what. Don't answer that. Pretend I didn't say it.'

Caleb couldn't tamp down his smile any longer, and he tightened his arms around her waist for good measure, pulling her up his body until she could kiss him without having to crick her neck.

'You're going to miss me when we get back,' he said against her lips. 'Admit it.'

She sighed. Because how had she ever stood a chance when he could just look at her and read her heart like that? Sometimes a girl needed a little dignity. 'Caleb,' she told him seriously. 'We live in the same city. You text me, like, a hundred times a day. When would I have the time to miss you?'

He bent his head and kissed the side of her neck.

'Just admit it,' he said again. 'All this can stop if you just admit you'll miss me.'

Ally sighed dramatically, letting her head fall to one side so that he could kiss up the side of her throat to her jaw. Not entirely sure why he thought that that was a threat that might work. Why on earth would she ever want this to stop?

'Fine. If you're going to miss me that much, you can take me out tomorrow night,' she said, relenting.

'Tomorrow night? Someone's keen,' Caleb said in a tone of voice that was far too smug for her liking. She planted both her hands on his chest and pushed him away, giving him the sternest look that she could manage while her body was half alight for him.

'Caleb, I have already spilt every bit of emotional drama I have going on into your lap. If the consequence is that I tell you what I really want now, you're just going to have to deal with it.'

'Tomorrow night?' he asked.

She groaned. 'Yes, tomorrow night. If, you know, that's what you want.'

He leaned in and kissed her on the lips. 'Of course I want. Stay over at mine?'

'You can't manage even the first night home without me?' she asked, part terrified, part ridiculously excited at the thought.

'Not if I can help it.'

'Good. Then I suppose you can have this back,' she said, reaching behind her for the T-shirt. 'I'll steal another of yours to sleep in tomorrow.'

'You know what, you should keep it,' Caleb said,

grinning and leaning in for another kiss. 'It looks better on you anyway.'

'You think all your T-shirts look better on me.'

'And we both know that I'm right,' Caleb said, with a smile so genuine that she couldn't help but think that he must be right.

As she leant in for another kiss she thought that maybe going back to London wasn't so bad. After all, this place boasted an infinity pool and a speedboat and a vineyard. But if London had Caleb, and an endless supply of his T-shirts to steal, she supposed she could probably live with that.

Just about for ever.

EPILOGUE

'WHAT DO YOU MEAN, Liv's gone?' Ally heard Caleb ask as she was putting the finishing touches to her hair. She poked her head out of the door of their bathroom. They'd been staying at the Cotswold manor house for a few days before Liv and Adam's wedding, and while it hadn't been the most relaxing few days— idyllic location notwithstanding—it had been so much fun to be back in the heart of the Kinley family.

'Is everything okay?' she asked, noting the concern on Rowan's face.

'I'm sorry to just barge in,' Rowan said, 'but I just went to Liv's room to see what was taking so long— because she said that she would be *right* down—and she wasn't there. The registrar is starting to get antsy.'

'When was the last time that anyone saw her?' Caleb asked the room at large. 'And has anyone spoken to Adam?'

At that moment Jonathan burst into the room and Ally resisted the urge to sigh or laugh. Did the Kinleys know just how *dramatic* they all were?

'Where the hell is Adam?' he shouted. 'I swear to

God, it doesn't matter how good a friend he is, if he leaves my little sister at the altar, I'm going to pull his guts out of his— What? What's going on?' he asked, when everyone in the room turned to look at him.

'Liv's missing too,' Rowan told him, and Jonathan rubbed at his forehead.

'So you're telling me that we're currently missing the bride *and* the groom for this wedding?' he said, with what Ally had already learned to recognise was more affection than exasperation.

'Seems that way,' Caleb said with a smirk, because it didn't take a genius to figure out what was going on here.

'Where would they have gone?' Jonathan asked.

Rowan reached for his hand and asked him, 'Does it matter? I don't think anyone's going to volunteer to go find them. We'll just have to wait until they're… done.'

'Only Liv would miss her own wedding because she couldn't wait one damn hour to have sex with the groom,' Jonathan said.

Ally grimaced, not sure whether this was the sort of family crisis where her intervention would be helpful, and then she caught sight of Caleb out of the corner of her eye. He was…pink. And getting pinker, passing through red, and onto something like…puce. She frowned.

'Right, well, if we're just going to wait,' she suggested, 'could we have our room back? I'm not quite done getting ready.'

Everyone made apologetic noises as they made

their way out, and she waited until they were alone to go over to Caleb. Was he about to have a meltdown? Because even with everything that they had gone through in Italy, she had never seen him as close to losing it as he looked right now.

'Caleb, is everything o—?'

He burst into howls of laughter, so abrupt and so loud that she actually took a step away from him and checked for the nearest exit.

'I'm sorry,' he said, through choking bouts of laughter. 'I just… This family—my family—they're just—'

Ally smiled back, his laughter infectious. 'They're what?'

'They're just so ridiculous,' he said. 'All of them. Completely ridiculous,' he said again, wrapping his arms around her waist and letting his forehead drop to her shoulder as he was wracked by another bout of hysterics.

'Tell me about it. What am I getting myself into?' Ally asked, laughing too and pressing a kiss to the side of his head.

'Absolute trouble, always,' Caleb answered, muffled against her shoulder. 'You probably should have run while you could.'

She felt him smile against her shoulder, and then he lifted his head for another kiss.

She kissed him back. Enthusiastically. It was always a joy to see Caleb smile, laugh. But to see him like this, with his family, when just a few months ago he'd barely been able to stand to be around them? It was magic.

'I meant it, you know,' he said when their kiss had slowed to something sweet.

'Meant it about what?' Ally asked, still thoroughly distracted.

'About not letting you go.'

'Good. I'm not planning on it either,' she replied, seeking out his lips again, but he pulled back, out of her reach, and she wasn't ashamed to pout about it.

'I'm being serious,' he said, cupping her face with his hand until she looked at him properly. 'I want you, this, for ever. I want what Ro and Jonathan have. What Liv and Adam are about to have.'

'Caleb, are you—?'

'I want to marry you. Here. With all my family getting in the way and annoying the hell out of us. I mean, not today, or this year, if you're not ready. I'm not going to rush you. But I want us to come back here every summer and get in Rowan and Jonathan's way. And I want us all to go on holiday and annoy the hell out of each other. And I want you with me for all of it. I can't imagine a future without you in it. What do you say?'

'I say I'm in,' she replied in a whisper, stretching up on tiptoes to kiss him. 'Yes, I'll marry you. In fact, if Liv and Adam don't turn up in the next five minutes, I'll do it here and now.'

Caleb's eyes widened, and so did his grin as he leaned in for another kiss.

'You know what, that's the best idea I've heard all day, and you had some really excellent ones before we'd even got out of bed this morning. Do you want

to know a secret?' he asked, after another ridiculous bout of kissing, and Ally nodded eagerly, a little
dazed from lack of oxygen and the fact that she was
fairly sure that she had just agreed to marry Caleb.

'I know where Liv and Adam are,' he confessed.
'Want to lock them in and steal their wedding?'

* * * *

COMING SOON!

We really hope you enjoyed reading this book.
If you're looking for more romance, be sure to
head to the shops when new books are
available on

Thursday 13th October

To see which titles are coming soon, please visit
millsandboon.co.uk/nextmonth

MILLS & BOON®

Coming next month

WEARING HIS RING TILL CHRISTMAS
Nina Singh

An older couple walking past smiled at them, then paused directly in front of their bench. Evan's response was a respectful nod with a slight bow. Chiara had no idea what to do so she followed his lead and mimicked the action.

But they didn't move on.

The woman pointed to the top of the pole behind the bench and said something Chiara didn't understand. Then she nodded enthusiastically. Chiara shrugged her shoulders and gave the woman a smile in return. Why hadn't she thought to learn a few words of greeting in Mandarin before coming to Singapore? Most of Singapore spoke English but it couldn't have hurt to learn a bit of the second most popular language here. Things had just moved so quickly after she'd yes to Evan's offer. In fact, time seemed to be speeding by since the day she'd met him. She leaned sideways in Evan's direction. "What's she saying?"

He turned to her. Their faces were inches apart. "She's pointing out that we happen to be sitting under some mistletoe."

Oh dear. The couple was still staring at them expectedly. Chiara froze in her spot, at a complete loss as to what to do.

But then, Evan lifted her chin with one finger. Suddenly, despite the chaotic fun and boisterous noise surrounding them, Chiara's entire focus narrowed to just the two of them. She gripped the cone in her hand so tight, it was a wonder it didn't break in her hand.

And she almost dropped it when she felt Evan's lips on hers. Soft yet firm, gentle yet somehow demanding in equal measure. She had no idea if he'd meant to deliver a small peck on the lips in response to a stranger's prompting, but this kiss was quickly turning into so much more than that. Heat and desire curled through her stomach as his mouth remained on hers. Every cell of her being vibrated with desire.

When she finally made herself pull away, she had to take a deep breath to try and regain some of her senses. The older couple wasn't even there any longer.

At some point, their fake kiss had become all too real. For her anyway. Maybe even for Evan...

Continue reading
WEARING HIS RING TILL CHRISTMAS
Nina Singh

Available next month
www.millsandboon.co.uk

MILLS & BOON

THE HEART OF ROMANCE

A ROMANCE FOR EVERY READER

MODERN

Prepare to be swept off your feet by sophisticated, sexy and seductive heroes, in some of the world's most glamourous and romantic locations, where power and passion collide.

HISTORICAL

Escape with historical heroes from time gone by. Whether your passion is for wicked Regency Rakes, muscled Vikings or rugged Highlanders, awaken the romance of the past.

MEDICAL

Set your pulse racing with dedicated, delectable doctors in the high-pressure world of medicine, where emotions run high and passion, comfort and love are the best medicine.

True Love

Celebrate true love with tender stories of heartfelt romance, from the rush of falling in love to the joy a new baby can bring, and a focus on the emotional heart of a relationship.

Desire

Indulge in secrets and scandal, intense drama and plenty of sizzling hot action with powerful and passionate heroes who have it all: wealth, status, good looks...everything but the right woman.

HEROES

Experience all the excitement of a gripping thriller, with an intense romance at its heart. Resourceful, true-to-life women and strong, fearless men face danger and desire - a killer combination!

To see which titles are coming soon, please visit

millsandboon.co.uk/nextmonth